A CROWN as SHARP as PINES

JENNIFER KROPF

MERRILY MERRILY

LIFE IS LIKE A DREAM

*Find this special Winter novella
at the back of this book*

Praise for The Winter Souls Series

"Wow, I loved this book! It was gripping, fast paced, and full of action, yet not lacking in heart. Highly recommend for young YA readers up-wards."
- USA Today Bestselling author Alice Ivinya

"It's the Chronicles of Narnia meets Harry Potter. This fantastic winter tale is the perfect blend of classic portal fantasy and the magic world co-existing with our own. It's a beautiful reminder of what is truly important in life."
- USA Today Bestselling author Astrid V. J.

"Fans of Chronicles of Narnia will be thrilled with this new wintery adventure!"
- Nikki Mitchell, author of *Nightshade Forest*

"Whimsical, action-packed, clean, and completely immersive."
- Goodreads Review

DEDICATION

For Austin Michael
The one who will see and know
The True King upon His throne

.

PART 1

THE

S T O R Y T E L L E R

PROLOGUE

A spark is how this story begins.

'Twas a glow of faith, no shinier than a silver spoon, no larger than a mustard seed, quiet for a measure until it was touched by a mighty spirit and given wings. The spark flapped to seek out the youthful heart for which it had been gifted, bringing with it the warmth of a new and glorious morn'.

When the spark landed, it got to work tugging the youthful heart this way and that, wrestling with opposition, calling wickets, and the sputters of doubt in the wind, and setting to lead the fair Trite girl into a destiny unrecognized by any wool-eyed, important theologian.

When little Kaley Bell awoke from the night's hushed middle, she felt a warm tug in her heart, a beat in her soul, and a purpose on her fingertips. She did not know what it was that had changed that morning, only that a thing had changed. She had the sudden and most unexplainable craving for sweets.

Dreaming of sugar, she climbed from her bed and followed the invisible string tugging her spirit out to her car.

An early-morning haze lingered in the streets of Stratford where Kaley stood a measure later, staring up at a candy store with big, forest-green eyes.

"Hello?" she called toward the dim windows in her birdsong voice.

Making a fluttery decision, she tugged the golden handle and found it unlocked, releasing the scent of sugar powder and maple sweets into the street.

The moment her spring sandals touched the hardwood floors, the quiet shop buzzed to life; candles lit and strings of bulbs spurted to a glow above, illuminating high shelves stacked with all the sweets one could dream of.

She searched the store for an owner, finding the counters left unattended and the maze of warm shelves absent of souls. Over by a decorative pine tree, a *toot* filled the shop, and an infant-sized toy train rounded on a silver track amidst the prickly branches. Tufts of glitter spat from the train's pipes as it disappeared back beneath a curtain of green needles and came out the other side, aiming toward a staircase at the store's edge.

Stealing one last glance at the empty Stratford street, Kaley followed the train.

The locomotive lit the way up the stairs with pea-sized headlights and into an unlit hall where a glow seeped beneath a large door. Kaley did not notice the train wander off, its horn disappearing from her mind. An embellished "W" was

2

painted on the door's wooden exterior.

For a reason she could not explain, Kaley felt she ought to knock. But the moment her knuckles tapped the wood, the door swung open, and light filled her vision. She shielded her eyes, peering through the radiance at the slender silhouette of a creature with violet wings. She was sucked in by a warm wind.

SEVERAL FULL QUARTERS LATER AND YET, ALMOST NO TIME LATER AT ALL (TIME IS A FUNNY THING)

Kaley flipped a page aged with water marks and crinkles. A low hum accompanied the book; constant, warm, and soothing. Her finger followed the lines best it could with the words hopping about and the sentences curling into twists, creating a path one had to turn the book upside down to follow.

"Have you heard about the magic cylinder that plays to the heartbeat of the Truth itself?" a book whispered from the stack to Kaley's right. "Painted red to hide its power and—"

"*Quiet*," Kaley scolded the book, for 'twas the seventh time that pesky thing had interrupted her reading that morning. Kaley was certain she would slap it across the time pocket if it did not shut up.

"Have you heard about the magic wreath that—"

"Un—*real*." Kaley dropped the book in her hands and reached to dig the chatty Volume out from the pile so she might stuff it under a blanket.

A sharp *pop* reverberated through the time pocket, and her fingers stilled. Kaley's gaze darted to where a smoky haze leaked through a fresh crack in the pocket's shell. This new crack was larger than the thread-thin ones that had appeared over the last two quarters. She jumped when it popped again, watching the crack channel across the shell. A shard of the pocket broke off and her heart stopped.

A breath of wind rushed in from the unlit basement beyond, brushing along Kaley's neck. She stared at the gap— just big enough for her to slip through, should she wish to try.

But she could not. Before Porethius Plum had left Kaley to read through the Volumes of Wisdom, the fairy had instructed, "*Do not leave this time pocket for any reason.*" For, as Porethius was not a true time overseer, she had not been able to stop time completely outside of the pocket she had created—only slow it down. 'Twas why the thing kept cracking.

The soft sound of distant shouts reached her ears, bringing Kaley to shift her footing. Her fingers fell from the book, and she moved to the gap, studying the jagged edges of the shell that looked as sharp as glass. But they felt soft and rubbery beneath her thumb. She tugged at them, finding them stretchy. She nearly had the time pocket yanked back together when a clang echoed through the dark room beyond, and a scream followed.

Kaley's attention darted into the dimness, to the breath of light curving 'round the staircase at the end of the room. The clanging continued, the shouts increasing. She let the fabric of the pocket slip from her hands and trained her eyes on the spiral staircase as she stepped into the dark basement, past the warm dome she had dwelled in for a good measure.

At the foot of the stairs, a *clang* and a *crash* from above drew her to creep up. 'Round and 'round she went until she came to a room of stained-glass windows and carved end tables, with an arched opening that reminded her of a modest church lobby. The clattering thrummed in Kaley's ears as she inched to the arch to spy into the next room. When she saw what lay beyond, her blood ran cold.

Six boys with pointed-toe boots and raven-black coats stood back-to-back among tipped over wooden benches and mounds of shattered stained glass.

Kaley stumbled back.

Limbs burst from a black mist overhead, lapping up boys like hungry tongues until only one remained. The blackness hovered over the last boy, and a low, beastly voice whispered from the darkness.

The boy tossed his staff to the floor, drawing forth a set of medallions with trembling hands. "Glory to Elowin," he gritted. He smashed the medallions together and popping sounds echoed through the room. White snow surged in through a broken window, covering the boy like a hand, and when it settled, the boy in raven-black had vanished.

Kaley couldn't breathe. The coil of blackness turned, and she felt a set of unseen eyes spot where she peeked 'round the arch. She fled, clamouring down the spiral staircase, hearing wind and shadow rage down the stairs behind her.

She raced across the basement floor, bursting into the time pocket and grabbing the jagged edges of the gap. She pulled the fabric together, releasing a cry until the ends sealed, halting the furious shadow that lay beyond.

Kaley tripped back a step, knocking over her chair.

The black cloud filled the basement, dark and infinite, tendrils curling slowly in sluggish time. At the cusp of the shadow, the edge of a large, engraved helmet peeked from the mist, with metal arches o'er the eyes. But there were no eyes inside.

All was quiet, apart from Kaley's heavy breathing. And then, from the back of the pocket, a Volume piped up:

"Have you heard about the broken star turned to fools' gold and guarded by eight hands or feet?"

CHAPTER

THE FIRST

O n the last day of June, there was a knock on Aunt
Sylvia's front door. I trotted down the grand stair-
case to answer it, expecting another parcel from
Quinn's shopping splurges. But when I opened the door,
Kaley was there.

"Uh…Come in?" I joked. "Did you forget how to walk
through a door since you snuck out at five o'clock this morning?"

"Five o'clock *this* morning? I've only been gone for a
day?" Kaley asked with a bizarre look, and I raised an eyebrow.

"What's wrong with you?" I asked, stepping onto the
porch. "You look like you've seen a ghost."

There was a crease between Kaley's brows, the edges of
her mouth were tipped down, and I glanced past her to the

street, wondering if she'd been followed home or was in some kind of trouble.

"Helen," she finally rasped after too much silence.

My sister burst into an elaborate story about how she'd been pulled through a shop door in Stratford by *wind* and had appeared in a basement. She spoke of a fairy named Porethius Plum who'd asked her to *read and remember* the Volumes of Wisdom, which she'd spent four months doing in a time pocket. It sounded like an impossible task she'd been given after an impossible story. Because *no one* could cross back over into Winter when the intersects were closed.

Even though the more she spoke, the clearer it became that what she was telling me was true, I couldn't get past the one thing that rang out from her story the loudest:

She'd been to Winter. *My* Winter. Without me.

After all these years, my aunt had finally found her brain and begrudgingly invited us to live in her enormous house *until we found something else,* after the region's health and safety board had deemed Grandma's house "unfit for occupancy" and forced us to leave last February. Moving day had been the worst. I couldn't have listened to Quinn's complaints or subtle jabs about us not belonging for a moment longer. I knew full well that the Bell children didn't quite *belong* anywhere.

"What did you do to your room?!" Sylvia's scold tore my nose up from the violet tome in my hands. Her horrified face took in the evenly spaced-apart papers that covered the floor, the half-filled mugs of cold coffee abandoned on my dresser, and the scribble-covered, coffee-stained napkins I had pegged to the walls.

"Uh…I'm doing a project," I lied, and added, "Science."

My aunt's face soured. "In July?"

The pause that came after was long and awkward. "Yep."

"Well, it can't be for school so what is it—"

"College. Prep." My eyes darted to the window like I'd spotted a bird, which I hadn't. "College prep. For college. To prepare."

Sylvia *hated* it when I talked about science. After she got back from her Costa Rican vacation, I'd tried to explain to her why the sea tides rose and fell, and she'd walked out of the room while I was still talking.

Sure enough, my aunt glared at my mess and pulled herself back out the bedroom door. I tapped a pencil against the cover of the Volume of Wisdom in my hands—the gift the library had left beneath our tree last Christmas.

"Did you just get one of Sylvia's epic scolds?" Kaley came in next. She eyed the napkins before heading over to the bed, and I rubbed my eyes.

"It was a mild one." I slapped the book shut and spun to face my sister. "I've been wanting to ask you: You said you felt a tug in your chest and then you followed it, right? That's how you found the door to Winter? And how exactly did you get it to show itself?" I asked.

Kaley pursed her lips. "I don't know, Helen. It was just there."

I glanced off, twirling my pencil. Kaley was watching the pencil when I spun back to face her again. Her gaze flickered up to mine.

"You have no idea how you got it to appear?"

"I don't think it was opened from our side. You should leave it alone, Helen. The last thing we want right now is to open another one. What if that shadow—"

"Nightflesh," I corrected. "It had to be him."

She shifted in her seat. "Okay. What if *Nightflesh* had chased me through the door? Do you really want to give him

8

another chance?"

I blinked and moved on.

"You said the Volume that spoke to you mentioned a drum, right?"

Kaley chewed on the inside of her cheek. "I'm assuming it was talking about a drum when it spoke of a *magic cylinder that plays to the heartbeat of the Truth itself*. It talked about a wreath and a star too. I don't know why that's important though, after what happened at the end of my time in the pocket..." I glanced up when her voice trailed off and I caught her staring at the wall. My hand tightened around the pencil.

"There had to be a reason," I said, tearing my eyes away. "The library gave me a book that had the story of Day and Night, right after Zane told me about the Triad of Signs and how the only way to make more Carriers is to put the Triad back together."

Kaley fell back on the bed. "I'm just supposed to store the Volumes in my mind, Helen. I don't think I'm supposed to read into that chatty book." She paused. "No pun intended."

"I think I figured it out," I said, and she lifted her head.

"Figured out what?" Her gaze darted warily to the mosaic of coffee-coated napkins.

"Think about it; Elowin created the Carriers of Truth when he was in Winter. That had to be his plan—to make Carriers to bring the Truth into every corner of Winter. Elowin also created the Triad of Signs; the one thing that can create more orbs, and thus, more Carriers." I paused as I waited for the gravity of this revelation to settle in her. "I think that's the way to overthrow Nightflesh, and that's why Nightflesh has been so intent on hunting all the Carriers down. It's why he tore apart the Triad of Signs; not just because he's trying to silence the Truth, but because he knows that Carriers are his weakness—the ones who were immune to even Mara Rouge's power." I twirled around one last time to look at my sister. "I think the answer has been in *me* all this time."

Kaley rolled onto her stomach and clasped her fingers together. "What does that have to do with the chatty book in the time pocket?"

"I don't think it was a coincidence that Zane told me about the Triad of Signs, and then the library gave me *this* book about Day and Night," I held up the violet tome, "and then that Volume in the time pocket told you those clues," I said. I waited, but she didn't reply, so I huffed and dropped the book onto my dresser, shoving an empty mug out of the way. "The Triad of Signs was made up of three things, Kaley. The Volume gave you three clues."

She blinked. My sister climbed up from the bed, her green eyes travelling back up to my soggy wall-napkins.

Kaley had this thing she did: she'd bite her lips together and blink. Just, *blink*. I knew she was holding things back, because it was the same face I used to make at Winston when I was trying to keep my thoughts about his ridiculous choices to myself.

In August, I sat across from Kaley and Emily—yes, *that* Emily—in a coffee shop we'd adopted as our meeting place to escape Aunt Sylvia, and I caught Kaley studying me. And she was making. That. Darn. *Face*.

"What?" I asked, snatching a sugar packet from the middle of the table.

"Nothing." Kaley gulped her coffee and looked out the window.

Thank goodness for Emily, who didn't know how to

keep her feelings to herself. "Have you been using that makeup I got you?" She took a long drink of her coffee too.

"I didn't have time to brush my hair today, okay? I got busy." I rolled my eyes.

"Too bad you weren't busy *showering*." Kaley finally said it, and I threw my sugar packet at her. She grunted when it bounced off her nose and landed in her drink.

My fingers found my hairline, and I scratched before I could stop myself. I realized my mistake when the two beauty queens before me winced. I dropped my hand back down and tightened my fingers around the mug that was rapidly losing heat. I forced myself to take a sip, making a mental note to shower when I got home.

The dynamic of my relationship with Emily Parker had changed drastically since our grade nine, catastrophic acquaintance. She wasn't afraid of anything, so it hadn't taken her long to find me at school a few days after she'd woken up to tell me, "I heard a ton of the things you said while I was in a coma, *Bell*." Of course, that had turned my insides into a raging inferno where I spent approximately a zillion milliseconds contemplating chucking myself in front of the next yellow school bus speeding by. But to my relief, she followed that comment with, "And I believe all those weird things you said."

In a bizarre twist of fate, the cannibalistic monarch I once knew as Emily Parker began following me around, beating away anyone who peeped a word of unkindness in my direction. And I got to watch as my high school's most famous social butterfly turned the bullies of my school back into the wide-eyed, whimpering caterpillars we'd all been on the first day of grade nine.

I was wary at first because it was *her*, but she and Kaley had things in common. So, I began to relax and accept that maybe Emily needed a friend after all she'd been through just as much as I did.

But with a new friend as blunt as Emily, it was like having a mirror held up to me at all times. If my hair was bad, her face would make sure I knew it. If I smelled like a three-day-old sweater, she'd fish a perfume out of her purse and spray it at me when I wasn't looking.

"I'll do your makeup for graduation," Emily said, tapping her long nail against her chin. "You're basically the smartest student in our school. You need to look the best."

"You can't dress me up if you're not coming," I decided. "We go together, dressed up, or I go alone and get to dress myself."

Emily let out a loud, throaty sound and a few heads turned our way from other tables. "They're only giving me a *participant's* graduate certificate out of pity. I'm not really graduating. It's humiliating, and I'm not going." She clanked the spoon against the edge of her mug after she stirred it. "I don't need to graduate anyway. My grandmother left me a ton of money for when I turn eighteen, which is in like three weeks."

"Seriously?" No wonder Emily had been buying me so much stuff; lipstick, clothes, false eyelashes I'd never wear...

"Yeah. My parents tried to access it a couple of times while I was half-dead or whatever, but since I wasn't *fully* dead, the lawyers wouldn't release the funds. Like, who does that to their own kid?" Emily shook her head and guzzled back her drink, but she kept talking the second the mug detached from her lips. "So now I have all this money and I don't know what to do with it. Mostly, I want to get away from my parents. My therapist said they're the cause of a bunch of my problems, and since I can't change *them*, I have to change *myself*, or something stupid like that." She rolled her eyes. "Anyway, now I'm stressed about having all this *money*."

Kaley's eyes flickered over to mine. "Aw," she said. "That's a rough problem to have."

I stifled a smile.

"Buy a house," I suggested. "It's a good investment."

"Well yeah, that's what I thought. I have enough for a down payment, but I'd still need to get a job to cover the mortgage payments," she grunted, "and who would hire the high school drop-out who was in a coma for a hundred years?"

"You weren't a *drop-out*," Kaley said.

My gaze drifted to my coffee as the girls chatted. Neither of them knew that this was my third cup today and that I'd sneak another few cups at ten p.m. once everyone had drifted off to their own rooms to go to bed. I knew the science of caffeine and how it was affecting my body these last weeks. I'd known how that would play out even before my hands had started shaking and my thoughts had started spinning.

Kaley snapped her fingers between the group of us. "Helen? Are you even listening?"

My gaze flickered up. "Huh?"

"I was telling Emily about that coffee recipe you made the other day with the orange—"

I stopped hearing Kaley's words when something moved in my cup. It took me a moment to register what it was. An *eye* opened in my coffee, bobbing in the liquid; a bright gold iris around a shiny black pupil. I thought I was imagining it, but then it *blinked*.

I screamed.

My chair toppled backward as I scrambled from the table where Kaley and Emily gawked. My back slammed the café window and all the chatter in the building went quiet.

"Helen...?" Kaley stood too.

Emily tossed a wad of bills onto the table and grabbed her purse. "Whelp. I guess we're done here," she said. But she paused to survey the other tables. "What are you all staring at?!" she snapped, and instantly the onlookers spun back to their own conversations.

I burst into my bedroom twenty minutes later, clutching

my thick leather bag of notes, and I grappled for the violet tome on my dresser, knocking a cold mug of coffee to the floor. I cracked open the book, flipping pages without stopping.

I'd spent the whole previous night hunched over, reading with my flashlight. I'd penned sixteen sheets of notes until I ran out of paper, and then I'd written the rest on my arm. Remembering, I paused to yank up my sleeve.

Right. That's why I hadn't showered.

I grabbed a pen and searched for a blank paper or unfilled margin. I pulled a messy page from the pile, barely recognizing my own scrawl, and my pen hit the blank corner:

AN EYE IS HERE.
IRIS: GOLDEN.
IT CAN BLINK.

I stared at my words for a moment, inhaling, exhaling. I scratched my hairline, then grabbed the pages I'd written the night before. The one on top—the last one I'd been focused on before I fell asleep on the floor at 4 a.m.—had bars of musical notation I'd sketched out. Below the bars, I'd scribbled:

Chapter 7 says the Guards of Doors were commissioned by the King of Truth during the first age of Winter to keep the intersects from being tampered with.

Only a Guard has authority over doors between the Trites and the Rime Folk.

I think they can make new doors too.

I dragged my Volume over and scanned chapter seven

for the part that explained how to get a Guard's attention. Finding the place, I read how a certain cherished, ancient hymn would scale the winds to find a Guard for anyone in need if it was hummed. I thought it was an outdated promise, because when I'd tried humming the music last night, nothing had happened.

"Good grief..." I muttered and paused my flipping to stare at the wall. Had I just gotten the attention of a Guard of Doors?

I nearly lost my voice over the next few weeks. I hummed that hymn so many times, I was hearing it in my sleep. But despite my persistent humming, I couldn't get the eye to come back. I sang, and sang, and *sang*, until I hurled the Volume of Wisdom against the wall of my bedroom and shouted at the sky, "I can't be away anymore!" After a moment of listening to my own breathing, I dropped to the carpet, chest heaving, hands shaking. "Elowin, can't you bring me back?"

The warm air began to cool in the evenings, and a crisp autumn crept in. I felt unusual sensations: frost on my knuckles, even while I was holding a piping hot coffee, and cool wind on my cheeks while laying in bed and staring at the ceiling fan. The familiar, hollow hunger began to spread through my chest; the yearning for a part of me that was missing; something that nothing in the Trite world could satisfy. I understood why Zane had been so determined to keep us on the same side of the intersect. When the ache was the heaviest, I wondered if he felt it too.

After my failed attempts to get the eye back, I entertained the theory that maybe sleep deprivation was to blame for it appearing in my coffee in the first place. It wasn't unrealistic to assume my own eyes were sending false signals to my brain. Grandma had warned me that I'd start to lose my mind if I didn't get some sleep. But what my family didn't realize was that I couldn't sleep even if I wanted to.

The eye reappeared in October.

I jerked to a halt when I noticed the golden iris hovering in the jeweler's window downtown. I blinked, worried it was my imagination. I leaned in to look at it, and I *poked* it. The eye jerked back and let out a muffled snarl. My jaw dropped.

Where the eye had just been, a peephole remained. I sprang forward, flattening my hands against the jeweler's window, and I stood on my tiptoes to see through.

A glittering, blue tent was on the other side, with star-shaped wind chimes. Through the open tent-flap I spotted other tents—some glittering and some striped, a white dancing monkey, and brilliant, chalky clouds of colour amidst it all. I could hear faint, metallic tunes from the glass stars clapping together in the navy tent. But before I could stick my finger through, the hole vanished and only the *Fall Sale* sign in the jeweler's window remained.

I drifted away from the window, my hands falling to my sides.

Striped tents.

Dancing monkeys.

"A circus," I whispered.

I looked down the street to see if anyone else had spotted the eye, even though I had a pretty good idea they hadn't. My gaze fell on a familiar lamppost at the end of the sidewalk by the old, boarded-up breakfast diner. The bulb had died out for good last year and no one had bothered to replace it.

November came with a grand sweep of bitter cold. I was too busy for a job, and since Emily was positive no one would hire her anyway, she refused to write a resume. She, Kaley, and I ended up spending far too much time together and the two of them finally stopped asking me if I was okay when I arrived places with bloodshot eyes and unbrushed hair.

We met at our café to keep warm when the weather plunged and left ice chips over the sidewalks. Kaley and Emily listened to me ramble on about the latest flavoured coffee drinks I'd designed. They exchanged subtle glances like they were asking each other, *"What time of night do you think she came up with this one?"* but I ignored them. Emily only ever half-listened anyway; she was always typing on her phone.

"Okay, so…I have a plan." I changed the subject, dragging a stack of notes from my leather book bag. I slapped them down on the table between us, making Kaley jump. But Emily perked up when she saw the title: *Winter-related things.*

"I've been doing some research based on the stuff you read about, Kaley, and then I cross referenced it with those maps you drew and my own experiences in Winter." My sister sighed and fumbled around for a sugar packet. "And I think I figured out where the first two pieces of the Triad are hiding."

Kaley's face changed.

I clicked the butt end of my handy pen and dragged the napkin dispenser over to free a fresh napkin. "The intersect is going to open soon," I said.

"How do you kn—"

"I can feel it." I began drawing. My artistry was horrendous, but I flipped the napkin around to show them. "Did you know that in the Red Kingdom palace, there's a museum with a painting of the Crimson Queen holding *this*?"

Kaley stared, but Emily tilted her head and decided to play Pictionary. "A drum?" she guessed.

I dropped the napkin onto the table. "A drum. I'm sure there are lots of drums in the Red Kingdom palace, but I think this one is it. It's been painted red."

Kaley looked at me for a long time without saying a word, but Emily slid the napkin over and tapped her long nail against it. "You guys are so weird. But this is cool." She grinned.

But I clasped my hands and waited for Kaley to respond.

Kaley glanced over at the napkin again, then slid it to herself to get a better look. "We'd never get to it, Helen— even if I did think hunting guarded Rime treasures was a good idea right now."

"But if my guess is correct, then we know where the first piece of the Triad is," I said. "And what's even better, is that the second piece I've located is one we might be able to steal." I squeezed my fingers. "But I need you with me on this, Kaley. I know you don't like that I haven't been sleeping much. So, before I tell you my plan, I need to know you've got my back."

Kaley blinked in surprise, the tension melting from her face. "Oh, Helen. You know I've always got your back."

Moisture filmed my eyes. "Good. Because we need to stop Nightflesh. He knows about you. He knows what you look like."

Kaley glanced at my stack of papers again, and this time she nodded. "I know." She reached across the table and took my hand. "Tell me your plan."

I started to feel the buzzing of the changing winds and the cold calling me from the other side three days later, when downtown Waterloo had transformed itself into a ribbon-covered city, ready for the Christmas hustle. And finally, that trickle of warmth I had missed beyond measure began to fill the terrible, hollow gap in my heart, telling me it was almost time to see him again. Zane was almost here.

CHAPTER

THE SECOND

The sign taped to the door of Grandma's old house was starting to crisp at the edges. That awful word I'd hated since the day it was spoken over our home stared back at me with no mercy:

CONDEMNED

I smooshed myself against the front door, but it didn't budge. Kaley burst out laughing.

"That was really pathetic," she said and took a step back. "Move." She twisted and thrust her boot against the door. Flakes of wood shattered around the handle and the door swung open.

"Show off," I muttered, clunking in and yanking down that horrid sign from the door as I did. I tossed my leather book bag inside the door.

Wafts of rotting wood and chilly air overtook my senses

as I entered the small kitchen with peeling wallpaper. Four chairs rested around the rustic wood table where we once sat: Grandma, Kaley, Winston, and me. A table that used to host plates of muffins every Sunday afternoon and pancakes during every holiday breakfast since we were kids.

I realized Kaley had stopped beside me. She let out a heavy breath, staring at the empty chairs too. This place still smelled of Grandma's love and a thousand warm memories, along with a few cold ones.

"Do you remember when we first came to live here?" I asked.

She shook her head. "I don't remember anything before this house."

My heart throbbed a little as I was reminded Kaley didn't remember our mother. I cleared my throat and tugged off my hat, knowing my hair was standing on end—adding to my madwoman allure.

Kaley kicked through the dust on the creaky floorboards and stopped in front of the hall closet. When she opened the door, some of Grandma's old, abandoned coats still clung to hangers. I looked away.

The sound of my sister shoving the coats aside and tugging the false closet wall free echoed through the empty house. When she came out, she had a smile on her face and my late grandfather's rusty shotgun in her grip. "Now we wait," she said.

"How are you so sure he's coming *here*?" I eyed the gun, wondering if she even knew how to use it.

"Because Porethius said he'll come looking for you, and this was the last place we lived before the intersect closed." She shoved an earplug into her right ear.

I looked at the gun again, sure that old, tarnished thing wouldn't be able to fire if it came down to it. I flicked it, but my hand froze in midair when the low, slow creaking of the turning doorknob trickled through the kitchen behind me.

Kaley's eyes widened. "He's here," she whispered, bracing the gun against her shoulder and aiming it at the door. "Hide!"

He's here.

Sweet mother of pearl...

I looked both ways and chose the path of least resistance. I'd barely ducked into the living room when the front door scraped open over the dirty floor. Cold wind flushed through the kitchen, along with the promise of an approaching presence that didn't belong, and my breathing hitched.

In walked Eliot Gray.

The fragrance of Winter flowers brushed in with him, along with an explosion of memories. He wasn't wearing raven-black, or curled-toe boots, or a jacket with a pointed hood. Eliot's jacket was fitted, silver velvet, with two vertical rows of pearly buttons up to his throat.

I inhaled through my nose, fighting the urge to show myself when his treacherous bright-blue eyes peered around the door and spotted Kaley there, fashioning her high wool socks and aiming a rusty Trite weapon at him.

Eliot opened his mouth to speak, but Kaley *fired.*

My sister flew back and caught herself against the wall as chunks of the doorframe burst above Eliot's head; wood chips sprinkling his curls. I gaped and winced at the ringing in my ears.

Eliot's hands flashed up in surrender, blue eyes wild. "Season's greetings, Trite," he said, not moving an inch now. A second of tense stillness buzzed through the kitchen until he tried to break the silence again. "I'm sure you don't remember me, but—"

"I remember you." Kaley's reply was as cold as the November frost, and a river of pride swarmed my chest.

"I see." Eliot scuffed his hair to shake out the debris as he no doubt thought about how to outsmart my sister. "I suppose you wouldn't mind telling me how to find—"

"She's gone. She's with *Zane.*"

I closed my eyes in disbelief. If she was trying to get a rise out of Eliot, it worked. For a split second, his bright eyes flickered green—the colour of his envious heart. He lowered his hands to his sides. The boy who had sold me out to Asteroth Ryuu, and was willing to let me wander the Midnight Forest for a thousand years, seemed to realize he'd wasted his time coming here.

The subtle, sweet scent of lilacs filled the air when Eliot took a bold step toward my sister. But Kaley re-aimed the gun at Eliot's chest, and he halted. I wondered if the bullet would even hurt him, being Rime. He seemed to think so.

So, the curly-haired ex-Patrolman nodded. "I'll scuttle off then," he said, turning for the door.

"I don't think so." Kaley came closer and pressed the shotgun's barrel against his bicep. "You're going to take me to the train, Eliot Gray. You're going to board it with me. And once we're in the care of Cornelius Britley, we'll have words."

Eliot's large lips tightened. "Ragnashuck, you're not like your frostbit sister, are you?" His eyes slid over to take her in.

"I'm more like her than you think. But you'll be staying far away from *her*." Kaley nudged him forward with the tip of the gun and shuffled back to the closet to steal one of Grandma's old coats. She tossed the coat over the shotgun but kept it aimed.

Eliot's nostrils flared but he turned toward the door, even raising his hands. Kaley stole one last look at where I peeked around the corner. She cast me a small nod, and I envied her confidence as she disappeared outside.

Porethius had given Kaley one single instruction and one single warning: *Read and preserve the Volumes of Wisdom,* and *Eliot Gray must not find Helen under any circumstances.* The time pocket had shattered a haunting second after the door back to our world had reappeared and Kaley had jumped through. It had sealed just in time to stop her from being followed.

But the intersect was open now. Which was why neither Kaley nor I could be anywhere near this house if that shadow came looking. I doubted Eliot would go to the train kindly, but I knew Cornelius Britley's rules would keep Kaley safe once they were on board—she just had to make it to the train.

I crept to the front door to get my leather bag, aware the neighbours had probably called the cops and I had to move. Every moment, warmth grew in my chest, and I found myself rubbing circles below my throat, smile spreading. I knew he was here—in Waterloo. I knew Zane had reached the intersect.

I took one last look at Grandma's abandoned house: at those four empty chairs. And then I raced out the door and banged down the front steps.

I didn't stop running when I reached downtown. I didn't look for the red-painted Steam Hollow or stop to study the towering Winterblood Elves in the streets. My orb necklace warmed at my throat, reaching for the other side.

I skidded to a halt at the field where everything had evaporated in front of me eleven months ago; the train whistle in the distance giving me hope that Kaley had made it. My eyes scanned the white drifts, the hills, the trees at the field's edge. I spun around, looking up and down, right and left. The weight of my book bag, combined with my poor-diet-dizziness, sent me toppling knee-first into the snow.

A loud laugh reverberated through the air, and I spun on my knees, a smile already stealing my face.

"Clumsy Trite," Zane muttered with a grin. "How have you survived all these quarters without me?"

There he was by the field's edge. Zane slid to his own knees and glided over to scoop me up, abandoning his Patrol staff into the drifts. I hugged around his neck, tears flooding my treacherous eyes. It felt like a dream, but I knew it was real because his heart hammered against mine. Zane wound his arms around my waist and held me there, his breath shuddering as we squeezed each other half to death. I felt his warm tear fall on my neck.

When we finally pulled apart, I huffed a laugh at his moisture-filled, flickering eyes that couldn't settle on one colour.

"Ragnashuck," he whispered, his hands sliding up to either side of my face.

"Ragnashuck," I agreed.

"You look terrible." He grinned, taking a lap of my tangled hair and lifting it between two fingers.

I grunted and lobbed a handful of snow onto his head. He bit his lips together as I patted it down, his gaze sparkling.

"If I didn't miss you so much, I'd toss you into a bank of flakes," he said, but his smile faded. He studied my face, my eyes, the rest of me. "What's wrong with you?" he asked, brows tugging together. "You look like you've battled the icewinds."

"That's a rude thing to say after you haven't seen me all year," I said, but I was still beaming, even as my hand came up to smooth down my unruly locks.

"Huh." His gaze followed my hand motions. "Anyway, there's no time to waste, Trite. We've got a sleigh to catch." He sprang back to his feet, pulling me up with him.

"A sleigh?"

"I raced Wanda here. She's snuffed I beat her, so I gave her a head start for the race back. But I can't let her win, or she'll never stop nattering about it." He extended a hand.

I looked at it. At him.

"Well. I'd hate for you to stop being the most over-glorified Patrolman there ever was," I said and took his hand.

"Trite," he warned, tugging me against him with a dangerous grin. "Careful."

"Zane," I said, and he paused.

My Patrolman bit his lip through a grin and brushed the tangles of hair from my face. "I know, Trite. I missed you too."

I closed my mouth, smile returning.

I grabbed my leather bag as he took off over the field and my stomach dropped. It took only minutes for us to catch up, and I nearly choked at the sight of the bell-decorated horses hauling a red sleigh full of Patrolmen.

Wanda slapped the reins as soon as she spotted us. I recognized Kilen and Mirkra in the back—Mirkra grinned and opened his arms wide, and I had a sinking feeling I knew what he wanted. Sure enough, Zane chucked me toward the sleigh, and Mirkra caught me, mid-gasp. The Patrolman set me on the bench beside Kilen, who rested an arm along the backrest and double-hopped his eyebrows in greeting.

"Wanda, if you lose, I'll toss your apprentice to the snow!" Mirkra called as Zane sped by.

Kilen shrieked when Mirkra tried to scuff his light hair. But my gaze lingered on the burn marks at Kilen's hairline where his fair curls didn't quite cover; a handful of memories reflecting along with the sun's crisp glow.

I tucked my bag into my lap, clutching it there.

The sleigh bounced and tilted, and I shrieked, finding nothing to hold on to. Kilen was no bigger than I was, but he wrapped an arm around my shoulders and pinned me against him when I was nearly tossed overboard. "Easy, Wanda! You're going to break Fred's sleigh!" he called.

"No, *faster!*" Mirkra howled as he reached to scoop a snowball over the rail. He threw it at Zane's back where it exploded, and Zane nudged his staff to send a wave of snow showering over us.

Their energy was beautiful; their laughter, intoxicating.

But my dizziness returned with all the motion, turning the white around me into a pale tornado. I closed my eyes to keep myself from tipping to the sleigh floor as I breathed in the Winter air I had missed so terribly for eleven long months.

WELCOME, A TIME AGAIN

PART II

THE FIRST INTERRUPTION

Kaley Bell flashed Cornelius Britley a caramel-candy smile as she boarded the train on the cusp of downtown Waterloo, nudging along a once-Patrolman on her shotgun's nose. The train conductor offered a pleasant smile in return.

"I have a ticket!" Kaley's high, sweet voice rang o'er the boxcar as she tugged down the collar of her shirt. A shiny, snowflake-shaped trinket glowed beneath the train's candlelight; one she was sure Cornelius Britley would recognize as he spied on them from where he sorted blankets. The doorwoman leaned in to see through her spectacles, but Cornelius chuckled and waved them through.

"Bring them tea," he told the doorwoman. "They'll need it to ease that spirited chill between them." He cast Kaley a long-lashed wink as she pushed Eliot Gray past, and Kaley thanked the train conductor with another smile.

Once the cabin doors were sealed, Kaley let out the breath she had been holding and tossed her grandmother's coat aside to reveal the weapon underneath. The once-Patrolman looked 'round the cabin and slumped into the seat across, settling his icy blue gaze upon his captor. "You're naive," he said to the Trite.

"You're wicked," Kaley said, with spice of her own.

"You're *small*."

"You're going to regret the day you sent the Greed to drag my brother and I from our home."

Eliot's jaw shifted left, then right.

They did not speak for the rest of the ride.

CHAPTER

THE THIRD

I tried to shake the chill on my spine as we rode further in, but the air in Winter felt sharper than I remembered. I studied the sky, wondering if it had always had a grayish haze to it. We passed a forest where glassy branches looked like they'd begun to crisp to charcoal at the points. My fingertips buzzed like the trees' ash was beneath my nails, and I drummed them against my knees.

On the ride, Mirkra handed out baggies of chocolates. Kilen tore his open and shook the bag over his face to dump them into his mouth, but I studied the bag I was given; the light-brown apple stamped on the paper, and the gold-brown ribbon that tied it shut. It had Apple Dough's style all over it, and I cracked a smile. But I set the bag on the bench, too worried about getting sick from the bumpy ride to eat.

An hour later, Kilen took my bag and dumped its contents into his mouth.

I stood when the spokes of the chocolate factory peeked over the snow. I wasn't sure what I expected—gray clouds? Ash? I shook my fingertips to relieve the numbness and breathed a sigh of relief when we plunged over the last hill and I saw Zane waiting, leaning against the factory's door with a smug grin.

My Patrolman glided over as we came to an unsteady stop. I was sure I would have barfed if the ride had gone on any longer—Kilen's face had paled in the last hour; his hand hadn't left his stomach.

Zane lifted me down, his brows tilting inward like he was seeing me again for the first time. I felt his gaze lingering even after I turned to accept Wanda's slap on the shoulder as a way of greeting. The bug-eyed girl went inside, and I readjusted my coat which fit looser on me this year than it had the last. I fished an elastic band out of my pocket too, so I could contain my hair and stop scaring everyone.

"Trite," Zane's voice rose to stop me when I tried to follow the others in. I turned to find him chewing on the inside of his cheek. "Anything we should...*talk* about?"

"I'm fine. I need to meet with everyone. It's important—"

He caught my hand and tugged me back to him. My muscles groaned from flexing, and I blinked back a rush of vertigo.

"Are you bloody joking?" Zane asked, all humour gone. "Helen, you're a spinbug. What happened to you over there?" He locked his gloved hand with mine.

"I haven't been sleeping well," I snapped. I didn't mean for it to come out harshly, but Zane blinked.

"Miss Helen!" Apple sang from the factory entrance. She was all bells and bows, wearing a dress made entirely of the same sparkling, gold-brown ribbons that had tied the bags of chocolates on the ride.

I untangled my fingers from Zane's and bit my lips together. "Sorry. I'm just tired," I muttered, mustering an apologetic smile. Zane put on a half-smile that didn't reach his eyes. His stare followed me as I jogged up the factory stairs to where Apple swallowed me in arms and bangles.

"I've been counting down the days until I could see you again, friend!" she gushed, linking her arm through mine. Her earrings had gotten larger, her lipstick deeper. "By the sharpest wind, you look exhausted! Perhaps an orange tea would do the trick. I'll brew one and you'll be feeling yourself again in a pinch."

Apple patted me on the hand, but I glanced back at Zane as I was pulled through the main space. He had already moved on to goofing around with Kilen. He scooped the boy up and tossed him over his shoulder while Kilen shrieked.

When I looked back at the factory, I halted. Hallways I swore hadn't been there before split off the main room with warm, golden torches flickering down the lengths, and crystal archways led to large rooms I also didn't remember. Above us, glittering, twisted staircases wove through the balconies, casting sparkles of light across the ceiling from the burning sun in the skylights.

"Ah, yes. Those have been showing up for a measure now," Apple explained when she saw me staring. "In the beginning it was fun—we would race through the new hallways and go exploring. I'm certain the spirit of the library has followed the Patrol here and is expanding this glorious factory of ours. But now we're used to new places showing up. I barely noticed yestereve when a door appeared across from mine in the hall. I haven't had time to check what's inside it yet."

A Patrolman went barrelling down the rail of the staircase on his rear, and a series of others bellowed in laughter when he tipped off the end and couldn't catch his feet. He tumbled right into the chocolate river. I recognized his fuchsia hair before it hit the brown liquid; he was the host of the competition Eliot had instigated last year to try and steal me from Zane.

35

My thoughts drifted to the new coat Eliot had been wearing when he'd arrived at Grandma's house, and for a split second, I regretted leaving Kaley behind with him.

"That's...*amazing*," I said to Apple, taking in the splatters of stained glass that seemed to have spread in patches over the tall windows at the back of the great room, and the bows that lined every balcony railing in sight. All that magic that had been stolen by Asteroth in the fire was crawling back to the surface. "How, though?" I remembered flames, burning shelves, and melting cutlery.

"Oh, I suppose it was inside the Patrol all along. Cora Thimble claims a church isn't a building, but a group of souls who come together. The church is here," she nodded to the Patrolmen. "It's inside of us. We are the library."

I smiled. "What have you done this year?" My chest tightened as I feared they'd been up to wonderful things that I'd missed while I was trapped on the other side.

Apple's deep lips curled up at the corners. "Well, my father and I aren't exactly the legends we were in seasons past, I'm afraid. We still make chocolates of course, but for different reasons now. We make them for the children in the Ten Towns over the hills. It gives the villagers something to look forward to, and now that I have several hundred delivery boys at my disposal, the job gets done quite well."

We paused at a table with a spread of chocolate treats, some with nut shavings, others with light pink hues and berries on top. I didn't realize I was so hungry until the scent of the velvety rose-chocolate reached my nose. Apple nudged me toward the table. "Eat something, friend. I'll brew you a tea. And then we'll talk of everything that's happened." Her face fell as she said the last part. "Now that you're here, perhaps we can come up with a thing to do about it all."

I nodded. But I already knew what I was going to do about it; about Nightflesh. If everything had gone according to plan, Kaley would be getting off the train soon.

The moment Apple stepped away, a dozen Patrolmen

inched toward me, some saying *hello*, others reaching to shake my hand, one bowing like a servant. Zane released his melodic laugh as he watched them flock me like seagulls.

"Ragnashuck sputtlepuns, mind your manners!" he said, but it was no use. As the news of my arrival trickled through the factory, young and old Patrolmen alike came to welcome me. Zane squeezed through the hoard and shewed them away, poking the closest ones with his Patrol staff. "It's like they all sipped syrup before we came in," he remarked.

"Well, *I'm* flattered." I reached to snag a chocolate from the table. Then another. And one after that.

Zane tilted his head as I shoved the handful into my mouth all at once, but I was too hungry to care. I moaned as the sugar and cocoa rolled over my taste buds. Apple had every right to brag about her skills as a Chocolatier—her treats were marvellous. I used my thumb to slide a pink chocolate into the pocket of my cheek around the others.

"Are you going to take a breath?" Zane made a face, tucking his staff into the crook of his elbow and folding his arms.

I answered him by holding eye contact while I stuffed another one into the wad of molten cocoa waste between my jaws. Despite my ogre act, he didn't look away. So, neither did I.

His mouth was twisted into a pinch when Apple returned with a steaming mug.

"Yum," I said through the brown fence on my teeth. Apple's eyes rounded when I reached for the tea and sipped it back to wash down my snack.

I didn't miss the look they exchanged. Though the tea was piping hot, I winced as I tried to drink back a current, using it to burn my brain fog away.

They were dead quiet until I finished, and I slammed the mug down on the table.

I fought the urge to burp.

"Did you two know that Kaley—my *sister*—came to

Winter several months ago?" I asked them point-blank.

Apple blinked in surprise, making it clear she knew nothing, but Zane's face tightened. It seemed the handsome, black-cloaked snow-shepherd had finally caught on.

"Your sister? She was *here*? I didn't realize that idea had taken flight." Apple's brown eyes grew wider.

I watched my Patrolman untangle his folded arms and stiffen his grip on the Patrol staff at his side. "The fairies mentioned a thing or three of it. I didn't know anything for certain. Cane was heading up that bit."

He couldn't be serious.

"Cane? The former *Red Prince*, Cane? Brother of the viper-prince who tried to kill me?" I snatched another chocolate. I threw the thing into the air and tried to catch it in my mouth. It was an epic fail, but at least Apple laughed when it knocked off the edge of the table and skittered across the floor, rolling to a stop at Zane's boots.

Apple wiped a bead from the corner of her lash before answering my question about Cane. "Yes, the one and only. He and the fairies have been staying with us since their ice caves were melted. In fact, Cane should be arriving in a measure. The other once-prince, Edward Haid—the *Green*—is with us too."

I was having trouble remembering who Edward Haid was, but I waited for her to finish her story, stealing a look at Zane in the meantime. His electric gaze was still leveled on me.

"Cane is safer here with us these quarters. You see, the Silver Jubilee Renewal has the whole Red Kingdom in a buzz, but it was Prince Forrester asking Holly Kissing to *marry* him that really put an unmerry rash on Cane's well-being," Apple explained, and I raised a brow. It seemed Apple had no trouble saying Cane's name aloud anymore.

"I think Forrester only did it to thrust a dagger of bad tidings into his renounced brother," she went on. "Cane revealed himself to the believers nearly four quarters ago, and though we are good at keeping our secrets, we couldn't stop the rumours from leaking across the Red Kingdom that Cane was alive and had befriended the Green once-prince, Edward. It's why Forrester decided to propose, I imagine. Gossip claims the Crimson family began to suspect Holly of lying about her true identity after our *heist* in the season past. Forrester must have guessed who she really was. It's all a pinch messy."

I'd stopped eating. A chocolate melted between my fingers as I absorbed this news about people I had danced and dined with at a time that suddenly didn't feel so long ago. Holly Kissing, despite her standoffishness, had tried to warn me at the Alabaster Ball. She'd tried to keep me from walking into a trap. Apparently, she found herself in one now.

I sighed, realizing my mind was sharper than it had been a moment ago. Apple's orange tea must have had magical powers.

"Anyway, let me assemble the group. Everyone has been waiting to meet until you arrived, friend. I'm afraid we have much to discuss," Apple said.

If only she knew.

The moment she fluttered off, my treacherous gaze flickered over to Zane again. He stared at me for a drawn-out moment before dragging a hand through his pecan hair. "I feel like I should know this but...are you upset that Porethius asked your sister for help?"

My answer was quick. "No." I turned away and focused on my teacup and the chocolates.

"You're lying." Zane stepped to the table. "What did you expect me to do, Trite? Did you want me to try and stop an ancient war fairy?" he asked, and my gaze darted back to him. He blinked. "Ragnashuck, you did."

I swallowed, the glory of my chocolate-eating-monster show wearing off. "We have nothing to discuss about it," I said. But Zane drew closer, stealing my view. A flicker of hurt crossed his face and a rush of guilt moved through me.

"Helen," he whispered. Though we were surrounded by background noise, I heard what he said next. "I missed you more these last quarters than I've ever missed anyone."

Anyone. The word struck a chord, and I thought of his first Carrier, and Mikal.

My attention flickered back. Good grief, I *was* a monster. Even before I'd attacked the chocolate. I opened my mouth to tell him everything, but my throat swelled, and I closed it again. Instead, I moved in and wrapped my arms around his middle until he relaxed, and his arms came around my shoulders.

"I missed you too," was all I said.

THE SECOND INTERRUPTION

'**T**was a steamy ride for a measure of reasons, and not one had to do with the translucent puffs of shimmer frothing from the train's pipes.

After bidding farewell to Cornelius Britley and watching as Cornelius conspicuously grinned at Eliot's situation, Kaley Bell led her captive off the train platform and into a town she knew only as an oval-shaped mass on a map she had glanced upon a quarter or three ago. Within slender hotels of shimmering red banners and pockets of tinsel, Kaley spotted a building with an ivory door, where pale steam painted the window's insides like milk.

"You can't possibly know where we are," Eliot Gray tried, grimacing at the flock of crystal toads hopping along the town's walkways, guided gently by an elf wrapped in crimson blossoms.

Kaley ignored him, yet still Eliot went on, "If you knew the rules of Winter, you'd avoid places like this. Places that are *red*," he offered. After another pinch with no response, he tried a time again. "It's not safe for us to be here, Trite. I'm on your side, you know. I went to the dead world to offer my apologies and bring good tidings to your sister."

Eliot Gray abandoned his natter as he was led into the building with the ivory door. He drew a puzzled face, taking in the hot drink tavern he had visited a time or three in seasons past. "How did you know about this place?"

Yet a time again, he was ignored. Kaley lowered her Trite weapon and scanned the bustling tables, grabbing faces she would never forget into her memories.

Silence often spoke greater volumes in her opinion. 'Twas in the silence Kaley was able to recall that morning of the not-so-distant past when pale-skinned monsters had come to her grandmother's house with their long bows and violet eyes. They had hovered over Winston as he ate his morning oats—Kaley had nearly jumped from her fair skin at the sight of them when she'd descended the stairs. One had leaned to whisper in her brother's ear, "*Season's greetings, Trite. Blink twice!*" The words still haunted Kaley's thoughts like a bitter whiff of smoke.

Eliot released a grunt when she did not say a thing. "Suit yourself. But if I have to let you drag me through the frostbitten snow, I'm getting a chocolate brew first."

Kaley did not stop him when he left for the counter. She laid the rusted shotgun against the wall, for it was out of bullets anyway. She patted the metal barrel in thanks, offering a thought to her grandmother who had once taught her how to use it. And there inside the building with the ivory door, she would leave the Trite weapon of her ancestors.

Kaley's attention travelled the misty room to a place Eliot had not bothered to look, where a rather charming boy in raven-black with a fur hood was flashing his strikingly wide grin all too carelessly. A sigh of disbelief escaped Kaley's pink lips, for the boy did not seem to have a clue that he made magic with that smile.

Kaley waited until the youthful Patrolman spotted her. The look on his face was confusion at first but turned to candy and stars as he rose from his seat, heating the air with that impossibly, dangerously infectious smile.

Lucas Leutenski sauntered through the tables. The rich topaz of his eyes glowed, but the colour fizzled when he spotted Eliot Gray at the counter. A speck of uncertainty blotted his light as he looked from Eliot to Kaley, then back to Eliot a time again.

"What exactly are *you* doing here, Trite? Nothing responsible, I imagine," Lucas said as he approached. He offered that treacherous grin again.

"You're right, nothing responsible." Kaley nodded toward Eliot who had gotten comfortable on a stool and was making a selection from the menu. "I've brought a prisoner here."

"Well, that's juicy. Please, explain that merry muddle to me," he insisted. "Unless you'd rather I drag him into a brawl on your behalf? I think we could get the rest of the shop to join in; break some perfectly good tables, maybe even shatter a window or three."

"As much as I'd love to see you two toss punches at each other to ease your inflated egos, I came here for you, actually."

"Really?" Lucas bit his lip through his smile.

"My job is done with Eliot. I need to ditch him," Kaley said.

Lucas's eyes transformed to golden suns. "I was hoping you'd say something like that, you perfect little Trite darling." His gloved hand came out. "Allow me to sweep you away on my steed."

They quietly slipped out of the shop and to the alley. Kaley's forest-green eyes rounded at the sight of that massive beast she had forgotten was so large and sharp. Helen's plan had seemed like a clever idea until Kaley was before Lucas Leutenski's reindeer again, and once there, she could not remember why she had agreed to any of it. The spears of its antlers sang a tune of death, slicing the air toward the pale Winter sky.

Lucas mounted the beast with a high leap. Taking a deep breath, Kaley approached on tiptoes, but Lucas snatched her by the arm and hauled her up, setting her in front of him atop the deer. Kaley tried not to react when he wound his arms 'round her waist to hold the reins at her sides. Though, she did notice that he was rather warm.

"Where to?" Lucas asked, breath steaming in the air.

"Just get me away from here," she said. "I never want to see Eliot Gray again."

"Ragnashuck. That's the loveliest thing I've heard all day," Lucas said. But the youthful Patrolman leaned over and hollered through the shop's cracked-open window, "Get frostbite, Gray! You positively scotchy rung-nut!"

And they took off.

A measure later, a windswept, rosy-cheeked Lucas brought the deer beneath a glistening, glass willow. The skies had creamed to soft white as a salty blizzard roared in. 'Twas there that Lucas decided to take shelter in a cove of muscled evergreens, slowing the creature to a modest trot.

"Though I'd never object to a pleasant ride through the Winter winds with you, perfect-little-Trite-darling, I wonder where we're really headed? You didn't actually come here *alone* with Gray, did you? It wouldn't make a pinch of sense if you did," he asked.

Kaley twiddled her thumbs before she answered. "Well aren't you clever, Lucas Leutenski. Alright, we're going to the Green Kingdom. You and I are going to steal something from Timber Castle."

At her back, Lucas yanked the reindeer to a halt, throwing Kaley off. He hopped down to catch her and plant her feet on the snow before she turned into a cranky, damp Trite mess.

Pinning Kaley against the deer's warm fur, Lucas blinked, all the fun and giggles gone from his face. "What was that, Trite?" he asked. "There must be frost in my ears, because I *thought* you said something terribly scotchy."

"I think you heard me," Kaley returned.

"Why would I ever *willingly* go to Green?" Lucas asked, blinking slow and deliberate.

"To steal a crown. It's the first step in Helen's plan," she said, but her voice dipped on her sister's name. She cleared her throat, and Lucas stopped his blinking.

"This is *Helen's* plan?" he prodded, and Kaley nodded, though she flicked her gaze to a passing bug in the air. "You must think me a spinbug," he said.

Kaley released a breath through her nose. "I'm here for Helen, that's all you need to know. And frankly, I'm starting to wonder why you still don't get why I came here looking for *you* of all the Patrolmen in Winter."

Lucas's topaz eyes narrowed. "Whose crown are you luring me to steal with you, Trite?" The daredevil himself seemed to fear the answer.

But Kaley spoke the words anyway. "I need to steal the queen's crown. The Crown of Pines." And then, "*perfect-little*-Rime-*darling*."

CHAPTER

THE FOURTH

Fred had gotten a new pair of glasses. They hugged his face as he rushed in a cocoa-stained apron to set out trays for a dessert feast. Pedestals filled the table in the middle of the room, a collage of autumn-coloured chocolates sprinkling every surface amidst the pinches of icing sugar he flung over everything.

Brass lanterns hung from the ceiling in this new room, turning the walls and tabletop to butter, and a bell hung over the door to alert those inside every time someone new entered. The Patrols had flocked in first, including Trevor and the rest of the Elders with their snowflake broaches. I realized I hadn't seen the elders since the library fire and my gaze flickered over the pale scars some had on their hands.

I grinned and waved when the dwarves came in, yarn dragging along the floor in fuzzy tentacles.

Then, in marched Porethius Plum, and the chatter in the room died down. The markings on her flesh swam, glittering dust swirling behind her. Another fairy followed; dark-skinned, male, muscular, with wild golden eyes. The mighty pair were a sight to behold, and I stood taller. I waited for Porethius to look for me, to nod in greeting or come say hi. But she headed across the room and began speaking to Trevor in a low voice. My shoulders lost their spirit and I slouched.

The bell knocked against the door again and I tensed when I recognized Cane. He couldn't be mistaken for anyone else with his rich mahogany hair, but I swallowed at the wild purple of his eyes, memories of the viper-prince slithering through my mind. If Cane had black hair, he and Quinten could have been twins.

A middle-aged man with dark hair and gold eyes walked beside the former Red Prince. I presumed he was the famous Edward Haid Apple had mentioned; the *other* once-prince. Edward whispered something to Cane, who suppressed a laugh.

"Season's greetings," Porethius called above the chatter in the room. I slunk to stand between Zane and Apple when I realized Porethius had other things on her mind than saying hello. Some of the Patrols continued to sneak to the table to fill their bowls with chocolates and mint-powdered popcorn, but everyone else hushed.

"More of the believers who were once safely hidden in the Red Kingdom and surrounding villages have now vanished, like the others." Porethius's wings shifted, her forehead creasing. "Gathadriel and I continue to search for the missing believers. But if our numbers persist to diminish at this rate, we'll be vanquished by—"

I suddenly burst out laughing. All eyes found me then, even *hers*. Zane looked at me like I'd started singing opera.

47

But everything Porethius said was so *depressing*.

"Carrier." It seemed Porethius had finally found it within herself to say hello.

"Sorry," I said, trying desperately to drop the laughter from my face. "But is this how we all give up? Is this how the sacred truths are wiped clean from Winter? Is this how my orb turns to a stone?" I looked around. "In a *meeting*?"

The violet-eyed fairy turned toward me. "No one said we were giving up," she said.

"Oh, really? I couldn't tell by all that awful stuff you just told us."

"*Trite*," Zane whispered. "Bloody drop it!"

But I looked around at the candlesticks on the shelf tops, the wreaths of garland, and the other festive remnants of a library that had once been. Everyone was quiet, and I knew they were waiting for me to explain myself, but I still took a moment to step to the large table and nudge a peppermint stick. It reminded me of my first visit to Winter. It reminded me of the simplicity of trekking across the snow, village to village, beside Zane. It reminded me of all that had happened since then.

"Do you have a thing to say, Miss Bell?" It was Trevor who finally broke the silence. The Patrolman had grown out his beard; the auburn limb reached halfway down his chest now.

"This is *my* plan," I started, and I picked up the peppermint stick to wave it like a wand before biting off the end. "You're right. Nightflesh is winning." I crunched the shards of peppermint, ignoring the shuffle of whispers that rose from me blurting out Nightflesh's real name. My gaze flickered up to Porethius, who faced me fully now. "Something is wrong with Winter. The sky is gray, and the trees are dying." My nails dug into my palms where phantom ash prickled my fingertips. "My job is to make sure the Truth doesn't die out, and to make sure the mountains and rocks aren't forced to sing in our place. So, *I'm* going to fix it," I told them. "Me and Kaley, to be more specific."

"Kaley *Bell*?" Cane spoke up for the first time. "Kaley Bell is in Winter?"

"She's on her way to get the first piece of the Triad of Signs," I told them. "We're going to put it back together."

A dead beat of silence thumped down on the room.

"Impossible." It was Trevor who broke it with his unwelcome negativity. "We gave up searching for the signs seasons ago. All who saw the Triad when it was first formed wouldn't recognize the pieces now—even Mikal had no insight into where they could be, or what they might look like."

"They *can* be found. By me and by my sister," I corrected. "She has dozens of Winter maps in her head, and a Volume woke up to tell her things about the Triad of Signs while she was supposed to be reading the—"

"Kingsblood, why in all of Winter is Kaley Bell *here*?!" Cane said again, purple eyes round as coins.

I huffed. "A wreath, a drum, and a star, right?" I asked Trevor. "That's what Mikal said the Triad was made of?" Trevor looked struck. He didn't deny it, so I turned to Porethius. "We don't need you to sign off on our plan. I really only came here as a courtesy. We'll be doing this whether we have help or not."

"Carrier," Porethius raised a delicate hand, her tattoos quivering.

"Don't '*Carrier*' me," I shot back. "You dragged my sister into this, remember? I would have done it. I would have come back here in a heartbeat. But you took *her*, and then she almost died in that basement! So now she and I are going to fix everything, because it seems like a hundred Rime Folk believers can't get it together long enough to rescue the sacred truths from going silent, and you've left it up to a bunch of measly, unimpressive Trite girls to *save your skins for you*!" I shouted it, flinging a tray off the table and sending truffles shooting for the wall where they splattered.

Zane appeared at my side, but I swatted him away. I

turned for Porethius again only to find her directly before me. Her hand took the side of my cheek, and then it was game over.

"Sleep, Carrier," she said.

And I dropped into Zane's arms.

I dreamt of the gardens surrounding Mikal's home. I absorbed the scents and beauty of the blooms, the teas, the vegetables, and all the other remarkable things Mikal had nurtured in his lifetime. It was the most peaceful sleep I'd had in months.

"She's lost her mind." I heard Zane's whisper between dreams. The corner of my eyelid peeled open enough to see his blur of raven-black, and the deep red of Cane's hair. Porethius was there too; they were gathered at the foot of my bed.

"She's exhausted." The fairy's musical voice drifted over. "She needs rest."

"Well, I'm merrily ubbersnugged. She's right, you know. We've put the fate of Winter in the hands of two Trite girls who never asked to be dragged into our muddle. Perhaps we were fools to think they'd stay in the dead world given all that's happened." It sounded like Quinten was in the room.

"I can't let her stay like this. She's madder than a bewitched snowsquatch," Zane said. "What do I do with her? I can't just lock her in the basement." A pause. "Can I?"

"Let her rest, Patrolman," Porethius told him again. "She needs to sleep and eat. Her state is muddling her judgment."

I fell back to sleep for the rest of the conversation.

When I finally awoke, I expected to find Zane by my bedside, but it was Porethius who remained. The room smelled of sugar and plums, fresh blossoms and early morning rain. I inhaled her scents.

Her feet were up on the edge of my bed. I'd never seen her lounge, but she still looked like a goddess when she did it. We looked at each other, neither of us in a rush.

Finally, she pulled her feet down and rested her elbows on her knees. "What did you mean when you said, *'a Volume woke up to tell her things about the Triad of Signs?'*" she asked in a soft voice.

I had to remind myself what I'd blurted at the meeting.

I rubbed my eyes. Above me, glittering butterflies moved in the rafters. Their lines were sharp and clear, and I felt like I'd been wearing glasses with the wrong prescription until now. "It's exactly how it sounds. A Volume whispered clues about the missing pieces of the Triad to Kaley while she was in your time pocket."

Porethius glanced out the window to where the rising sun cast pink and yellow hues over the hills. My fingers traced Apple's quilt. I was in the same bedroom as last year. There were a few decorative changes, but the rest was still the same—the faded mirror by the door; the wiry nightstand beside the bed.

I sighed and ran my fingers through my tangled hair. I couldn't make eye contact with Porethius, but a warm breeze flitted through the room and covered my shoulders, and I knew it was her.

"I could say a lot of things about what you did," I began. "Kaley was nearly taken. On *your* watch."

Porethius looked to the floor. "I had no idea what would happen to that cathedral. It used to be fostered by one hundred and thirty plus eight believers in our fold."

"What happened to them?" I crossed my arms, and she glanced at me.

"The same thing that happened to the Patrolmen we sent

to check on them after we didn't hear from them for a measure," she said. "They vanished."

My skin pebbled as I thought about how Kaley had described the Patrolmen being swallowed by a shadow. "How many believers have gone missing?"

"Many."

"Are they alive?"

"I don't know."

Soft sounds of laughter drifted up from downstairs. I stared at the fairy, at her drooping wings and tightly gripped hands. "You pulled Kaley through a door into Winter while the intersects were shut. How did you do that?"

Her brows tilted in. "I opened an old door with Elowin's blessing, but it was sealed once it served its purpose."

I chewed on the inside of my cheek.

Porethius stood and sighed. "You should know that I did not choose your sister over you; your sister was needed *in addition* to you. And I knew the risks of giving her that assignment in the basement, but so did she. She did it for *you*. Because she wanted to help you."

I looked off at the mirror by the door. "She shouldn't have."

"She's braver than most."

"She's only sixteen."

"So were you when you came."

A long pause hung between us. Porethius came to my bedside and extended a tattooed hand. "Come, Carrier. I'd like to show you a thing." Her other hand flicked the latch of the bedroom window and shoved it open. I released a heavy breath and lifted my hand.

The moment my Trite flesh touched her fairy skin, I was whisked through the window, and I gasped as we propelled faster than a jet through the Winter sky, the factory turning to a speck below. The fairy glowed, spiralling against the wind like a shooting star. We burst through cloud and gale, leaving no shadow, icy landscapes and deep green forests glimmering under the flecks of golden sunlight slipping by us.

After taking in Winter's glory, my face fell as we descended over a dark, metal gate surrounding a kingdom with ruby statues; a misty city in the middle of it all.

"Porethius, why are you taking me here?" I called over the howling wind.

She didn't answer.

We broke from the clouds and my stomach tried to scramble up into my throat as we dropped. The fairy repositioned her legs and hit the ground, snow rippling away from her sabatons, and a deep echo reverberated through the frost-kissed trees. Pure white apples clung to the branches around us. I spun to Porethius.

"Why did you bring me *here*?!" I shrieked. I'd aligned myself with Quinten in this orchard. Jolly Cheat had handed me a white apple in this orchard. I'd fooled Red Princes and the Crimson King in *this* orchard.

"This way." Porethius turned for a snowy path, reaching into a satchel at her hip and tugging out a furry corner of fabric. The fabric kept coming; she pulled until she held a full-sized red cloak, and she extended it to me.

I held it up, knowing there was no point in asking about the science of the gaps and nooks in Winter. Porethius pulled out another cloak and flipped it over her shoulders as she walked. I scrambled to follow.

We ventured down the path out of the orchard and made our way through a maze of buildings with narrow alleys. Porethius marched on light toes, barely making a noise, while I clunked along. We slowed at a wide, round, crowded pavilion. The Red Kingdom dwellers chatted and pointed, some laughing. In the middle of the pavilion, two men were in an open, cobbled space. The first sat upon a chair with a large feather pen; his chin tilted up, showing off his yellow eyes. He looked bored, but occasionally he scribbled something on the parchment before him.

The second man reminded me of the pirates I'd met the first year I came to Winter. He had a few flashy trinkets—a silver earring, a gold tooth. He was red-faced and *shouting*.

"Who are those two?" I asked Porethius.

"The scribe is Sullen Sprit-Spellborrow. He's the editor-in-chief of the Natter Nugget, the Scarlet Post, and the Pebble Paper." She glanced at me as she said the last one.

My gaze returned to the man in the chair. So, this was the guy who'd written all that garbage about the fight in the courtyard last year—blaming it on the believers, calling us *dangerous*.

"The other man is a fisherman. He is a believer in the Truth," she explained.

"Well, if he's a believer, shouldn't we warn him? He could get snatched up by Nightflesh's shadow for revealing himself with such a scene."

Porethius watched the fisherman start off on a new tangent, shouting even louder than before. He called the people names, and I winced when he shouted in a mother's face and her baby began to cry.

"Nightflesh doesn't need to take this man," Porethius said, her irises turning grape. "This man is doing Nightflesh a favour. He is making the Rime Folk despise us, and he is making the Rime Folk despise Elowin too, by representing him with hatred on his tongue," she said, and I watched her shoulders sag. "Cruelty rarely convinces anyone of anything." She looked at me. "Anyone can yell and argue."

My eyes found the ground at my feet. I hoped I hadn't looked as ridiculous as the fisherman when I'd been the one yelling in the middle of the meeting.

"But only the believers can pray for a miracle on a silent night. That is our weapon, Carrier. Prayer is our one advantage in this war."

I watched the fisherman raise his fist; an accusatory finger pointed toward the people gathered. None of the Red

Kingdom dwellers seemed to be listening anymore. A mocking smile traced the edge of Sullen Sprit-Spellborrow's mouth, and he went back to writing his article.

"Take me back now," I said. "I'm convinced."

Without another word, Porethius headed back to the orchard.

The ride back felt longer. But when we got to my bedroom in the factory, Porethius headed for my nightstand and lifted the lid of the silver teapot resting there. A faint wisp of steam curled out. "Eat. Rest. And grow merry again," she said, sliding the tray off the nightstand and setting it on my bed. Fruit slices and warm bread with chocolate syrup rested on the wooden platter.

When Porethius headed for the door, she cast me an unexpected smile. "I suppose I should have said this before, but welcome back, Carrier."

It took some self-coaching to be able to leave my room, but when I finally worked up the nerve to open my door, Zane was standing there like he'd been ready to knock. He was sporting a white t-shirt, of all things. It was so *normal*, and for a moment I imagined him standing amidst a Trite Waterloo crowd and fitting in. But I shook the thought from my mind.

"Zane—"

"It's alright, Helen. I know you're upset—"

"I'm—"

"—and after the meeting, I'm going to find a way to cheer you up." His hand came out, ushering me into his minty presence, and I glanced at his skull tattoo he no longer hid.

I looked at him, *really* looked at him for the first time

since we'd collided on the field in Waterloo. I hadn't been able to focus then, but now I realized his hair was different—longer. His electric blue eyes were as remarkable as always, and he'd gotten a smidgen taller. There was a new scar on the side of his neck, below his ear. I reached to touch it, and he went still.

"Where'd you get this?"

Zane's mouth tightened at the edges. "It's an unmerry story for another day, Trite. We have scotchier troubles to face presently."

I glanced past him toward the stairs. "Does everyone think I'm crazy?"

"Yes," he said, and my face fell. "I mean...No?" he tried again.

I shot him a look, but the corners of my mouth betrayed me and curled up.

"Ragnashuck, Trite, what do you want me to say?" he grinned. "You pitched a bloody tray at the wall!"

My hand came over my face. "The Patrol are going to abandon me."

He peeled my hand away from my eyes and chuckled. "The Patrol might. But I would never."

The sound of conversation lifted up the stairs and I swallowed. Zane put an arm around my shoulders and guided me toward it. "Anyway, they want to meet again. I came to get you," he said.

"They still want me there after what I did?"

"The meeting is about all that stuff you nattered, so I'd say so."

My plan. "Wait!" I sprang back to my room, looking for my leather book bag, hoping someone had brought it up while I'd been sleeping. I spotted it against the nightstand, and I hauled it over my arm.

I'd hoped we could stay hidden at the back, but when Zane and I slipped into the meeting, Cane spotted us.

"Ah. The cheery maiden herself," he called from where

he was sprawled sideways over a chair. I wondered how he was conducting a meeting like that. "Shall we duck and cover?" he asked, and that beautiful, princely smile of his tugged wider.

I felt warmth meet my cheeks; Zane couldn't conceal his laugh.

"Maybe just *you* should." I flashed a smile back at Cane.

Cane slid to sit up straight, surprise in his burgundy irises. "Kingsblood. You're trouble," he decided. "I think I like you."

"You like anything that causes trouble," Edward Haid piped up from the corner where he stood, adjusting the collar of his jacket in front of a mirror.

"Well. 'Tis the season." Cane said, casting Edward a devilish grin. The Green Prince bit his lips to stifle an inside-joke-type of laugh and I sniffed princely mischief in the air.

"Why don't we let our Carrier tell us what she knows?" Porethius interjected. The dark-skinned fairy she'd called *Gathadriel* stood beside her.

I swallowed and stepped forward. "Well, first, obviously I should apologize for my..." I waved toward the table, "*thing*. But yes, I'd like to tell you what my sister and I are up to, if you'll hear me out."

Hundreds of eyes blinked in my direction. This was the moment I had planned for. Regardless of what I'd said at first, if this group wasn't on board, I knew we couldn't pull off the plan.

I took in a deep breath, inhaling the warm peppermint and pine scent at my back. "I think Mara Rouge requested to have the Triad of Signs given to her as a gift in the beginning because she recognized what it was. When the Crimson Court handed it over, the Beast within her ripped it apart into its original three pieces—the signs bearing evidence that Elowin was the Truth itself, and thus, the real King of Winter. I don't think Nightflesh *could* destroy it completely. I think ripping it up and hiding the pieces was the best he could do. It took some time to figure out, but Kaley and I have a good idea where two of those three pieces are."

Cane was standing now, arms crossed, a finger tapping against his mouth as he paced. "I've studied the Volumes of Wisdom too, and I found nothing about the location of the signs," he said.

"I don't know what to tell you about that. But I have all the notes to back up our theories." I hauled my book bag onto the table and tipped it over. Papers dumped in every direction, some slipping onto the floor. People inched in, picking up sheets to examine for themselves.

Zane had an odd look, but he pegged a page with his finger and dragged it to himself. When he lifted it to read, his brows pulled together. His gaze darted to the other pages on the table.

"You see, all the evidence is right here." I rapped my knuckle against the notes. "Mikal would have known that the Triad was made up of a drum, a wreath, and a star, but he wouldn't have known that the drum was painted red without the clues, or that the—"

"Helen…" Zane pursed his lips and extended his page to me. "We can't read this."

My brain halted. I grabbed the page from his hand. "What do you mean? Don't the Rime Folk know how to read cursive?" I scanned the handwriting, but when I glanced up at the others, everyone had the same look.

"I mean, you've clearly taken a good measure of notes, Trite," Zane made a face at the paper-heaps, "but what are we to do with this?"

I blinked at the filled margins, the arrows connecting the research, at my writing between the lines of other writing. "I mean, I know I didn't cross all the 't's or dot all the 'i's but…" Spilled coffee had washed the ink away in spots. "I mean, I was a little tired when I wrote it," I admitted, lowering the page. I swallowed. "Well, I'll just have to read it to you then." I tried to calculate the time it would take based on the number of pages and my reading speed.

"Why don't you just tell us where you guess these signs to be hidden, Carrier? Maybe that would help," Porethius offered. "Surely if a Volume woke up to speak, it was for a purpose."

I stared at the pages for moment. And I let the one in my hand fall back to the pile with the others. If I'd been able to come to Winter months ago when I needed to, I could have told them all this in person.

"The wreath is in the care of the Evergreen dynasty," I rasped. I took an awkward gander at Edward Haid. "The wreath was Elowin's original crown of pine needles. I think Nightflesh twisted it into a garland and placed it upon the head of the Queen of the Pines. It's been hiding inside her crown for almost twenty years."

Cane's gaze flew to Edward who'd gone as still as a statue, but I went on. "The second sign was the drum. In the story of Day and Night, the Volumes say a drum was used to soothe Elowin himself on the day he was born into Winter. Its beat mimicked the True King's heartbeat, thus giving its rhythm power. But I think Nightflesh painted it red, covered it in jewels, and passed it off to the Crimson family through one of his vessels, pretending it was a gift."

Cane paled. He looked at Porethius. "Kingsblood," he rasped. "I know that drum. My mother used to bring out a magic drum for the seasonal Red Holiday," he said.

"No," the fairy objected, seemingly before he could ask the question on his mind.

But Cane marched over to her. "I have unfinished business in the palace anyway. You know that," he said in a loud whisper. "Plum, I can get to that drum. Our Carrier is *right*— we have no other ideas, and our people are vanishing. We need to do something!"

"Even if we did put the Triad back together, used it to make more orbs, and then trained more Carriers of Truth, Nightflesh would just hunt them down like he did with the others," Trevor piped up, bad memories flickering across his eyes.

"Not if we did it in secret." Cane was still looking at Porethius.

"Exactly," I chimed back in. "Elowin came to Winter to spark a great commission that was meant to grow an army. That army got destroyed over time, but Elowin left the pieces here. We have the tools we need; we just need to find them."

Porethius glanced over at me, at the Patrols, at the dwarves.

"Let me get the drum, Plum," Cane begged, pulling her attention back.

I held my breath. The last time I'd asked Porethius for help, she'd made it clear she wasn't supposed to get involved.

"If we don't do something, we're going to lose everyone," Cane added.

The fairy looked off. I wasn't sure what she was doing, but her lips moved silently.

"What do *you* think, Cohen?" Trevor asked, hugging his arms to himself. The rest of the Patrols looked at Zane too.

I realized Zane had found a chair at the side of the room. He was slouched back, his head leaning against the wall. "If the Trite is set on this unmerry thing, I'm sure I'll probably die trying to make it happen. If I don't, I'll be beaten to death with a truffle tray anyway." He shrugged and I made a face when Patrolmen around the room snickered. Zane's gaze flickered over to mine. He couldn't fight his smile and I had half a mind to pick up a *truffle tray* and fulfill his destiny right then and there.

Finally, Porethius looked back to us, and the giggles ceased. "Yes. I think this is the only way," she said, and Cane cast me a victorious look. "But it will be no easy task to face Winter kings and queens," she added. "The Beast is coming for you, Carrier. Do you understand what will happen to the believers, to this band of brothers standing with you, if you're caught by Nightflesh a time again? He will not use you as bait a second time. You will be a martyr."

I didn't want to think about that, but I nodded.

"Then I'll support you in this," she said. "Cane and I will fetch the drum. I made a deal with the Crimson King to be granted an audience, one time. I will bring that agreement to fruition for this cause. But I cannot allow Edward to go to Green for the Pines's crown."

Edward's head snapped up. The flesh around his eyes looked swollen, and I wondered if he wished she'd come to another conclusion.

"My sister is already going to the Green Kingdom for the wreath," I told them, and Zane choked.

"She's bloody what?"

"Alone?" Cane turned to me now.

"No. She went to sniff out Lucas."

Zane stifled a moan. "Great," he muttered. "She's doomed."

"Leutenski is on sabbatical." Trevor's arms tightened around himself.

"Whelp. Not anymore," I said apologetically. "I sent Kaley to get the easier sign of the two. The Crown of Pines was the only one we knew the location of for sure, and I figured Lucas would help her pull off a simple snatch-and-run. I was originally planning to go get the drum myself."

But Porethius shook her head wildly. "The Green Kingdom is on the cusp of losing the war. Your beloved sister should not be there!" Her violet eyes swam with colour. "I'll send Gathadriel to fetch her while Cane and I secure the drum, and we'll make a new plan. *Do not* go to the Green Kingdom at this time, any of you." She looked around the room.

Something sank in the pit of my stomach. The Green Kingdom was on the cusp of losing the war?

I looked at my notes on the table. My hands shook as I began scooping up the papers, shoving them back into my leather bag. I hadn't come across any evidence suggesting that the Green Kingdom might be in turmoil.

Kaley. Kaley. Kaley. Kaley.

"What of the third sign, Carrier? What do you know of the iron star?" Cane came to the table, snapping me out of my self-loathing. He leaned forward on his fists, his purple eyes swallowing me into a memory of someone else.

"I don't know where that one is," I admitted. "I know it was turned into 'fools' gold.' I know it shines but its *gleam* is an illusion. I know it was swallowed by the snowseas and is guarded by eight hands or feet, which seems weird that it's not one or the other but could be either. Kaley redrew the maps though, and the star could be anywhere. There are dozens of seas in Winter, not to mention the dunes which some maps referred to as seas."

Cane began to pace again as I gathered the rest of my notes. I hugged my packed leather bag to myself when I was finished, and the former Red Prince slumped into his chair. "It is riddlesome that the books gave you two clues you could solve, and one you could not."

It took me a moment to realize Zane had gone rigid in his chair, bright eyes glued to the floor.

My fingers kept brushing over the orb necklace at my throat, my heart silently asking it for a douse of strength so I wouldn't go bolting out into the snow and racing to the Green Kingdom myself.

"You'll never guess what your Patrolman did a quarter plus a half ago. Mr. Zane created a *costume* while you were gone," Apple said as she brushed my freshly bathed hair.

Theresa came into Apple's room carrying a tray of sizzling baked white pears with sugar and my stomach growled.

"A costume? Zane?" I reached for a pear, trying to imagine Zane fashioning his own getup. I couldn't. But when I glanced up, I realized Apple's face had fallen; she bit her lip.

I dropped the pear to my lap. "What happened?"

"Oh, friend. I'm not sure I should have said a thing," she admitted.

Theresa sighed and slid the tray onto the dresser to leave it with us. "Share your heart, love. It may bring a good tiding or three," she said to Apple. The dwarf patted my hand and left without another word.

When the door clicked shut, Apple slid the brush into her pocket.

"Well, we get the Pebble Paper delivered here every morning. Sometimes it skips a day or three, but..." She released a loud huff. "That rancid *sea-cow*—Sullen Sprit-Spellborrow—has been making dreadful claims about the believers. And with the way he so eloquently crafts his words, it's no secret who's to blame for the Red Kingdom's loathing of us." Apple pulled the brush out in a fidget and started re-brushing my wet locks. "Anyway, the *sea-cow* wrote an article about the Crimson Court's prophetess and her plans to marry a rich Red Lord in these next quarters. But that isn't the point. The prophetess was married to Mr. Zane's *father*, which puts her in a bind by Winter's rules. If she's preparing to enter into a Winter oath, the only explanation is that Mr. Zane's father must be..." The brush stilled, and I stared at Apple's reflection in the mirror.

"Dead?" I finished for her, my heart dipping cold.

"I'm afraid so." The brush began moving again; Apple's eyes were trained on my hair.

My gaze found my somber reflection. "He didn't tell me," I rasped.

"Well, that's the thing; he didn't tell *anyone*. Wanda spotted him slipping out on a cold eve after the publication, wearing a red costume. It was so riddlesome that she followed him. Your Patrolman wandered the Red Kingdom streets in disguise, right to the Hall of Knowledge. Wanda found Mr. Zane flipping through the Records of Confessions. When Wanda revealed herself, Zane admitted he was looking for a name, but had just discovered that the man he was searching for was dead. Murdered a good measure of seasons ago—by his mother."

"You're kidding me." A set of pure white eyes and a grotesque ashworm tattoo flickered through my mind.

"That's not all. It was a good thing Wanda followed him, because Jolly Cheat strolled into the Hall of Knowledge a pinch later. And as you can imagine, your Patrolman was not at his best. The two quarrelled right there in the lobby, and Mr. Zane nearly killed the court magician. Wanda had to drag Zane away before he would have been surrounded by Legionnaires. It's a miracle the Ruby Legion's elites aren't currently hunting him down for his crimes."

My jaw tightened. I wished I'd been in Winter.

"It's why Mr. Zane has that scar. It was the one hit Cheat managed to land." But Apple released a light laugh. "It seems we finally know who'd win in a true duel between Mr. Zane and Mr. Cheat. We've all been wondering."

I shook my head. "I just don't understand why he wouldn't tell me."

"He won't talk about it to anyone, I'm afraid. Wanda only told us because she feared a retaliation might be coming from Cheat."

I gripped my fingers on my lap, appalled with myself. Here I was throwing truffles, and Zane was mourning the loss of his father.

"Let's not have it spoil our day, friend," Apple said with a dark-chocolate smile. "Your hair is finished. Let me make you some tea."

Downstairs, Apple had another orange tea between my fingers in minutes, ever determined to nurse me back to health. The grayish Winter sky hovered over the skylights, stealing the glow from the main room. My fingertips buzzed in response to the ashy veil over the factory that still hadn't left, and I pressed them against my burning tea mug.

I smirked at the Patrolmen around the room; hollering, competing, and in some cases, getting on each other's nerves. Occasionally, one of them would turn and look around the main room, then pause to stare off like they realized the person they were looking for wasn't there.

My smile faded and I took an unsteady sip of my tea.

Zane sneaking into the Red Kingdom.

Believers vanishing without a trace.

I tightened my fingers around my steaming mug until they burned, accepting the pain. If I'd been here when the believers had started to disappear, maybe I could have done something. My hand found the Revelation Orb at my throat, and I tapped it.

Another group of raven-black jackets flooded in from a hall, and my eyes narrowed on a head of fuchsia hair amidst them. For the life of me, I couldn't remember the pink-haired boy's name. Tumblebee? Timblewood? Wonton?

I spent several minutes watching him while I tried to sort it out. His theatrics hadn't diminished in the slightest since last year.

"Why are you looking at Timblewon like that?"

Timblewon. That's what it was.

I turned to Zane and my eyes settled on the scar by his jaw.

"You said Timblewon used to be in the circus, right? Does the circus ever pass by here? Or is it always in the same place?" Kaley had never told me much about the Winter circus, even when I'd asked. And I'd never been able to find it on her maps.

"It just arrived over the hill a pinch away," Zane said, his blue eyes lighting. "Do you want to go?"

"Yes!" I practically shouted it. "Are we allowed?"

"Not likely, but we can sneak out as long as we're quiet. Trevor will burn my scotcher if he catches us." He grinned, dimples showing. "I promised I'd cheer you up, didn't I, Trite?"

CHAPTER

THE FIFTH

Stars peeked from a blanket of navy sky, trying to break through the ever-present wool of shadow haunting Winter's heavens. Fred's sleigh was packed; Zane, Apple, Timblewon, Wanda, Kilen, Mirkra and I had all wedged in. At first, Timblewon had insisted he shouldn't come, that the white lions would sniff him out. But Apple had been persuasive; she'd powdered his hair dark with cocoa and insisted the chocolate scent would fool the lions. She'd fixed everyone else with robes and coats, and Zane and I with large, preposterous hats—fake apples and berries sewn together with ribbons.

Apple giggled and hooted the whole way, exchanging wild banter with Wanda whose cackling howl echoed to the sky. I found myself laughing, especially when Zane mimicked Wanda's laugh twice as loud and her smile dropped.

The circus glowed below a radiant halo of stardust when

we arrived, casting visions of gold waters across the under-side of the dark clouds. Zane chucked Kilen out of the sleigh first, right into a heap of snow.

Sky-high tents bloomed up from the ground, heavy-drummed music boomed through the fabrics, and dancing elves entertained the crowds. Multicoloured, sparkling fires breathed up from glass barrels to light the paths through the circus, painting the air with turquoise, sour pink, and dusty orange.

"Ragnashuck, it's like being under a rainbow sea!" Kilen gushed, flicking a bulb-ornament.

"You've never been to the circus before?" Timblewon's cocoa-dyed brow arched.

"Never," Kilen replied. "I haven't travelled anywhere apart from my birth village, the old library, the factory, and that one time we all went to the Scarlet City and Cohen started yelling at the Ruby Legion, and then we had to fight for our lives. You remember that, right, Timbie?"

Timblewon made a face. "It's hard to forget." He shuddered, no doubt remembering the viper's bite.

"Cohen wasn't yelling at the *Ruby Legion*," Mirkra corrected. "He was yelling at the frostbit Crimson King, the Red Princes, Asteroth Ryuu, a measure of other scotchy fellows, *and* the Ruby Legion." Mirkra jabbed Zane with his elbow.

"By the sharpest wind, was there anyone you *weren't* yelling at, Mr. Zane?" Apple murmured, and Wanda snorted a laugh.

We ventured onto a misty path, warm with the fires' glow. The banter faded amidst the folds of chatter and music as we braved the metropolis of brilliantly coloured tents. I scanned the paths, the creatures, the jugglers, the musicians, the acrobats on round stages. But I looked at the shadowed corners too. My gaze travelled past open tent flaps, along narrow drapery alleys, and into the crevices of the stages most would ignore.

Apple appeared at my side with a wand of sticky bubbles—bright gold and glittering with sugar crystals. She handed it to me, keeping a metallic blue one for herself. She bit into it and blue crumbs tumbled down her chin and into the snow. "I do love this stuff. I wonder if I can make a bubblebaker-stuffed chocolate tray. It would be excellent for the village children."

My teeth cracked into the fizzy treat, and warm, sweet vanilla tickled my tongue. I nodded, "Yes, you should definitely make a chocolate tray of these." Good grief, I was in love. But the candy paused on my lips when I saw something shift in the dark behind a tent.

I turned, gazing through the sheer fabric, unsure if I was imagining the set of bright eyes and white beard. I pushed into the tent and peered into the darkness; shoulders tight.

"Have you come to see the future?" A voice tore my focus down to a table where a tattoo-faced woman eyed me. Before her, a glass ball with a roiling haze rested on a pedestal.

My gaze flickered back to the shadow behind the sheer tent, but my shoulders dropped when I saw just another hollow corner.

"Helen, what are you doing in here?" Zane cast the woman a scowl. The woman released an unfeminine sound and began to examine her nails, seeming to grasp we wouldn't be paying customers.

"Oh, um..." I took in the odd symbols dangling from strings above and the scatters of tea leaves in glass jars around the tent. "I...wasn't looking where I was going." I forced a laugh and turned to leave.

Outside, Zane eyed me as he stuffed the rest of the bubblebaker candy into his mouth.

Zane had downed three of the bubble wands before any of us had finished our first. It seemed to rush straight to his brain, and he bounced into the sky to see over the tents, his hat catapulting halfway across the circus and revealing his pecan hair for all to see. Kilen sprang after him, and it quickly became a contest to see who could jump the highest. "Save it for the records testing, sputtlepuns. We don't have our weapons," Mirkra scolded them, eyeing the crowds.

When Zane landed, I snagged his blue imperial coat and dragged him to my side to end his shenanigans. He flung an arm over my shoulder, laughing at himself and tousling his hair.

"He almost beat you, you know." I nodded to where Kilen was pushing through the crowd to play a game.

Zane's smile fell. "No, he bloody didn't."

I laughed.

"Don't be so ubbersnugged. Kilen has a top-quality mentor!" Wanda called as she kicked a wad of snow at us. Zane slapped it out of the air before it hit me.

"There's a merry show up ahead!" Kilen rushed back. "It's about to start!"

"Wait." Timblewon snagged Kilen's sleeve. "Should we be going in there?" He made a face at the big tent.

"Why ever would we decline an invitation to a show?" Apple fanned her grinning cheeks.

"It's a show put on by untrustworthy ring-hungries, that's why." Timblewon folded his arms and stood tall.

"Oh come, Mr. Timblewon. Let's have a pinch of fun before we're forced to endure more factory *meetings*," Apple rolled her eyes and pranced toward the show.

"Don't say I didn't warn you," Timbelwon muttered as he followed, but he smiled at Apple's back. I barely caught the look before he recomposed his face.

Inside the show tent, spectators squeezed into rows of satin-coated bleachers, some eating bubblebaker treats, others chewing on white-pearl candies, and still others consuming dark green strings like licorice. The crowd cheered when a man with silver-streaked black hair spun his way onto the stage. Behind him, pure-white lions waited in gilded cages. A chandelier lowered from the ceiling, and I gaped at the four slender elf women draped across it, waving with glittering smiles. When the chandelier reached the stage, the elves climbed off and danced, claret skirts billowing.

"Welcome Rime Folk, wide and tall! Come inside and be enthralled!" The dark-haired man twirled back to centre stage, and Apple squealed down the row.

"I'm your ringmaster, Sigrion Mellstellie! And you've just entered a night of fascination, enchantment, and *chaos*!" the man went on, and the crowd roared. The ringmaster pulled a glass ball from his pocket and tossed it. The ball whipped around, soaring over the seats like a wingless bird. People reached to try and catch it from the air, but it darted left and right, evading everyone.

When the ringmaster lifted his hand, the ball came back, but his eyes stayed on the crowd. His gaze narrowed, head tilting slightly.

Down the row, Timblewon sprang to his feet. "No..." The Patrolman spun to the rest of us. "He knows."

The ringmaster flicked his hand. We'd barely had a chance to register Timblewon's warning when the boy gasped like something had hit him, and suddenly, Timblewon *disappeared*.

The crowd around us gasped and clapped, but Zane, Mirkra, and Wanda jumped from their seats, Mirkra jabbing the empty space where Timblewon had just been.

"Well, what a turn of events this is," the ringmaster cooed. His fingers grappled at something in the air, and he tugged.

Suddenly Timblewon appeared on the stage, stumbling to catch his footing. His cloak was off, his disguise dissolved, his hair *fuchsia*.

"Frostbite!" Mirkra leapt over the row before us toward the stage, and Wanda tugged Kilen down the aisle by his sleeve to the exit.

"Time to go." Zane took my arm and reached for Apple, but Timblewon held up his hand at the front, halting Mirkra halfway down the rows and stilling Zane's grip on me.

The whole tent was quiet. Timblewon was still half hunched from catching himself, but he glanced up at the ringmaster.

"I thought I spotted tulip hair beneath that patchy disguise." The ringmaster's hand remained in the air; his fingers pinched together like they held a leash.

"*Patchy*?!" Apple whispered.

"What a merry trick," Timblewon said, finally standing. "Smoke and mirrors, strings and stars...You always had flair, Sigrion." For once, Timblewon's voice wasn't theatrical.

"That's what the folk remember me for. Isn't that right?" The man took a bow as people clapped again, likely assuming this was part of the show. "Same as your tulip locks. A folk like you can never hide. Not without *real* magic." The ringmaster's grin spread—too wide to be natural.

But Timblewon smiled and offered a shallow bow to the audience as well. When he came up, he lifted his hands at his sides. "I'm not you, Sigrion. I'm a good measure *better*." Suddenly Timblewon yanked his hands together and disappeared into thin air.

The ringmaster's brows furrowed. He spun once, his hand coming up to swipe at nothing.

A loud screech echoed through the tent and chatter lifted from the crowd as one of the white lion's cage doors slid open. Then another, and all the rest followed. The ringmaster spun on his heel as the lions emerged, barring their teeth, growls rumbling through the tent.

Timblewon suddenly appeared back beside Apple, and Apple screamed. He slapped a hand over her mouth and pulled her down the row toward the exit. I was hot on his heels, Zane dancing backward down the aisle, casting his electric-eyed glare at the intrigued audience. Wanda fidgeted by the tent flap; I fell into step beside her, and we broke into the cold night, the coloured smoke gliding over us. I glanced back to find Zane waiting for Mirkra. Flowery security creatures rounded the path just as Mirkra burst from the flap; Zane grabbed his shoulder and pushed him down a different path than us.

Apple craned her neck toward me. "Hurry, friend!" she called. Kilen appeared from a tent across the pathway and walked parallel to our group.

A figure shifted at the edge of the path, mostly shadowed by a tall checkerboard tent. My heels skidded to a stop. The others didn't notice—Timblewon led them around the snowy bend toward the field where we'd left Fred's sleigh.

The figure crept from the shadow, and my breathing stilled. The firelights illuminated his white beard, his droopy eyelids, and his bright, *golden* irises.

"Helen!" I heard Zane somewhere at my back.

The man with the white beard glanced behind me toward Zane's voice, then back to me. He raised his hand like the ringmaster had done, and he flicked his wrist.

It was so quick; I almost didn't feel the tether wrap my waist. My body was sucked forward like I was speeding through a straw.

I vanished.

CHAPTER

THE SIXTH

My gasp filled the air as I landed on my feet. My wide eyes looked around the cozy space.

A tent. I was still at the circus.

I turned, hands balled into fists. The navy tent fabric rippled in the breeze coming through the open flap, silver star-shaped wind chimes clattering overhead.

There the man sat, fiddling with a mechanical gadget and not even paying me any attention. The table before him was covered in metal pieces, like oddly shaped bolts and gears.

"Excuse me?" I said, snapping my fingers in front of him.

The man shot me an annoyed look past his droopy eyelids. Then he went back to his fiddling.

I huffed. "I know you saw me," I said to him. "In the Trite world. I know it was your eye; I recognize your tent."

The man only shrugged. "What of it?" He looked up

again and raised his brows.

"Uh…" I blinked. "*Why*? Aren't you even going to tell my *why* you've been watching me?"

"You tell me." The man finally put down his gadget. "I'm busy, as you can see. So. Out with it."

I made a face. Good grief. "You were watching me in my world. Not *helping*, I should clarify, just *watching*. If you're a Guard of Doors, you should at least have the decency to ask why I needed help in the first place."

The man huffed and stroked his white beard. Then he picked up the gadget again and rattled it. "I haven't been called upon to guard the integrity of the intersects in eight full seasons. Then a song rings in my ears right in the exact middle of the midday feast at my mum's seasonal birth celebration. And now, I must be dreaming a thing or three, because it seems as though you're blaming *me* for it."

"So you *are* a Guard of Doors." I stood straighter. "Did you open a door to my world?" I blurted, dropping into the chair across from his table. He picked up a tool and began twisting something on the side of the gadget.

"No. Not a full one. Just one the size of a button, really. Just big enough to see what the trouble was." The man set the gadget down and reached for a needle and some thread. "Now tell me, girl, what in the name of tooting-tootlebees do you want?"

His fingers worked as he asked, and I clasped my hands together below the table.

"Well, I want to be able to come and go between the Trite world and Winter whenever I need to. I want a door."

The man slowed his stitching. He set the needle down, and when he looked up, he blinked. "Impossible."

My chest deflated. "I'm the last Carrier of Truth in Winter. I'm—"

"Yes, yes, I know what you are." The man waved me off. "Still. Impossible. I was instructed never to get involved in personal interests. Otherwise, I could be bought off, and there are rules to uphold, you know."

"So…you're a follower of Elowin?" I asked. "Did he give you that rule?"

"It's not my place, girl." The man smacked his hand on the table. "I'm not to speak of such things, and you are not to know them."

My jaw tightened and I strangled my fingers below the table.

"Well, if you change your mind…" The man chuckled when I didn't finish the sentence.

"I know where to find you." But it was clear he never intended to come looking for me again.

"What's your name?" I asked anyway.

"Questions, questions." The man shook his head. "I'm Obb. Now, out that way, if you please. Left, then right a time or three. You'll find your way out if you keep moving and don't stop to think." He nodded toward the tent flap.

Realizing our chat was over, I reluctantly rose from my seat to follow his instructions. I glanced back at the white-bearded man before I left, but I couldn't come up with any more arguments. He was back to studying his gadget, my plight already forgotten.

"If you change your mind," I said again, interrupting his work, "please find me."

I went left on the path like Obb said. I took a few right turns, but I doubted the vague instructions would lead me out. When I took my third right, which should have taken me back to where I started, I saw what the old man's instructions were really leading me to.

Zane stood at the end of the path in his blue imperial coat, a hand holding tightly to his pecan hair. When he saw me, his greying eyes fired to life, and he broke into a jog.

"*Ragnashuck,* Trite!" he called on his way.

I thought he would be relieved to see me, but as he drew closer, I saw the scorching sparks in his eyes, and the tight twist of his mouth.

He looped his arm around my shoulders and ushered me through the twists of the circus to where the others were waiting in the sleigh. Mirkra squirmed, and Timblewon was tapping his foot against the sleigh floor. The sleigh began moving before Zane had even climbed all the way in.

Minutes into the choppy ride, Wanda and Kilen seemed to forget what had happened; they whistled in off-key harmony. Timblewon was fidgety, looking off at nothing, stealing a glance at Apple, then at Zane, then at me, then off at nothing again.

"I'm so sorry, Timblewon. I'm heartwrenched," Apple finally said. "I truly thought they'd never recognize you with my costume."

Timblewon surprised us with a laugh. Then he laughed again, louder, until he was hunched forward. The sound echoed over the hills, warming the cool night.

Mirkra laughed too, crossing his burly arms. Kilen burst into giggles, and Wanda chuckled. Apple relaxed, her dark lips pulling into a smile, and *finally* Zane—who'd been snobbish and tight-lipped the whole ride—cracked a smirk, his dimples showing.

I couldn't help myself when I saw them all howling at the Winter stars. My laughter mixed in with the choir, and I slouched back against the bench, dragging the horrendous fruit-basket hat off my head.

"How are we going to sneak back into the factory?" Kilen asked when we slid down the last hill.

"Not to worry, friends. Everyone should be in bed at this hour." Apple stole another look at Timblewon when he wasn't looking, regret flickering across her brown eyes.

But Mirkra still smiled. "Did you spot the unmerry look on the infamous Sigrion Mellstellie's face when Timblewon let the lions out?"

"I did more than that. I snatched the ashworm's pocket watch too. Look!" Timblewon yanked a bronze chain from his jacket and a heavy pendant unrolled, dangling in the moonlight.

Mirkra threw his head back and roared, driving everyone back into a melody of snorts and giggles.

But my smile melted away as I observed the snowy night flakes wandering from the heavens, adding new layers to the drifts.

Kaley would have found Lucas by now. If Lucas had agreed to go with her, they'd be arriving at the Green Kingdom soon enough.

THE

STORYTELLER

AN INTERRUPTION

A certain hum reverberated beneath the reindeer's hooves. Kaley had been listening to it for a measure of the ride until the sparse trees thickened to a congested garden of pines. Though she had never been told, she had read about a breathing song such as this one: a tune the Volumes of Wisdom affectionately called *"The Song of Winter."* She swore she had heard Helen hum it a time or three while folding socks or scrubbing a dish.

Kaley found the tune a soothing medicine for her weary bones now, and when she hushed her thoughts to listen, she imagined mountains, hills, and a message being told. She could see the bar in her mind's eye, exactly as it was in the psalm book, each note glowing as it was touched by sound:

"There's a village past this stretch of trees. It's the first of many in the Green Kingdom," Lucas interrupted her serenity. "But because I'm generous and gentlemanly and all sorts of other endearing things, I'll give you another chance to abandon this riddlesome mission of yours, and I'll offer to take you to *anywhere else* in Winter you wish to go," the youthful Patrolman promised as he slowed the deer to a stop. He dismounted and raised his arms to Kaley. But Kaley made a face at his offer and slid off the steed herself.

Lucas exhaled, "Too proud for help, Trite?" he asked. "You seemed to be implying the opposite when you showed up at my merriest brew room back there, *begging* for my assistance." He tied the deer's reigns to a branch and patted its burly rump.

Kaley eyed the creature, its prickly antlers glistening. "I needed a ride and you provided that. If you don't want to go the rest of the way with me, that's fine." To prove her indifference, Kaley marched toward the sounds of a village beyond the web of branches that shrouded them.

Lucas's fingers flashed out and caught her hand. "Ragnashuck, I never said I *wanted* to abandon you. I have a good measure of souls who'd send scotchy tidings my way if I did such a thing, including your beloved sister," he said, and Kaley's gaze flickered to him at the mention of Helen. "Just trying to change your mind before we go in."

Her stare fell to where Lucas held her hand. His did too; he grinned.

"Fine then. Come with me, but don't get in my way, Lucas Leutenski. Helen has a plan, and we need this crown." Kaley tugged her hand free, blushing a pinch.

"Yes, yes, yes. Helen's merry plan." Lucas dragged his Patrol staff from the reindeer's back and led the way into the woods. "Steal the sacred crown off a blood-hungry monarch's head. For *Helen*."

Kaley's jaw stiffened.

"Let me see if I've got this right. You're to distract Eliot Gray, steal a heavily guarded trophy, and then...?" He waited, and Kaley glared.

"It's none of your business what comes next."

"Oh, but it is." Lucas shook a finger. "I've muddled up a thing or three in seasons past by not asking questions. Which is why I'll *help you help Helen* on one condition: You need to tell me everything, even the naughty little secret you're hiding from your sister."

Kaley's wide doe-eyes flickered back to him. "I don't have secrets from Helen."

"Rubbish. It's been all over your face since we left the brew room. I'll not take another step until you tell me."

Kaley opened her mouth and closed it again. She huffed, and for a moment, she almost spoke but...nothing.

Lucas sighed. "Your beloved sister was flimsy and hungry all the time when she arrived here—a real peg out of its shell, you know. But you're different." He tapped a finger against his Patrol staff, caramel gaze flickering over her legs, her posture, her shoulders. "You're fearless. So, I'm inclined to believe you're either more of a daredevil than I am, or you're just terribly stupid."

"What? I'm not stupid. And I *am* just like Helen." Kaley stabbed her forefinger against Lucas's chest, and he winced.

"Well, I suppose. You're both mean for no reason," he muttered, rubbing the spot.

Kaley moved for the curtain of crisp vines again, but she paused when she realized Lucas had not followed. He cast her a forced smile.

She released a heavy breath and tossed her hands. "Fine! I told Helen what happened to me in the time pocket, and it changed her. It's my fault Helen is on this mission in the first place. That's why I'm here. Because I have to help her finish this to repair what I did."

Her heavy breaths steamed the forest, and the soft hums of birds flitted through the branches above. A crystal bug scurried up a trunk.

Without a word, Lucas sauntered forward and used his Patrol staff to part the pine curtain.

"Let's go steal a crown," he said.

Garland-embellished, wooden pillars were wrapped with twinkling lights throughout the village. Wreathes hung on every shop door, dripping wax candles ran along each rail with sparkling yellow flames, and rustic boardwalks weaved between each dwelling.

The boardwalks bustled with a current of creatures—humans, dwarves, and elves—many with wreaths atop their heads; some of forest branches, others of garland vines. Some had wooden armour or olive-green coats with wood toggles, and an elf passed by with branches fastened to his head like the antlers on Lucas's reindeer.

"Time for noonday-feast," Lucas announced as he slipped into the river of bodies. Kaley's pulse sputtered and she jumped in, trying to keep an eye on his raven-black uniform. But his hand came out and found hers; a warm clutch, even through his gloves.

"How will we find something to eat?" Kaley ducked to avoid a folk's swinging stick-antler.

"Not to worry, darling." Lucas latched his staff to the contraption on his back and swivelled around, brushing against coats and capes. His free hand came down to press something into Kaley's palm. She glanced down at it, and her eyes widened.

"Did you just…"

"I was a child-thief. Purchased straight from a den of ring-hungry bandits," Lucas bragged.

Kaley held up the gold ring as Lucas turned again, arms and fingers brushing scarves and pockets. "Purchased by who?" She slid the ring into her pocket, but not before Lucas displayed a handful more.

"By a sturdy, wise, cunning folk named Mikal," he explained, tossing the rings to her one by one. She missed catching the last one and it rolled away.

"Yes, I've heard about him. Helen had some good things to say about your old mentor."

"Well, she'd better have. And he wasn't just my mentor." Lucas stopped talking, the sparks leaving his eyes. He turned away, his knuckles grazing a burlap satchel as a richly dressed lady pushed past.

Kaley cleared her throat and decided on a subject change. "It's wrong to steal. You know that, right?" But she still took the four more rings he passed along.

"Oh, I'm sure the Volumes say a thing or three of that sort. But don't muddle your buttons over it; I thought you said you were fearless." His twinkle returned as he nodded toward the crowd, and Kaley slowed.

"Wait, you don't actually want *me* to…" She looked at the bustling creatures, at their pockets.

"I dare you, daredevil." Lucas bit his lower lip through his grin. "Unless you're not really fearless after all."

Kaley stopped walking. Her eyes caught a man with a large pocket coming her way. "I'll rob him," she decided, nodding.

Lucas's grin widened. "Excellent."

Kaley slowed her breathing as the man came by. Just as she lifted her fingers, Lucas stuck out his foot and the man tripped. Kaley found herself catching the folk instead, her eyes as round as saucers.

"Pinespittle…" the man cursed, not even thanking her as he regained his footing and shoved his way back into the crowd.

Lucas's laugh was loud and raspy. He slid an arm 'round Kaley's waist to weave her out of the rush.

"Stealing is wrong, Lucas Leutenski," Kaley stated as she composed herself. "I don't care what you think it proves."

"Well, frostbite. You want to eat, don't you?" He drew her to a porch where a dozen plus two candles cast traces of light against a spruce-branch awning. There, he let her go, and Kaley shuddered at the sweep of cold that came after. Scents of cooked vegetables and spices leaked from the cracked door to her right.

"Of course I want to eat," she said.

"Well quit your nattering, and I'll buy you a feast." But brassy-orange swept over Lucas's irises, and he glanced at the road. "Or perhaps we ought to scuttle back into the forest. We seem to have a pesky ashworm on our trail."

Kaley turned but saw only commotion, antlers, and green coats. "Wait…" she tried, but Lucas was already trotting down the porch stairs.

When she followed, Lucas rounded and placed a hand against her shoulder. "Stay, Trite," he whispered and pulled up his hood.

"I'm not a *peg out of its shell*, Lucas. I can keep up." Kaley's words faded when a figure appeared in the village crowd, marching headstrong in a silver, fitted, velvet jacket whose pearl buttons looked ready to pop off over his tight chest. In fact, one of Eliot Gray's buttons was missing already.

"Should we run for the trees? I bet I can outrun you," Kaley whispered in challenge.

The corner of Lucas's mouth curled but he stayed put. "I don't think so. To both."

Kaley fought the impulse to act as Eliot strutted past. She

turned her face away, and Lucas slinked around, tugging Kaley with him. His hand swiped Eliot's pocket, and their mutual foe did not bat an eye.

The pair moved in silence down the road, past the veil of pine ivy, and back into the forest.

Kaley sighed in relief as Lucas turned and splayed his hands to show all that had been in Eliot's pocket. A pearl button rolled around amidst the collection of lint, rings, two brass tins, and a crumpled paper.

"I guess we know he wasn't carrying any weapons." Kaley reached for the button and laughed as she held it up. "Should we hold this ransom? Tell him he won't be able to wear his stupid coat anymore unless he leaves us alone?"

Lucas grinned, but the smile fell away when he unwrinkled the paper and read its contents. "Ragnashuck," he whispered. And with a flick of his wrist, he had the paper folded back up and tucked away in his own pocket.

"What was that?" Kaley tossed the button into the snow.

"It's not a thing," Lucas swore, shaking his gloves to rid himself of the rest of Eliot's pocket-contents—except for the two brass tins. He raised one to study it.

Kaley tilted her head. "Why don't you want me to see that paper?" She tried to lunge for his pocket, but Lucas caught her 'round the waist and spun, wicked smile returning.

"It's a secret for now, Trite."

Kaley pushed him off. "I thought we decided to air out all our dirty laundry back there," she said.

Lucas made a repulsed face. "Air out our what?"

"It's an expression. It means we decided to keep things out in the open. What's on that note?" she asked again. "Does it involve me?"

A twitch of his mouth. Another of his left eye. "No."

Kaley drew back. "What does Eliot Gray want with *me*?"

"Well, I'd like to have my frostbit *things* back, for starters." Kaley and Lucas jumped at Eliot's voice booming through the trees.

Kaley pressed a hand against her settling heart as she took in Eliot's dark, furrowed brows and his mouth tipped down in an ugly scowl.

"Apologies, Gray. She threw your button over there." Lucas nodded in the general direction.

But Eliot's eyes sank to murky blue. "Give it back, Leutenski."

"Hmm," Lucas thought about it. Then, "*No.*"

Kaley looked between the two and backed away a pinch.

"I'd fancy a quarrel," Eliot said, gripping a Patrol weapon he had not been carrying before, and Lucas smiled.

"At last." But Lucas's jests turned cold as his eyes dipped to rust. He unhooked his staff from his back. "For Mikal," he added, and Eliot's hard face drained of colour.

"Leutenski...I didn't have anything to do with the unmerry tidings that befell Mikal." Eliot's words had less steam now.

"Scrape his name from your tongue." Lucas's staff exploded with silver hairs of ice. "We'll settle this as Patrolmen. We'll settle this the way *my* mentor would have proposed."

Eliot's shoulders tightened. "*Fine.*" Icicles grew from his weapon too.

"First to drop the other in the snow?" Lucas proposed.

"First to draw blood," Eliot countered, and Lucas's topaz gaze narrowed. "And you'll wish you'd given me my belongings back when I asked."

"What's the prize? Your creepy letter?" Lucas braced himself on his heel.

"The prize is a visit with Helen."

Kaley's attention fired to the curly-haired ex-Patrolman. "You're not going anywhere near my sister."

"That's all I want. I'll take nothing less."

"Ragnashuck, I guess I'd better win, then. And when I do," Lucas cut in, "you must stay far away from *both* Trites."

Eliot's face changed. "For how long?"

"For the remainder of your unmerry timestring. *Forever.*"

Eliot's Patrol staff dipped, and he raised a flat hand. "Wait. I cannot agree to that."

"*You* raised the stakes."

"No, Lucas. You don't understand—"

"That's him!" A new voice entered the woods, and an elk-antlered woman pointed at Lucas with a crooked finger. "That's the sputtlepun who stole my rings!" Ten plus one men blocked the path back to the village. They wore long, emerald capes and wood armour with silver axes and tight-strung bows in their grips.

"Well. Frostbite," Lucas muttered, and the ice slithered back into his Patrol staff.

The men's eyes fastened on Lucas as they came, but Eliot rushed between them, a single finger raised, nose in the air.

"Halt. I demand it," he said, and the soldiers slowed. "I am an emissary for the Second King of the East. I'm expected at Timber Castle in an hour or three, so I forbid you from arresting my guardsman and…guardslady. A simple apology from my sticky-fingered guard should do, even if his actions are," Eliot risked a glare at Lucas, "revolting."

The woods turned quiet, and Eliot raised a brow at Lucas.

It took Lucas a pinch. "Oh…" he said when he realized his part to play. "Yes. I apologize. Though, unmerry lady, you should consider carrying your rings in a satchel next time, not in your wide open, gaping *pocket*—"

"There you have it. Now, the snow globe has been shaken, so we'll scuttle off now before the storm rolls in," Eliot stated.

"*You* are the emissary for the Second King of the East?"

one of the men asked, tapping a large finger against his axe and eyeing Eliot's expensive coat. "You do not look like a folk of the East."

"I *am* the emissary. My guardsman is carrying the two tins of frankincense I was given by the Second King as gifts for the Queen of the Pines." Eliot's words were clipped, and Lucas reluctantly reached into his pockets to produce the brass tins.

"How about a personal escort to the castle, then?" the man said. Men moved in and took Lucas and Kaley by their arms as Eliot fumbled through an indecipherable protest.

CHAPTER

THE SEVENTH

The last time I spoke to my brother, Winston, was Christmas Eve last year. He hadn't been with us for Christmas day, he hadn't been there to receive his blanket knitted by Theresa, he hadn't come home for Christmas supper. In fact, he hadn't come home at all.

The last words he'd said to me before he disappeared into the night on Christmas Eve were, *"Stay away from me."*

I thought he was just in a bad mood and was annoyed that I'd been right about Winter. I didn't realize that when he told me to stay away, he meant, *"Don't follow me. Don't come looking for me."*

For the first few weeks I'd been restless. I looked around for him at school, but I never saw him there. I risked my own humiliation by approaching his friends to see if they knew where he was, but they'd scowled at my proximity and told me they hadn't seen him, either. So, I'd hustled over to the police station, and I'd tried to explain to a chubby police detective that my brother was missing. The man—*Jeffrey Stromer*—had the audacity to roll his eyes. He'd said, *"You Bells always seem to have someone missing."*

I didn't know what he was talking about, but when he flipped open a box of jelly doughnuts and started eating them in front of me while I was still talking, I decided he was the most useless detective in the world. After I left, I tried not to think about how much his words stung. Yes. We were a family who had started as five, but who would always have someone missing. Then, for a while it was two *someones*. Now, it was three.

So, in September, when I saw a boy with shaggy, blond hair and a tacky guns-crossing neck tattoo at the end of the junk food aisle in the grocery store, I felt a fireworks show of emotions: relief, worry, confusion, anger.

Winston had a new girlfriend—she hung off his arm with half-closed eyes and I tried not to cringe at how they both teetered. Winston stared blankly at the chip options for a solid two minutes before he came to his senses and grabbed one.

I thought about approaching him. I imagined confronting him for bailing on us at Christmas, and for never coming back. Because for someone who spent so much of his childhood angry about how our father had left us, I wanted to point out that he'd done the *exact same thing*.

I'd abandoned my half-filled shopping cart, left the grocery store, and drove back to Syliva's in silence.

That was the moment I realized I'd lost Winston for good.

I sipped a steaming mug of hot chocolate at the breakfast table as I scanned the Pebble Paper: Prince Forrester and Lady Holly Kissing had an upcoming engagement party, Prince Driar was coming to the end of his research trip in

Polar Territory, the Crimson Queen was extending her vacation, *again*. Zane found me when I was halfway through the last page.

A glass plate piled with my favourite chocolates—smooth mint, white-vanilla-stuffed frosting, butternut crunch—slid out in front of me, pulling my attention from the paper.

When I glanced up, Zane was folding his arms.

"What's this?" I nudged the plate, trying not to get too excited about the butternut crunch candies.

"It's a bribe, Trite."

Suddenly the butternut seemed less thrilling. "A bribe for what?"

Zane slid into the chair beside me, his hickory hair falling out of place, his knuckles rapping the tabletop in a fidget. I felt like I was back in the detective's office, being assessed by jelly-filled Jeffrey Stromer.

"Something is still bothering you. I was going to wait until you were ready to tell me yourself, but I can sniff it on you, Helen. Trust me, you're even less inconspicuous this season, which I didn't think was possible."

I set the newspaper on the table.

"Why did you really want to go to the circus?" he asked.

I bit my lips. "I don't know what you're—"

"Oh, come on, Helen. You weren't running away from that bearded man. I watched you *let him* take you. Who is he?"

When I didn't reply, Zane slid the plate of treats back to himself where I couldn't reach, and my jaw dropped.

"That man is no one. I wanted something from him, but he couldn't help me." Before Zane could retaliate, I grabbed a butternut crunch candy and shoved it in my mouth.

Zane huffed. "I thought we learned not to keep secrets from each other. The last time you shut me out, you got bitten by an ashworm snake-prince."

I bit my tongue so I wouldn't bring up what Apple had

told me about Zane's secret visit to the Red Kingdom.

"The circus was a mistake, and I shouldn't have asked you to bring me." I glanced down at the table and pushed the Pebble Paper aside with my knuckle. I was done with it anyway. "Thank you for the chocolates, but I'm *fine*." I lifted my gaze to prove it, and I smiled. "I'm fine."

"You're a scotchy liar, Trite."

I threw up my hands. "How about you tell me how *you're* doing, Zane? Let's start with that."

He folded his arms and leaned back a little. "This isn't about me."

"Sure it is. You go first." I tried again, and his jaw hardened.

"I'm fine."

The silence that followed was crisp with cheery background noise and brick-solid willpower. Finally, Zane reached over and tugged the Revelation Orb necklace from beneath my shirt. He studied the glass ball and sighed.

"I suppose we're being petty with everything that's going on," he said.

I glanced past him to where Patrolmen were packaging chocolates with Apple. I looked down at my hands, then at the orb in Zane's fingers.

"Do you think the believers could use a reminder of the Truth?" I asked. "If we're waiting for Gathadriel to bring back Kaley, and for Cane to get the drum, shouldn't we be doing something to *help*?"

Zane's shoulders relaxed and he dropped the orb back to my chest. "I thought you'd never ask. I'll take you to Wentchester Cove if it'll help you shake whatever unmerry thing that's got you muddled."

Joy filled my chest at the thought of putting a message of hope across the smokey Winter skies. "How far is it? I want to be back here when Kaley arrives."

"It's a good measure closer than the last time." He cracked a smile. "I can have us there and back in a pinch."

"Perfect. Should we bring more Patrols?"

"Halt your scotcher, Trite." Zane stood. "I said I'd take you, but Porethius will never let us scuttle off with the Beast on the hunt," he said, and I stood too.

"So how do we get her to change her mind?"

"We don't," he shrugged. "She and Cane are leaving in an hour or three to go to Red. We'll sneak out as soon as they're gone, but you and I will be doing this alone."

PART 111

A Measure of Seasons Ago...

Once upon a Winter's eve
A young Red Prince was vastly naive
With cruel jests and the sweetest of tunes
He sang his own praises in sugary croons

Only one girl did not applaud him as great
And for it, he chased her out the iron gate
But when she was gone, the prince felt alone
He secretly wished that she might come home

On the cool Winter's eve before the prince broke
He lost his cruel heart to a great bout of smoke
To get his heart back, the prince had to be clever
"Fetch five golden rings or lose it for forever."

But on his great quest, the prince learned a thing
'Twas a thing that thwarted him and lost him a ring
The mean Red Prince was forced to change his song
Or live without a heart, and never truly belong

The clever prince battled wind, wall, and wave
And with hope in hand, he stole his heart from the grave
And when he returned; stale, princely heart beating
He found the girl he had hated for leaving

And so, after all his conflict and follies
The prince kissed the girl beneath a bough of hollies
But before the girl turned to look upon his face
The prince with a heart disappeared without a trace

THE

STORYTELLER

THE NEXT INTERRUPTION

Presently...

C ane considered himself a clever fellow—the cleverest of his brothers, in fact.

Of his siblings, Tegan had been the bully.

Forrester had been the quiet, cruel one.

Quinten had been the manipulative tattletale.

And Driar...Oh, how Cane did not want to think of Driar now. The young Red Prince who loved books more than his own family might have enjoyed the journeys Cane had found himself on—reading, studying and consuming ancient texts. Cane was a pinch relieved Driar was not at the Red Palace when he and Porethius arrived, for Driar was the one brother

Cane had struggled to leave.

The rest of the unmerry band of nattery whipsteamers Cane had wished good riddance to on his way out the door.

Cane spun the ring on his forefinger as he and his fairy were led through the palace halls, smoky with dark dreams and twisted memories, where false prophets crept through the basement and a gluttonous court feasted on truthspire and misplaced hope. He twisted and twisted and twisted the ring a time again, until Porethius reached over and slapped his hand.

"Kingsblood," Cane cursed in a low tenor so the Ruby Legionnaires might not hear. "It's not my fault it muddles my buttons to be in this dreadful palace." Though, it was his fault. All the fruity faults were his. "He won't give us the drum," Cane added now that they were talking. "As soon as the king realizes we want it, it'll become a bargaining tool. The cost for us will be high in the end."

"I'm certain it will be," Porethius said.

"You might not enjoy what he asks for," Cane returned.

The fairy stopped walking, bringing the Legionaries to a halt, also.

"What is it? Better to be out with it now, Plum. You'll be trapped in silence the moment we're through those repulsively decorated doors."

Porethius blinked a time or three. "I'm not certain. The Winter wind has changed directions."

Cane sighed. "*Perfect.*"

The fairy resumed, followed by the once-prince, and behind him the Legionnaires, until the tetrad passed through the doors that were, in fact, overdone with gaudy decorations. They came before the Crimson King and Cane sent his burgundy eyes to the tile floor. He had thought it would be a private meeting, but it seemed his once-father had other plans. The throne room was a packed pen of pudgy, Red-painted nobles ogling at Cane in his black mask.

Upon the dais, each of Cane's brothers rested in their

thrones apart from the empty throne of Driar, and one for the absent queen who was rumoured to have been on a mysterious holiday for nearly two full seasons. Cane's throne had been removed, along with Quinten's. How much smaller the line of the royal family looked now.

"This meeting makes my deal with you complete, fairy. I'm to host the Crimson Court soon. I will not keep them waiting." The Crimson King's voice carried the roughness of his seasons, a sound cracking at the edges. 'Twas a voice that had disciplined Cane with iron and ferocity in his early seasons; one Cane had heard command enemies to their deaths more times than he could count.

"I come in search of a special drum whose rhythm makes the Winter snow dance. I think you know it." Porethius got right to it.

The king's glower sharpened on the pair—Cane's hair was stained cocoa, and he wore a hood to cast his masked-face in shadow, but even so, he cringed under the scrutiny of the king until it settled back on Porethius. The king and the fairy chatted a measure more, but their words dropped from Cane's awareness when a door opened across the room, and in walked Scarlet Strange.

Or, as they called her now in this dreadful palace, *Holly Kissing*.

The obsession of his childhood paused her step when she saw him standing in the middle of the throne room. He knew she recognized him; he could not breathe.

A braid of honey-gold locks rested aside her neck, smooth and lovely. Too treacherously lovely. A lovely girl who was betrothed to Forrester.

Cane tore his stare away. He glanced to where Forrester sat in his second-prince's seat, bored. The ivory-haired *bear of battle* looked deadly, even while he sat doing nothing at all.

"…and what can I offer you in exchange for a glimpse of this ancient drum? I have myrrh, pirate loot, rubies, or rings," Porethius was saying.

The Crimson King leaned back in his throne. "I do not need more riches. My wish is the same as it was in the season past. I wish for you to join me in my war against the Evergreen Host. I wish for you to fight for *me*."

"My assignment is elsewhere." Porethius did not bat an eye.

"To which Winter king do you belong?" the king challenged. "I shall pay you more than he."

At that, Porethius went quiet, and Cane shifted at her side.

"We serve the King who once owned the drum. Perhaps you've heard of him? Elowin, *King of Truth*," he blurted.

Whispers erupted through the throne room; the Red Princes leaned in closer. Though it would ruffle Porethius's delicate, violet wings, Cane went on, "And if you will not suggest a *reasonable* deal, we will come back with another offer," Cane added, lowering his voice lest his sound be recognized. "Please allow us to stay a short measure while we sort it out."

Porethius's head tilted toward the once-prince, her expression alone reminding him that it was not her plan to stay.

But the Crimson King let out a merry, raspy laugh. "Don the ancient yuletide carols!" he invited the bandsmen with sinister, dark purple eyes. "We're to have guests who represent the Dead King!" Then to Porethius, he said, "Yes. I should very much like you to *stay*."

"We cannot be here overnight," the fairy whispered to Cane.

"Then I suppose we'd better come up with something to trade before the eve arrives," Cane whispered right back.

Porethius and Cane bowed as Legionnaires came to escort them away. They were led from the throne room, down a hall or three.

When they rounded a corner, Cane spotted a lock of honey hair in the mirrors' reflection. "I'll meet you in the guest chambers," he said to Porethius.

"*Cane*," Porethius warned, but Cane had already slipped into a servants' tunnel.

He waited until the girl came 'round the hall's corner. Then, he swung open the door, took her wrist, and tugged her in with him.

The slat metal door slapped shut and Cane tore off his mask.

Scarlet Strange mimicked a rigid, porcelain statue.

"Hello." He smiled, handsomely.

"You shouldn't be here," she said, though it did not sound like a threat.

"You should not be here either, Scarlet."

"Don't call me that," she whispered. "Why are you trying to get to that drum? You know it's behind lock and key until the Red Holiday."

"I need it." Cane swallowed his nerves. "Help me," he added.

Scarlet's brassy eyes tightened. "Help you, what?"

"Help me get it. And then I'll scuttle off and you'll never have to see me again for the remainder of your timestring."

The metal door swung open, and an elf trudged in with a stack of baskets. Scarlet froze to the wall, but Cane tilted his head, trying to recall the elf's name. "Shnuckle," he guessed. The elf paused, blinking in surprise. The creature glanced back toward the hall, then at Cane a time again, and with a dip of his head, he whispered, "Your Highness."

The elf continued down the tunnel with his baskets, and Cane released a breath.

"Kingsblood," Scarlet breathed. "You've been discovered, and I've been discovered with you!" she chided.

Cane cracked his beautiful smile. "You have a lot to learn, Scarlet—"

"I said, don't *call me that*."

"—the first thing being that a measure of the servants here are still loyal to *me*."

Scarlet Strange stared at the once-prince for a long, heart-thumping measure. She lifted off the wall and exited the servants' tunnel without glancing back.

CHAPTER

THE EIGHTH

This past summer, I realized I'd forgotten my wallet on my way to meet Kaley and Emily at our café. I didn't think it would be a big deal to run back and grab it from Sylvia's house, but lucky for me, it started to pour. And when I say pour, I mean the sky split open and unleashed a furious ocean of tears upon Waterloo.

I was drenched when I finally stopped my ridiculous rain-run and jogged up some stairs to hide beneath an awning. I was leaning back against the brick when I realized the windows were stained-glass. Remnants of good memories bleeding together with bad ones rose to the surface, until a guy with a black umbrella trotted up the stairs too.

"Hey," he said, closing his umbrella and shaking it out.

I looked both ways. "Do I know you?" I'd asked.

The boy shrugged and patted rain off his shoulders. "Don't think so."

"Then why'd you follow me up here?" I crossed my arms, stifling a shiver.

The guy stopped. A slow grin spread across his face.

"You must not be part of this congregation." He nodded to the doors at my back.

I blinked. Then I turned to look at the building.

Good grief, it was a church—an old, architecturally stunning cathedral I'd somehow never paid attention to until now, even though I must have walked past it a hundred times on my way downtown.

"Uh...no. I'm not part of this congregation." I apologized. "I'm not homeless or anything. I was just trying to get out of the rain."

He laughed. "I didn't think you were. I'm Stephen and I work here." He smiled again. "And you're welcome to come inside. I have coffee."

My breathing wavered as I tried to deduce whether he was just being nice to a stranger or if he was trying to flirt. I realized he had to be a few years older than I thought if he worked here.

"No pressure," he added when I didn't reply right away. He pulled out a set of keys and turned the lock in the doors, then hauled one of them open.

Inside the building, I saw pale wood structures scattered across the unlit rooms: pews, balconies, and a platform at the front. The stained-glass windows lined the walls of the sanctuary, and colourful paintings crawled over a domed ceiling. I realized I was holding my breath. The sight came with a flood of warm feelings, feelings I knew were from another place. And I found myself answering before I could change my mind.

"Sure. I love coffee."

Zane raced the wind; my hair spun into knots as I held on, wishing this was all we ever had to do. The quivering, grayish sky stretched for miles; new clouds toiling with an oncoming storm, growling with heavy wind in their sails. I watched it warily.

When the storm thundered in and drowned us in a sea of white, Zane ducked into a cave. After digging a handful of caramels from the Patrol bag, he said, "Now, tell me why you wanted to go to the bloody circus."

Icy air swept in. When I shuddered, Zane dragged over dry branches from around the cave and tossed them into a pile.

"Come on, Helen, out with it. I'll be up all night if you don't tell me, and trust me, I'll pitch snowballs at you from across this cave until first light if that's the case."

"What do you want me to say?" I asked. "I missed you. There, happy?" He slowed his movements, flicking twigs into the fire and blowing on the flame to spread it. A moment later, he dropped down to sit across from me.

"I missed you too," he said.

"I missed you...*way* worse." It sounded like a lame joke, but I wasn't smiling. "Didn't you struggle with being separated this year? You sure seemed like you wanted to be spared from it when you asked me to stay in Winter with you."

A drizzle of snow brushed across the cave floor. Zane studied my hair, eyes, mouth...When he dropped his gaze to the twig between his fingers, disappointment sank through me.

"Helen," he whispered, tearing brittle pine needles from the twig, "you can't blame me for wanting you to stay here. I'll always want you to stay. That will never change."

I unclasped my hands and leaned back on my palms, biting my lips together.

"What?" he asked, brows tugging in. "Ragnashuck, I've muddled your mood again, haven't I?" He picked up his Patrol staff. "What did I do *now*?" He tossed a handful of snow at the cave wall and lifted his staff. The snow spiralled like a flock of butterflies that evaporated and sprinkled me with snow.

"I don't care that you want me to stay. I care that I have to choose a side to stay on at all," I said.

His face changed. "What do you mean?"

"That man at the circus was a Guard of Doors. I wanted him to make me a door."

I watched paleness bleach his cheeks. "You bloody what?" Zane scrambled to his knees. "You *can't*, Helen. If Elowin has closed a door, you're not supposed to try and force it open!"

"How do you know Elowin doesn't want me to have a door?"

"If he wanted you to have one, he would have opened one."

"He did open one!" I sprang to my feet, kicking snow. "And *Kaley* went through it. So now, I need to stop Night-flesh before something happens to her. That's why I need a door; so I'm not stuck on the other side every time I need to be here!"

Zane looked struck. "Helen...you can't. If it was an option, I would have done it by now."

I sighed, and an untimely laugh escaped me. "Let's just forget it." I scrubbed my eyes and slumped back to sit. "I'm too tired to deal with this right now."

Zane's lips twisted like he'd eaten something sour. It brought my gaze to his mouth, and when I didn't find anything else to look at, a slow smile spread across his face. A blush soaked mine. I forced my eyes back up to his and kept them there. "Do you want me to kiss you, Trite?" he asked. "Will that make you better?"

"What?" I scrambled to reposition my legs. "No. That's not what I was..."

His smile grew, irises lighting. Zane dropped his Patrol staff and leaned forward, bringing his face before mine. I stopped breathing but he waited, mouth hovering, his lashes nearly brushing me. "You do want me to, but you also don't," he said. He bit his lip and pulled back, draping an arm over his knee. The space between us felt like a cavern that had appeared too fast.

"Good grief, Zane. I never said I wanted you to do that." I hugged my arms to myself.

"You're all wishwashy." Zane tapped his fingers on his legs. "I'll kiss you when I know you want me to, Helen. That's a Winter promise."

I huffed. "You're so..."

His dimples appeared with his smile. "I certainly hope so. I'd hate to make things too easy for you, grumpy Trite."

I reached to shove him off balance, but he snatched my wrist and tickled inside my elbow. I released an unfeminine shriek-laugh before tearing my arm away.

"You're frustrating too, Helen Bell," he said. "You don't know the half of it."

A pair of snow rabbits rolled from beneath a log when we emerged from the cave the next morning. They grinned, eyeing our backpacks with their greedy blue eyes.

"What are we going to do if we get to the key room and it's guarded by an army?" I asked Zane as we trudged over snow-dusted logs and rocks.

"I suppose we'll turn back." He tugged on his gloves as we walked, glancing up at the hazy heavens. A moment later, he extended a hand to me. "Enough walking."

After hours of gliding over white dunes, things started looking familiar. I could almost hear Mara Rouge's snow-pups howling from Wentchester Cove, the gnomes clashing their weapons against their armour.

I shuddered when we reached the valley. I forced myself to face it—the cove where it all began for me. But I blinked.

"It's empty," I said.

Zane eyed the landscape; the pillars, the glassy rink, the beige cliffside. "Maybe the Beast doesn't believe this place is a threat anymore."

"Well, he's wrong," I said and began marching down the slope into the valley. The warmth of my orb promised as much.

The glassy ice crunched beneath our boots. There were so many things I wanted to say about this place, but we walked in silence, each reliving our own nightmares and victories. Halfway across the rink, Zane took my hand.

My Patrolman stopped in the tunnel's entrance, but I kept moving, anticipating the large, golden sun-orb bursting to life in the key room. I couldn't wait to feel its glorious message sink into my skin. After the year I'd had, I *needed* a win.

Zane caught up as I swept through the curtains. I smiled and breathed in the fragrance of life, flora, and unity, studying the hundreds of Carrier names on the walls as I pulled off my necklace. This was for them.

"I think we should get back to the factory," Zane said, glancing back at the tunnel with a peculiar face. I slid my orb into the nearest key slot just as the next word cracked from his mouth, "*Wait!*"

Frazzled, I tore the orb back out, but it was too late.

The golden sun burst with light, just like I'd imagined. But it *flickered*.

My hand tightened around my orb. The golden sun blinked out, then sank to dark black like molten ink. "W…what's it doing?" I breathed, raising my orb. A crack popped upon the surface of the glass, a spear of smoke digging its way in. The gold and ivory retaliated, trying to smother it out.

"What did I do?" I croaked, dragging it against my chest.

The cave walls began to twist like an illusion of mirrors. The names carefully penned over so many years began to melt, their ink dripping down the walls. Flames burst from the sun, slashing at whatever names remained like they were crossing them off a list.

Zane grabbed me and tore into the tunnel. "It's him!"

Ice needled from his Patrol staff as an eruption rattled the room behind us. "*Run!*" he shouted, and I gasped. Smoke rushed from the key room curtains, turning like a giant snake head and slithering after us.

Snow flew in from the tunnel entrance like birds pumping their wings and fused together to create an ice-wall at our backs, but the smoke split into three tentacles and leapt around it.

It got Zane first; a hand of smoke coiled around his neck and smothered his eyes. His Patrol staff clattered to the ground, and I screamed. He was dragged into the blackness; I grabbed his Patrol staff and slashed at the smoke.

My Revelation Orb burned with light, and I shouted at the darkness, "Let him *go!*" Heat filled my veins and I tossed the Patrol staff to go in, following Zane's anguished shouts.

The orb was a lamp in the storm, illuminating my path until I found him shuddering on the ground. I grabbed Zane's arms and dragged him with me as cracking echoed down the tunnel.

Zane tried to help; he clambered to his feet and stumbled along, running into me. I could hear his raspy breaths. I grabbed his arm and pulled it over my shoulders to guide him, shuffling step by step. His other arm wound around my waist until his toe hit his Patrol staff. He fumbled to scoop it up.

Boulders caved in around us; flames erupted out of nowhere. I jogged for the light at the tunnel's end, putting every ounce of gusto I possessed into pulling Zane with me.

We shot out the tunnel's mouth and fell into the snow as the cliff crumbled, loose rocks tumbling in every direction. I scrambled back, yanking Zane's jacket so he'd follow. He fumbled behind me as we put distance between ourselves and the exploding mountain.

When we stopped, panting, I turned to see the cliffside of Wentchester Cove spill in, crushing the remnants of the key room to dust and exploding into a mass of flames. I glanced over at Zane and found him...*not* watching it.

He stared straight ahead, blinking, crawling back on wobbly limbs. His gloved hand came against his face, feeling his cheeks, his eyelids. Still staring off at nothing.

"Zane," I whispered as the last of the roaring cliff began to hush. "Are you..."

His head tilted in my direction, and I swallowed at the absence of electricity in his eyes. Just pale irises remained, and moisture in the corners. "Trite..." he said. His hand came out in my direction, not finding me.

My stomach tightened, and I crawled over.

Zane wasn't quite looking at my face, but I felt his spirit reaching out. The tune that normally sailed from his heart was quiet, like a music box that had been stomped upon. My Patrolman felt around for my wrist. He slid his hand up my arm when he found it, and he clutched my bicep.

"I can't see," he rasped.

Zane would have heard the grinding of rocks, and he would have felt the flying pebbles. But he didn't see the last breath of the cliff. Only I had witnessed the death of Wentchester Cove.

I didn't know the way back to the factory. It was going to take days to get back to the others on foot with me whispering landmarks in Zane's ear.

My Patrolman gripped me with one hand, and his Patrol staff with the other, holding it ahead to bump against uneven spots on the path. With verbal directions alone, he steered us toward the nearest village in between raspy coughs.

"Which inn should we go to?" I whispered as we inched over a cobbled road. Dusk has swept over the village, transforming the hazy sky to charcoal. Strings of flickering lights dangled from branches curling over the street, slipping down like glowing vines. The tallest elves brushed them aside to avoid walking into them. The street was mostly empty, but those who walked it wore red.

"It doesn't matter. Pick one." Zane reminded me of a cracking marble statue without the spark in his eyes, the flush in his cheeks, or the vibrance in his words. In fact, with his pale irises, he looked like...

I swallowed. He looked like his *mother*.

A carriage crunched over the ice-patched street. As it passed, I caught a glimpse of metal cages filled with snow rabbits. The creatures' ears were wilted as they huddled together, their mouths tipped into frowns. It was the first time I felt an ounce of remorse for the obnoxious little critters and my gaze followed the cages until they disappeared around the bend.

I guided Zane to the nearest inn. A collection of bells sang when I pushed the door open, and the spicy scents of citrus and holly berries engulfed us. Candles rested atop a long beam-countertop where a Red elf was sorting room keys.

"I'd like a room, please." My request brought her head up from her work. She looked at me oddly, at my dull Trite eyes. But she nodded and picked up a key. I reached for it, but she drew it back, laying her other hand flat. I was a breath away from offering to clean her lobby as a trade for payment when Zane slipped his arm from me and drew a satchel from his pocket.

"How many rings?" he asked the elf, then coughed.

The elf looked us up and down. "Ten plus six," she decided, revealing a cringingly high voice.

"*Ten plus six?*" I objected.

But the elf shrugged, bunching her puffed sleeves. "Our taxes to the Red Kingdom were raised this quarter past. Bad tidings befall us all."

"This is all I have. Take it," Zane said, handing the woman the satchel. The elf raised a brow, but she grabbed the satchel and stuffed it into her dress pocket. With one last look down her nose, she slid a copper key with a threaded ticket over the wood counter. I scooped it up, biting back my complaints.

Zane linked his hand through mine, and I guided him past the lobby and down the hall until I found our room.

The room was the size of a closet. There wasn't enough space for one of us to lay on the narrow bed and another to lay flat on the floor. A chair took up the corner, and when Zane realized what it was, he slumped down into it, padding his hand along the wall to find a place to rest his Patrol staff.

"Don't be ridiculous. You take the bed," I said to him.

When he smiled—the first smile since we left Wentchester Cove—it warmed my whole body. "Helen, I've learned that you turn into a grouchy polar creature when your mind is muddled. Go to bed, Trite. I'll wake you if I hear anything troublesome."

There was no way I'd sleep a wink after what happened, but I knew he would argue me to death over it, so I sat on the bed to pull off my boots and laid back on the mattress. "It smells like dust and claustrophobia in here."

Zane was resting his mouth against his fist, but I saw his smile spread past his knuckles. I tilted to study him. "You don't seem upset about what happened," I added.

His smile did slide away then. He shifted in his seat and folded his hands on his lap. "I'm unmerry enough for the both of us," he admitted.

The chain of my necklace rattled as I lifted my orb, studying the crack in the glass where a smoky stain had scorched it. The ivory and gold toiled, restless.

"It's a sign," Zane said. "Nightflesh is trying to get in—the way he got into the Cove. The way his blackness got into your orb."

"It's a sign he's trying to get into what?"

"He's trying to get into *you*, Helen," Zane said. "He's burned the Volumes, the library, the key room, and the hope in most of Winter's villages. You're the last thing he needs to stop the Truth from spreading."

THE

STORYTELLER

THE FIFTH INTERRUPTION

A Measure of Seasons ago...
(Twenty plus five, to be precise)

It was an unofficial crime in the Green Kingdom to *not* hoot and holler and fuss over the banquets. Young Edward Green knew as much, yet he often could not find himself lured in by the sugary nectar drizzled over hot, roasted bird, or the cooked citrus slices layered upon the sizzling forest boar. The fermented ciders did not entertain him, and the heaps of smoked sausages dunked in olive butters did not get a second glance from the young prince, either.

The spoon between his fingers felt colder than the frost outside where the royal family dined at the long, lumber table along with the Council of Pines. The place settings stretched further into the forest than Edward could see, and he often wondered how long it took the servants to prepare such large feasts at every sunrise and sunset, and how they kept the birds from swooping in to eat it all before the guests arrived.

The king was a large man, as muscled as any Green huntsman. His dark beard dipped into his steaming berry soup with every bite, and Edward winced. The King of the Pines was praised by the inner-woods cities but hated by the villagers beyond. Though, in the king's defense, the man hadn't a clue how the villages felt about things.

Across the table, Edward's sister laughed at the gory stories—ones of hunting and slaying large animals, of tracking the snowsquatches, and of the iron-clashing war on their kingdom's brink that never slept. Ever Green was not shy or unsure like Edward; she kept her chin high and her eyes bright, her laugh loud and her skin thick.

"To the King of the Pines! May his victory in the Silver Jubilee Renewal tomorrow change the course of the war!" The general's wooden armour clapped at his elbows. Edward tasted bile in his throat as fifty soldiers plus five raised their glasses of fermented cider and cheered for the king, who bellowed a laugh and raised his own glass to himself too. Cups were smashed down the table, bits of glass or clay spilling away into the grassy forest carpet. All were certain their king would still be alive after tomorrow.

But Edward twisted in his seat, his eyes flickering past the gingerbread sculptures dotted with mint twists, and he found his sister across the table, cheering along with the men. What would it do to Ever if the king did not live through the Renewal? What would it do to all of them?

Edward excused himself; rising with the grace of a young prince, but his feet were cold, his heart heavy, and his mind pulling in a multitude of directions. He fastened his cloak and slipped away from the banquet, unnoticed by the Evergreen Host soldiers at the table.

He moved quietly through the curtains of silver-bell

studded garland and from there, the prince chased the wind through the trees.

The Silver Jubilee Renewal would arrive at noon whether Edward was ready for it or not. Two kings would fight until only one lived, and Edward would either be forced to become one of the youngest kings in the history of the Pines, or he would be able to stay a prince for a measure longer.

Sweat clung to his neck when he arrived at his destination, where patches of ice floated on the ever-rippling waters of the Fountain of Wishes. He pulled down the hood of his cloak and watched the clear waters swirl in the bowl. The statue of the white bird in the centre was chipped in so many places, it hardly resembled an animal anymore.

The quiet forest hummed as Edward reached for the ring on his forefinger and slid it off with care. He eyed the silver piece, inlaid with a band of wood. And he tossed it to the water.

"I'm not religious. I have not prayed before," he admitted to the fountain, so it would not think him a liar or trickster. "I simply need help."

That was all. Edward watched the water bubble in silence, though he thought he heard a giggle-snort in the air, and he swore he saw a flit of light galloping away.

The morning skies clouded with gray as heavy air swept in, splitting the day.

Edward had to decide before tomorrow who he was: Edward Green—Prince of the Pines, or Edward Haid; a man of no title. Stay and be a king or run and be a coward.

Either choice would cost him.

Presently...

Green was a fool's colour; the brand of pride and greed. Edward Haid knew as much. Green was a shade of the envious, the gluttonous, and the feasters. And emerald was the cover of its false strength.

The snow slid into shapes atop the table in the empty meeting room. Edward tilted the Patrol staff, watching the flakes dance into the forms of people he once knew, ones he had once loved. The face of a young girl looked back with gray eyes and dark hair the pure white snow could not show. The girl had done a good measure of things Edward had not as a child. She had yelled and cussed and slayed forest animals, yet for all her bravery, she had never overcome her fear of glass beetles.

A dull chuckle tickled Edward's throat as he watched the snow-form girl run from a sputtlepun boy chasing her through Timber Castle with a beetle in his fingers. She burst from the doors and flung herself over a balcony, catching herself on her feet and racing into the woods where he had not been able to catch up. Edward's laugh fizzled away, and the quiet meeting room felt empty again.

The meeting room door squeaked, and Edward cut the snow from the air, watching it fall into a pile as heavy footsteps entered the room.

"Did you know Cohen was leaving with the Carrier?" Trevor South marched to the wardrobe and flipped it open.

"No, of course not." Edward took a long look at the lifeless pile of snow, then turned on his seat to face the interim Patrol Commander. "Did you find out where they went?"

"They went to the cove. So, now I need to go after the sputtlepuns before they get hurt or snatched." Trevor brushed his fingers down his beard. "Cohen is going to get a righteous whipsteaming when he gets back," he added with a mutter.

"I could come help look," Edward said, gold eyes locking upon the auburn-haired man. His fingers tightened around the Patrol staff, his toes curling in his boots. "Please," he added.

"And leave me to deal with the fairies for it? I think not." Trevor went to the cupboard next and pulled out an armful of backpacks. "Sorry, Edward, but your fairy left you in my care. You belong here where it's safe."

Edward stood with a clatter. "And what about Cane? Why has he been sent to help while I'm trapped here?!" But the once-prince steadied himself. "Pinespittle. Apologies, Trevor," he cursed when the Patrol Commander looked at him in surprise.

"We're ready to go." Mirkra stood in the doorway of the meeting room with his pointed hood up. He looked between Trevor and the once-prince. When the room rang with warm, tense silence, Mirkra slid back a step. Then another, and another, until he had disappeared back into the hall.

Edward sighed and folded his arms. "Go, then. May the forces of Winter aid you on your journey."

Trevor came 'round the table, fastening one of the packs to his back. The man was a mere quarter or three older than Edward. They had aged together this last season, both sprouting gray hairs beneath the pressure of the darkening Winter skies.

"Stay put," Trevor said with apology. "The Patrol will be back by nightfall."

Edward sat upon his quilted mattress, gripping the sides of his salt-streaked hair as he threw his legs over the bedside.

"Pinespittle," he muttered as he stood from the bed to

roam. The moon's glow leaked in from the factory's sky-light.

"What am I to do?" he asked the silent night, for an eve or three had passed since Trevor had promised to return, and it had been even longer since Cane was supposed to be back.

Edward fidgeted with his fingers, pacing a measure. Finally, he spun and flung a bowl from the nightstand, which clattered against the wall and rolled across the hardwood before clunking against the door. His clamouring could not wake an empty factory. Edward looked at the stars past the murky gray haze cloaking the skylight.

Each folk who left had promised to come back.

Edward grabbed his cloak from the dresser, pulled on his hood, and set out through the metal hallways to the factory's front door.

The night's chill was harsh, but he walked and walked and walked as the skies lightened, the gentle fall of snow kissing his shoulders. He strode through a sleeping village, keeping to the alleys and travelling below bridges, and came out to a tree-scattered forest where the trail of blazed snow picked up, half muted by the morning's snowfall. Edward hiked through the cold until the trail stopped in a vast, snowy meadow. He halted, gold eyes darting over the surface. The meadow was a disaster.

Edward inched toward deep divots of footprints, scattered ice chips, and trinkets of belongings strewn across the plain. By a large blade of ice, a raven-black outfit lay flat in the drift, and Edward's eyes froze on the snapped Patrol staff stabbed into the snow beside it.

"By the sharpest wind..." His throat constricted; he moved for the cloak, tugging it flat to reveal the golden flake brooch, and Edward's hand slapped o'er his mouth.

A gap in the sky's haze released a ray of sunlight upon the destroyed meadow, and something above the jacket glimmered in the snow. Edward's quivering hand dug it from the drift. He raised a pair of medallions, just as the sunlight was suffocated again and the meadow grew dim.

With heavy breaths, Edward slid the medallions into his pocket and stood, looking 'round at the wind, the skies, the trees. There was no indication of where the Patrol had gone from here, as though they had vanished into thin air.

CHAPTER

THE NINTH

Zane tried to lead us through as many villages as possible, but there were times we had no choice but to brave the fallen logs and slippery brush of the forest. Nighttime caught us again, and we found ourselves tucked in an alley to escape the cold wind, just off a street dotted with giant-bulb lampposts of live flames. Zane coughed, and coughed, and *coughed* until he flopped back against the wall. I expected him to fall asleep when his eyes slid closed, but he spoke between shivers. "Did I ever tell you the one about the ice tower the Rime Folk built so they could get to the White Kingdom without Elowin's blessing?" he asked.

I leaned against his shoulder to share my warmth. "No, I don't think I've heard that one," I said. "But Zane, you don't have to tell me a story right n—"

"Shh. I'm storytelling, Trite. It started with an ancient king in Polar Territory. He'd collected riches from across Winter, stealing a measure of it, swindling the defenseless folk for the rest. He refused to recognize the Truth as a living, breathing being." He paused to cough again. "The king commissioned a thousand plus five hundred more Rime Folk to help him build a mighty steeple of ice ladders. He planned to climb over the barrier into the White Kingdom to live eternally among those who had been faithful to the True King since the first age. But sometimes Elowin has a sense of humour about these things."

I glanced over at his bluing lips. "What did Elowin do?"

"He changed their tongues—all the folk began speaking in different languages. I wish I could have seen the spinbugs all nattering at each other." He leaned his head against mine. "Anyway, they didn't finish their tower. The snow globe was shaken the next day, and the ladders shattered. The tower became a monument of ice rubble that still sits in the Polar snow to this day."

I smirked. "That's a good story."

Zane looked at me. At first, I thought he was just staring into darkness, but his eyes settled on my face, a miniscule dot of bright blue shining through the slate on his left iris.

"Can you see me?" I shifted to face him.

"No." He chewed on the inside of his cheek, shoulders dropping. "I don't know how to be bloody blind, Trite," he admitted.

I held his arm tighter, wishing I could give him knit blankets, warm tarts, and bedtime stories. I stared ahead at the cold stone wall across the alley.

The factory appeared over the hills, its front lights glowing against the whipping flurries, but the rest of the factory looked unlit.

A cold tear bit at my eye. "We made it." I huffed hot air on my knuckles to warm my hands so I could drag Kaley into a hug. It had taken us another full day to arrive, and my bones felt like mush.

We clamoured inside. The doors slammed behind us with an echo as cocoa and nut fragrances hit my senses, and I breathed in a lungful. I glanced up at the ramps and balconies, and I spun to see the halls. "Where is everyone?" I reached to stop Zane before he tripped on anything.

"By the sharpest wind!" Apple flew down the staircase and bounded across the main room. She swept me into a hug, her bangle bracelets clapping at my ear. "Helen! Mr. Zane, I'm so relieved," she said.

"We got delayed."

But Apple spoke before I could tell her what had happened, "There's trouble, I'm afraid."

I realized her lipstick was smudged, and her irises were splotchy like she'd neglected her eyedrops. Theresa came from the hallway; she stopped in front of Zane, taking in his blank stare, his fingers hovering in front of him. Her earth-brown eyes filled with remorse.

"Come, love. Let's get you settled." She took Zane's hand and led him away.

"I'll make you cocoa..." Apple spun around, frazzled like she couldn't remember which way the kitchen was.

I stood in the empty main room and looked around, wondering why no one had bothered to light a candle or start the fireplace. I went to the stack of logs and lifted one off the pile, but a voice came from the unlit corner, "You'll just waste the firewood."

Edward Haid was half blanketed in shadow. His dark hair and jacket mostly hid him, but his gold eyes glimmered from where he sat at a table in the corner.

I glanced the way Apple had disappeared, then back to the former Green Prince. Abandoning the fireplace, I headed to where he twirled a silver spoon in a mug that had lost its steam. I slowly lowered into the chair across.

He said nothing to elaborate, so I leaned back and folded my arms. "Why is Apple being weird? Where is everyone?"

Edward's gaze met my eyes. "You're the only ones who came back."

"What are you talking about?" I looked over my shoulder, scanning the slat hallways. "Where's my sister?"

"I don't know. I don't know where any of them are." His gaze dropped back to his mug, watching the cocoa twirl.

I leaned forward. "What do you mean, *any* of them?"

"Gathadriel, Cane, Porethius, The Patrol. Everyone left, and no one came back. Except for you."

My hand flashed out to stop Edward's stirring and his stare lifted. "My sister isn't *back yet*?!"

"I don't know anything of her. I just know the Patrol left to search for you after you didn't return, and they vanished like all the others."

"They bloody what?" Zane's voice lifted behind me.

The Green Prince shoved his mug away. "Trevor's been turned to snow."

The large clock at the end of the room released a metallic cry, eight beats long. No one spoke as it clanged.

I stood, palms flat on the table.

"I need to go to Green," I whispered, and Edward's gold eyes flashed.

I turned for the doors, but Zane caught me. "Wait, Helen, think this through! The Patrol aren't here, Green is in danger, and I can't *see*—"

"I can't lose her too, Zane." A rough whisper.

"Please, friend, don't go." Apple followed me toward the factory doors. "Helen!" she shouted, moving to block the way and flattening a hand against my shoulder. "*Listen!* I'm not a warrior like the fairies, or a guardian like the Patrols, but I've lost people too, so *please*, as your friend, I'm begging you, *please don't go*."

There was a pause. Apple's big brown eyes pleaded.

"Thank you for being my friend, Apple."

I pushed back out into the cold.

CHAPTER

THE TENTH

I could have gotten it together at home. I could have taken sleeping supplements and seen a therapist—it wouldn't have been the first time. I could have been content with my weekday meets at the café with Emily. Why, why, *why* did I drag Kaley back here?

I was reminded of my old ankle injury when I left the factory. A volcano of molten lava shot up my leg in greeting. "Peg out of its shell," I muttered, caving to a limp after the first hour. I walked straight through the night.

When dulled morning light burned against the snow-peaks, I heard music lifting in the distance; a collaboration of high bird songs. I listened to it for hours as I ventured through the woods and arrived at a glassy cove.

My footsteps slowed, my ankle crying in relief, and I studied the deep blue cliffsides that looked like sparkling quartz towers. The smooth ice below had the same cobalt hue, and gemstone spots like stardust had been scattered over a silk evening sky. I marvelled at it as I came to the edge of a turquoise pond.

I sighed, trying to determine the best way around. Also, I was completely lost.

A bird tweeted overhead, and I glanced up as two more cascaded from the sky, sweeping into the glass branches above me. My eyes narrowed on the glints of silver in their feathers.

Something slammed into my back, and I spiralled face-first into the pond. Icy water stunned my senses and filled my ears, but I still heard Zane's muffled voice yell, "Trite?...Trite? *Helen*?!"

My head flung up and I gasped. Disoriented, I scrambled from the water and scooted up the shore.

Zane dropped to his knees and smacked the snow with gloved hands in a clumsy search. I watched, baffled.

"What the heck, Zane?!" I shouted, and he jumped in surprise, his hand flying over his heart.

"Ragnashuck, you startled me," he accused.

"Yeah, so we're even. Only difference is I didn't knock you into a pond!"

He slumped to sit. "Well, you don't have to be grumpy about it. You know I can't see, right?"

"Why are you here? You're just going to slow me down." I hugged my legs, trembling with shivers.

Zane laughed. "Will I? Because it seems to me like you haven't a bloody clue where you're going. Even without my eyes, I can tell the birds led me in a giant circle."

I smacked him. He grunted and swung at the air to try and get me back. I waited until his aimless hand was out of the way, and I smacked him again.

It was all the invitation Zane needed to lunge, push me into the snow, and pin me down. "*Trite*," he warned, but his dimples gave him away.

"I'm going to start throwing rocks at your birds," I threatened.

"Please do. I can't wait to discover what they'll do in return."

My face fell.

Zane bit his lips, cloudy eyes roaming.

I didn't swat at him again. I was so cold—the only warm parts of me were the ones he leaned against. "How did you even follow me?"

"The birds led me with a merry tune." He rolled off to lay beside me and pointed toward the sky, nowhere near the direction of the birds.

"I'm not going back. My sister needs me."

"I know, but I was never going to stay back at the factory, Trite."

An easy silence fell between us, and I noticed the sound of water trickling into the pond. My cold bones rattled beneath my skin.

Zane stood and tugged off his jacket. "We'd better get moving." He tossed it to me and peeled off his gloves while yanking a brown paper package from his pocket. Everything landed on my lap. "You can eat on the way."

Zane's birds led us until thundering drums resonated through the woods.

"War drums," Zane whispered. "The Red and Green Kingdoms' border is just a pinch away."

My eyes scooted toward the sound. "They're fighting right over there?"

"Ragnashuck, I hope your sister isn't here," was his only response.

I blinked at the villagers hauling stick baskets and herding species of forest animals. A dwarf was playing a wood flute on his front porch. Their tense gazes flickered to the woods every few seconds.

Mulch paths wove between dark lumber boardwalks.

There was no iron gate or wall stopping us from walking in like in the Red Kingdom. I'd expected creepy statues, smooth roads, and tricky Court magicians hiding around the corners, but the Green Kingdom didn't look complicated.

As I stepped onto the boardwalk, everyone in the village stopped what they were doing, and I froze.

People dropped to their knees down the path until only Zane and I were left standing. I pulled Zane down with me, keeping my fingers locked around his sleeve as two pure-white polar bears burst through the trees, cracking branches and overturning stones. The sleigh they pulled was flanked by six muscled men with silver axes, riding bears of their own.

In the sleigh stood a woman whose garland dress filled the chariot with bristly green piles. She took in the village with solid, glassy gray eyes. A wreath glistened atop her head; spindles of branches sprouted like wood horns, wedged between wax candles and icicles.

The group halted at the village's edge.

"What's happening?" Zane whispered.

"It's..." A second sleigh plunged from the brush and my words faltered. When its bear came alongside the others, it whispered something and the rest of the bears released low, growly chuckles.

But I stood, glaring at a curly-haired traitor in a silvery jacket, whose large lips had once made me promises and told me lies.

From his sleigh, Eliot Gray spotted me in the crowd.

Zane stood beside me. "Trite, what's going—"

"The two with scotchy manners are with me," Eliot's voice boomed over the village, and Zane tensed.

The Queen of the Pines stared at us before giving a small nod. "You have unusual traditions in the East," she said to Eliot.

"Come on," Eliot called to us. "You two can ride to Timber Castle in my sleigh."

CHAPTER

THE ELEVENTH

My jaw was sore from clenching.

"Calm your scotchers," Eliot said when the grunting polar bears and grinding of the sleigh-runners made a commotion. "You would have been bear meat without me. When we get to the castle, just do as I say, for frostbit sake."

Zane tilted his head toward Eliot. "You and I have matters to settle first, Gray."

"You don't look to be in a position to settle matters at present, Cohen."

"How is your friend these days, Eliot?" I cut in to ask. "What was his name again? *Nightflesh*?"

Eliot's shoulders tightened, but he didn't glance back at where we were huddled on the sleigh. "You're meddling with a thing you don't understand, Helen," he warned. "If you and your beloved sister want to get out of this muddle, you're going to have to *trust me*."

I shut my mouth as we pulled up to a magnificent mansion of spruce-scented timber beams. Twinkling lights and silver bells wrapped carved steeples, cutting the sky with their stature. Everything was sprinkled with snow and steam that curled out the archways.

I tried counting the chimney trunks amidst the winding tower of wood rails and curved walkways in the forest heights.

"Have you ever seen this castle before?" I asked Zane, debating how I'd describe it to him.

"A time or three," he said. "My first Carrier, Thomas, was from a Green village."

"Harmony was too. A place called Belbun." Eliot glanced off, and a strange current moved between the three of us.

The Queen of the Pines glided past, crunching ice-crowns beneath her boots. She stole a look at us, gray eyes fastening to me.

Eliot took my hand. "This is my *wife*. And the folk with her is her guardsman, though he befell bad tidings on their trek and needs a guide to his sleeping quarters."

I tugged my hand away.

"Your beloved wife seems rather *common*," the queen said, and Eliot's throat bobbed when he swallowed.

"That's a merry story…" He tugged at his curls, turning to Zane. "Guardsman, you'll sleep in the village with the other guards of the East," he instructed.

Zane released a quiet laugh as the wide castle doors were hauled open with ropes. The queen cast us a look, then left with her Axemen a step behind.

"Gray," Zane said. "I'd really love to destroy you right now."

"Off to the village, guardsman." Eliot had the audacity

to flick his hand. "If you want to frostbit *live*, that is." He reached for me like I was some puppy he expected would follow, and I smacked his hand away.

Eliot's large lips pinched together, but he turned and marched into Timber Castle without another word.

"Just do what he says," I muttered, taking Zane's arm to lead him inside. "We don't have a choice if we want to find out what happened to Kaley."

"He's going to regret this." Zane blinked his pale eyes.

A feast of woodwork lay inside the castle; carved pillars and a glorious spiral staircase at the back of the foyer. Cherry and maple tones mixed with birch and oak in the details. Flames roared from oval fireplaces in the walls where men hauled in logs, and the foyer smelled of freshly crisping woodfires, sweet apple cider, and the nutty aroma of gingerbread.

I glared at Eliot's back as he strutted with all the authority of a fake noble. Then I looked at Zane, holding his fingers ahead like a shield, and during the walk through the main space, I took a deep breath to remind myself that even though Winter had briefly granted me a bad Patrolman once, it had also granted me a good one too.

I kept my eyes on Zane at the foot of the stairs as the Axemen led Eliot and I up the grand, creaking, spiral staircase to *our room*. Zane stared straight ahead, jaw solid. He waited there until I was halfway up the masterful twists of steps.

The rail was wrapped with emerald taffeta and studded with rustic pinecones. Names were carved into the wood; some ancient-looking and some crisp. It gave off the feel of quaint magic and the scent of pine needles. I halted when I saw a freshly carved name:

Edward Green
Prince of the Pines: XVI

"Does that name mean something to you?" Eliot asked over my shoulder. I spun away from the Green Prince's name. Without a word, I marched past Eliot the rest of the way up the stairs.

The moment the door to our room closed, I turned to face him. "I won't listen to you, Eliot."

Circular windows lined the walls, ovals of early moonlight puddling across the floor. Bushy pine features filled the sills with an ivory candle in each bunch. I went to stand by one and plucked the needles.

Eliot was quiet. His curls had been knocked off balance by the sleigh ride, but his eyes were as vivid as ever, even as the colour flickered.

"Helen," his throat bobbed, "I need to make things right between us."

I studied his hunched shoulders and tilted brows, but his terrible last words to me in the Red Kingdom palace dungeon rang in my ears:

They turned me.

"You were going to let me marry Quinten, that *monster*. I'll never trust anything you say while you're pledged to Nightflesh," I said.

He frowned but didn't deny it. "I've pledged myself to you too."

"That's not true."

"It is. I didn't know things would be like this. I'm still your Patrolman—"

"Just *don't*." I rolled my eyes.

"—and I know that because my heart turned to a frost-bitten *ice-block* when the intersects closed and you weren't in Winter anymore."

"What a poetic sonnet." I shook my head and began to pace, but I stole a peek at him when he shut his eyes.

"I need you to forgive me," he whispered.

"You're going to have to be more specific. Exactly which thing are you asking for forgiveness for, Eliot? Lying to me since the day you showed up at my school? Trying to get Zane killed by a snowsquatch? Luring me to the Red Kingdom where Quinten was waiting? Letting me get thrown into that *horrible* forest?" My voice shrieked by the end. "You were my *friend*! I don't have a lot of those, but I actually cared about you. And it was all fake."

"It wasn't *all* fake." His eyes flew open. "Ragnashuck, Helen. You were my friend too."

I folded my arms and dropped my gaze to the hardwood floor. After a pause, I dragged my feet to stand before the ex-Patrolman in the silver jacket. "Are you here to trick me again?" I asked.

His brows tilted in. "No! How can you ask me that after what I just said?"

It was odd, and possibly a smidgen frustrating, but I had to admit he seemed sincere.

"Where's my sister?" I asked.

Eliot cleared his throat and released a heavy breath. "They'll be at the Gingerbread Feast at midnight. They're not prisoners, so try to find a pinch of cheer in that, for frostbit sake."

"They?"

"Leutenski is with her."

Thank goodness.

"The queen knows I'm a Trite," I said. "This cute little act of yours isn't going to last."

"It doesn't matter what she thinks you are. The Evergreen Host is crumbling beneath the Ruby Legion's might at the border. She's desperate for help, and the Three Kings of the East have armies. She wouldn't risk offending an emissary, whether she's certain of me or not."

"How convenient."

"Helen..." Eliot stepped in, throat bobbing again. "I tried to get back to you. Even before the intersects were open. I couldn't stand the way I felt..."

My bitter thoughts slowed. "What do you mean you tried

to get back to me...?"

"In the dead world." He hugged his arms to himself. "I was trying to find a way across. I know it was a spinbug idea, but I had to see you."

"Did you?" I stepped in too, my hands falling at my sides. "Did you find a way to get through? Did you learn how to make a door?"

Eliot blinked. "I found a thing or three of it. It's not a merry quest, but by that reaction I can't imagine you would care about the scotchy sacrifices it would take."

I clamped my mouth shut.

Eliot took me in with a long look before sighing and dragging in another step. There was barely an inch left between us and I watched his bright blue gaze sink to gray. "If you take me back, I'll tell you all I know of it. We can figure out how to make one together."

I glanced off, finger tapping against my leg.

"How do I prove to you that I'm on your side?" He dragged a hand down his cheek, leaving a red mark. "Tell me what to do, Helen, and I'll do it. Ragnashuck, do you want me to hand myself over to the Patrol to face their judgement? Do you want me to be your spy these next quarters and bring you details of Nightflesh's plans?" He looked back and forth between my widening eyes. "I'll do it," he promised.

I blinked in surprise. "There isn't anything I want you to *do*..." I caught myself as a thought filled my head; one I shouldn't have even considered. But once it was there, I couldn't get it back out again.

"You thought of something, didn't you? Tell me." Eliot stepped in, and I realized his jacket was missing a pearl button. He still smelled of lilacs and roses, like the scent was branded into his skin.

"Eliot Gray," I said, knowing I wouldn't get a chance like this again. I looked into his sapphire eyes. "I want you to steal the Queen of the Pines's crown."

Hot cider was passed to us as we descended the spiral staircase. The main level of Timber Castle buzzed as elves prepared for the Gingerbread Feast. The miniature houses they carried made me look twice; spiral candies, deep chocolate squares, sugar-coated caramels, and peppermint flakes sprinkled the cookie-sheet artwork.

I held Eliot's arm as we came out to the snowy landscape of glowing lanterns illuminating the branches above. A massive table stretched deep into the woods, hosting log pedestals for the gingerbread houses to sit upon, along with platters of chocolate bark and assorted candies.

Eliot was stone-faced the whole walk, and I hoped he would keep it together long enough for me to find Kaley. I sipped my cider, but my eyes never stopped moving, searching faces.

The Queen of the Pines appeared to the thundering roar of a dozen drums, and I felt Eliot flinch. His eyes fastened themselves to her as she draped herself across her wooden throne. The ice sprouts of her crown glistened beneath the lanterns, and I wavered when the steeples of candles burst to life with flames.

"Isn't she worried about her hair catching fire?"

"Not likely. The crown is magic. I imagine that's why you want it?" Eliot's gaze flickered to me.

I didn't grace his question with an answer.

The scent of pumpkin pudding washed over us as we sat, and I peered down the table at the city of geometric gingerbread houses, the piles of sugar-coated candy, and the bowls of multicoloured gourds. Bronze cutlery glimmered beneath the fairy lights; seven different pieces at each place setting. I picked up a fork and studied the antique spirals in the metal.

For people who would rather smash drums than play any song with a melody, it was surprising they chose to work such artistry into their *cutlery*.

"Helen." The sound of my sister's voice slammed into my chest and my gaze fired up from the fork.

Kaley was in a suit of wooden armour.

"Thank goodness!" I wanted to leap over the table.

"Actually, you can thank *me*." Lucas was smiling beside her, dressed the same and looking another half-inch taller than the last time I'd seen him, with a full head of wispy hair.

Zane approached the table too, Lucas's hand guiding him by the shoulder. They were on the opposite side of the table as Eliot and I. Lucas glanced at the empty chair beside me and muttered something into Zane's ear.

"Sit down," Eliot instructed them. Most of the feast's guests had already taken their seats.

"I'll walk around," Zane decided, turning to feel his way down the table, knocking a guest's cider into the snow. Heads down the line turned in our direction; people leaned to see what the commotion was.

"Just sit *down*, Cohen," Eliot snapped. Zane's tight-lipped face flickered back in our general direction.

"It's fine, Zane," I said to spare him having to poke his way around the whole gathering just to sit with me. Zane reluctantly hobbled back and lowered into a seat across from us.

I thought that was the end of it, but something brushed my leg and I shrieked, springing to my feet and nearly careening backward. Lucas crawled out from underneath the dining table and climbed to his feet on our side, patting forest brush off his knees.

"Ragnashuck, Leutenski." Eliot placed a hand over his pink face while guests murmured and pointed.

Lucas grinned and dragged the spare seat a little closer to mine. "Nice and cozy," he said. I shrank back into my own chair beneath the watchful eyes of the Greens. Lucas flung his arm across my backrest.

"Is everyone merry now?" Eliot glared at where Lucas's fingers brushed his shoulder.

From across the table, Zane smirked with satisfaction. "Quite merry," he said.

My sister cast me a small smile. "Look." She raised an arm to show me the dark-wood pauldron at her shoulder. "I feel like I could take on a snowsquatch in this."

"You look awesome." I leaned in to ask her more questions—

"They took our weapons," Zane said as he carefully accepted a glass of cider from an elf. I closed my mouth, shooting Zane a look he couldn't see. Zane took a sip of the cider and made a sour face. "Needs more sugar."

"I like it." Lucas reached for a glass from a passing tray. "It reminds me of the apple juice we'd make at the garden house with Mikal. Cold and crisp."

Beside me, Eliot shifted in his chair.

"No, it's nothing like it. I had Mikal's apple juice a time or three and it tasted a good measure sweeter than this rubbish." Zane turned his cup upside down and dumped the rest of his cider into the snow. I flinched as guests down the table scowled.

"That's because we added blue wasp nectar, you syrup-sipper." Lucas tilted back his glass and swallowed the rest in one long, dramatic gulp. Eliot gripped his hands until his knuckles turned white. "And as for the matter of weapons," Lucas slammed his glass down on the tabletop and released a horrid belch, "perhaps we ought to take a lesson from the dwarves." He lifted a bronze fork and turned it in the moonlight.

"Frostbitten thief," Eliot muttered through his hands which he'd placed back over his face.

"That I am," Lucas agreed, and slid the fork into his pocket along with three knives, two spoons, a triangle server utensil, and an oversized meat fork.

"You look ridiculous," Eliot grumbled.

Lucas patted the misshapen angles of his coat. "You won't be nattering about it when I save your scotcher with a spoon."

I laughed. "Well, if I need a fork for something, I know who to…" A chilly wind swept through the forest, leaving a frosty taste on my tongue. It brushed along my neck and shoulders, like spiders rushing across my skin.

I caught the Queen of the Pines watching me. I thought she was somehow summoning me with an icy gale. But looking into her eyes, I realized it wasn't her trying to get my attention.

I searched the table as the air dipped colder. My Revelation Orb became a hot flame beneath my clothes. Frost formed on my fingertips, and I pulled my hands into fists. The table chatter continued, but a blanket of darkness swept in like a wave, suffocating the lanterns and fairy lights, blotting out the candles.

Somewhere in the black haze I could hear Kaley asking me if I was alright. The place where she'd been at the table had turned into a hollow black hole, and I gasped, fumbling for a butter knife and tripping out of my seat.

I could see the edges of dim trees and elves serving food. Laughter from the feast echoed, the animals in the forest growled and sang. But everyone I'd been with had become gaps of darkness.

"Don't you see, Trite? Don't you see that I can take them from you?"

I felt a scream pulsing in my throat; that beastly strand of coaxing echoed with the cries of fallen saints.

I spun, eyes darting from shadow to shadow in the forest, smoke and torment burning my lungs. The wind picked up, and I was sure I would get sucked away into the abyss the sky had become.

"Where are you?" I called to Nightflesh.

"Helen! You have to fight it!" Kaley's voice was beside

me now. Everything spun and I swatted through the blackness to find her. Her hand grabbed my shoulder and instantly, my legs lost their feeling.

I was sprawled on the ground in a fitful sleep a second later. The last thing I heard was Eliot shouting, "My wife is ill! I demand assistance!"

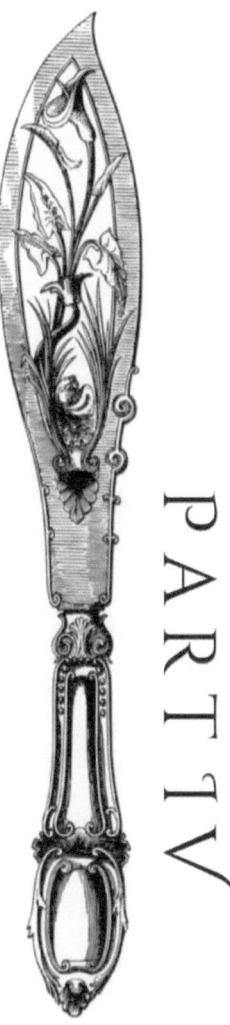

PART IV

THE

STORYTELLER

ANOTHER INTERRUPTION

A Measure of Seasons Ago...

The Red Holiday marked a full seven days on the season's calendar. Prince Cane anticipated sweet bread and warm vanilla pudding with ice berries. He pressed his nose up against the glass to spy upon the bakers in the city, biting his lip in agony that he would have to wait until the Red Holiday began to be able to taste the treats. How unfair it was, that he should be forced to wait like the peasants.

"Leave it alone, Brother." Forrester rolled his eyes as he passed, his ivory hair ruffling in the wind.

Cane grunted and left the bakery's window. "They would hand over their pastries to us if we commanded them to," he pointed out. "I don't see why anyone would have to know."

"What are you afraid of, Forrester?" Quinten adjusted his sliding coronet, scuffing his crow-black hair as he huffed to catch up.

"Snow frogs," Cane answered, and Quinten snorted a laugh. "Forrester is afraid of snow frogs. I've seen it."

Forrester glared back at Cane, purple eyes deadly. "Watch yourself, Brother. I know your fears too."

Cane's smile vanished.

"Now quit your nattering. We're late for the draw." Forrester broke into a jog past the last of the reindeer sleighs and reached the palace entrance first.

"Who do you think you'll get?" Quinten asked. "I hope I get Driar. He'll be easy to find a gift for. I'll just take a book from the palace library."

Cane rolled his eyes. "Don't get him a book. He already reads too much."

The ballroom smelled of cinnamon toast and hot jams as the boys trotted through, turning it into a race. Forrester breezed into the draw room first in complete silence, not bothering to hold the door for his brothers.

The Crimson Queen had already begun instructing the noble sputtlepuns on how the draw worked—as if they did not know the tradition from every single merry season past. Cane sighed and glanced at the clock upon the wall. He wondered if there was any cinnamon toast left.

Driar sat in the corner by himself, nestled into a pile of pillows as if he wished to vanish beneath them. His nose was shoved far into a book. "The boy hasn't a clue how to have fun. Kingsblood, he *deserves* to be alone," Quinten murmured when he saw Cane staring.

The lights dimmed and a flame flickered to life where the Crimson Queen stood, holding a candle. The room hushed and the nobles scattered to find seats as the queen lifted a red-painted drum covered in rubies. When she patted it, sparks flitted into the air above them. Snow began to dance across the windows as if overhearing the rhythm inside...

Presently...

Cane rolled his eyes at the pair of conspicuous Ruby Legionnaires trailing him and Porethius—two of his former
personal guardsmen; men he used to train alongside as a boy
but never fully got along with.

The once-prince followed Porethius to the dining room
where they would certainly not drink the king's drink, or
taste the king's luxuries, or be persuaded by the king's
mighty hand.

"I fought against the Crimson King's sons in the season
past to aid the Patrol. He would be foolish to trust us,"
Porethius reminded him when she caught Cane glaring at the
Legionnaires.

The large doors swung open, revealing a glistening table
of fruit and drinks, teapots, and fire-roasted cave-bird eggs
balanced into piles upon silver trays. Through his embellished, black mask, Cane's eyes found Scarlet-Strange-
Holly-Kissing when he stood behind his seat. Her lovely
eyes avoided his.

Another entered the room from the side opposite—all
white clothing; crumpled and un-ironed. The court magician
did not wear *his* mask as he came in. Jolly Cheat moved rig-
idly to a chair, a prickly hat with bells rattling atop his head.

"How was your time in Polar Territory, Cheat? Did
Driar bore you to death with his studies?" Prince Tegan
asked the magician, who stripped off his gloves.

"It was *fine*," Jolly Cheat muttered, eyeing Forrester
across the table.

Forrester was preoccupied with the stacked rings on his

fingers, so he did not notice the magician's nickel irises sharpen to silver daggers. Cane looked between the magician and Forrester, and for a moment, he missed being in on the nobles' drama.

"Why does your ally hide his face?" the king rasped to Porethius, and Cane's curiosity ripped from Jolly Cheat, finding the Crimson King staring straight at him once again.

"He has been burned hideously in a fire," Forrester piped up, purple eyes lifting to absorb Cane with a peculiar fascination. "Didn't you read the message, Father?"

Warmth crept into Cane's fair cheeks as the king looked him over. Ideas flooded Cane's mind—ones of excusing himself, ones of escape. Porethius could not start a war with the Crimson King by trying to save him if the king got too curious.

But the Crimson King rounded his white-bearskin chair, and he sat. The rest of the guests followed suit. "Have you come up with a better offer to see my drum?" he asked Porethius.

"I have. I shall grant you tactical advice for your wars, since that appears to be what is most important to you," Porethius stated while everyone reached for tea and drink.

The Crimson King did not blink.

"I see no value in advice. I have enough advisors. I would be swayed by a deal, if such a deal involved you fighting alongside me at the border. I would also require you to slay the Green heir once I beat the Queen of the Pines in the Silver Jubilee Renewal in a few days' time." The king leaned back in his chair, a shadow spreading o'er his brow.

Cane shifted in his seat. The movement tore the king's eyes from the fairy and back to Cane.

"My assignment is elsewhere," Porethius said. Again.

"Remove your mask, boy." The king's command startled Cane from his thoughts. "I'll not have you keeping secrets at my table. Take it off or my Legionnaires will do it for you."

Ruby Legionnaires shifted from their posts 'round the room and Cane's stomach dropped. He sprang to his feet, raising a hand. "Of course!" he agreed. "I have nothing to hide. I wouldn't want you to think as much." He swallowed, certain his hands were unsteady as he reached for his black mask, mind racing.

Porethius's eyes grew round. "If you do not trust us, King, we have no reason to stay." She lifted from her seat.

Suddenly, Cane bellowed a laugh. The Ruby Legionnaires slowed their step, the king's dark brows lifted, and Scarlet Strange's eyes locked onto him, finally.

"My apologies, King. I did not mean to offend. I simply cannot get the mask off without the key I've left in my chambers. I'll go fetch it immediately and remove the mask for you—no need to grow unmerry."

Porethius's tanned flesh was tight, tattoos glowing. Nevertheless, she lowered herself back to her seat.

Cane nodded to the king, to his once-brothers, and left the table. He could hear the Ruby Legionnaires creeping behind him as he exited the dining room.

"Perhaps I will think about your offer..." Cane heard Porethius's voice fade into the distance.

When Cane rounded a corner, he swept into a servants' tunnel, latching the metal slat door a mere moment before the Legionnaires whisked into the hall. The brutes spun, then split into different hallways, and Cane released the breath he had been holding.

The metal door flung open and his blood cooled to ice, his hand flattening against his pocket to search for a dagger that was not there.

A pair of brassy eyes pinned him to the wall in the dimness.

"Scarlet," he greeted and tore off his mask. He straightened himself, tugging at his shirt, smoothing down his mahogany hair. Shuddering.

"That is not my name," she said.

"What shall I call you then?" he whispered back.

"Nothing."

"Alright. Why have you followed me in here, *Nothing?*" He fought an untimely smile.

Scarlet's lovely eyes flickered to that smile, but she dropped her gaze to the tunnel floor. "You're going to run, I imagine. Now that the king has demanded you reveal yourself."

"Yes." The merriment left Cane's face.

Scarlet nodded. "Farewell, then. If you're not here to interfere with the marriage, then I suppose we have nothing further to discuss."

A well sprang up inside the once-prince, and he caught her arm before she might leave. "Kingsblood, Scarlet, don't marry him. Forrester will ruin you. We both know it."

But Scarlet tore her arm away, eyes flickering with hurt. "*You* ruined me, Cane. Not him."

The floor tipped beneath Cane as she took the door's latch. "I did not just come to steal a drum," he confessed, and her hand slowed against the handle. "I came here to steal a heart too."

When Scarlet glanced back, Cane held out his hand. 'Twas the same as the last time when he had offered her another way to live, an offer he had promised he would not give to her again.

"Shall I beg?" he asked in earnest. "Would that make you change your mind?"

It took her ten plus five heartbeats to utter a response, and even then, it was so quiet Cane nearly missed it. "He moved it," she whispered, and Cane stepped in to hear. "The drum. As soon as your fairy asked about it, the king moved it to his bedside table so it might be in the most heavily guarded room in the palace. You'll never get to it."

Cane found he could not stop blinking. "But you can," he realized.

Scarlet's cheeks blossomed.

"Do you know what the kingdom would think of me, what the Crimson Court would *say* about me, if I snuck into the king's chambers?" she accused, and Cane nodded.

"That's not a *no*, then. You could do it," he said. Scarlet shut her mouth and he drifted a pinch closer, studying the face he had dreamt of for too many seasons. "They will say vile, cruel, untrue things, I imagine. It's up to you, Scarlet. Fetch the drum and leave with me, and I'll hide you in the cracks of the globe for the remainder of your timestring. Or stay with them—" he nodded toward the dining room, "—but aren't you tired of caring what they think?" His burgundy eyes traced the speckles of light burning through the slats of the door and spotting her cheek, reminding him of a time when she had scars there.

A single, silver tear tumbled down the canvas of her skin, and he reached to brush it away.

"I'll try to fetch your drum." Her voice was rough, but it was stars, sunlight, and music to Cane's ears.

Noises erupted in the hallway—palace slippers slapping tile, and silver spears clattering. Cane found Scarlet's arm and he tugged her the way opposite. "Run! To the end of the tunnel!" he whispered, nudging her ahead. "I'll distract them. And Scarlet…"

Her silhouette went still in the darkness. Cane realized he had no words. But he smiled, hoping that would say enough. A mere tug appeared at the edge of Scarlet's mouth.

CHAPTER

THE TWELFTH

I spun. *Fingers and claws pushed me right and left; low growls and high shrieks stung my ears. I tried to grapple onto a solid picture, a solid floor, a solid* anything, *as lights flashed in my vision. I saw faces. Webs of ice and iron trapped those faces in cold cages where groups huddled together.*

My feet slammed a stone floor and the smoke vanished.

I could hear my own loud breathing in my ears. Other noises trickled in; snarls and whimpers. The cages sharpened in my view.

Gnomes rattled the spokes, releasing growling laughs and scratching at the ice with grey fingers. The potent scent of damp soil and rotting hope was familiar, and so were the low cries of the fallen Carriers of Truth that leaked up from the ground, mixed with the horrid, crazed laughter of the witch who would never leave me alone.

I'd been in these dark tunnels before. I'd drank Mara Rouge's poison in these tunnels. Wren Stallone had died in these tunnels, along with dozens of Carriers before my time.

The Dungeon of Souls was laced with a chalky haze. Through it, I saw throngs of people trapped down here, and I had a sinking feeling as I realized who these people were.

My gut tightened as I looked down the hall where rows upon rows of wiry ice and iron cages held more groups, groans seeping from their cells. Tiny sparkles of light fell from their chests, drifting into the sky like gold paint being washed away in water—something I'd never seen before.

"No...No, don't give up!" I tried to yell.

A gnome reached through a pair of bars and poked a woman with a long branch of ice. He pinned one of her pant legs as she tried to scramble back.

"Stop it!" I shouted, but the gnome laughed and banged his fist against his red breastplate as though he couldn't hear me. "Stop!" I shouted again, and this time, it echoed through the pit.

The gnome paused. He looked over his shoulder with the most peculiar face, searching the space where I stood.

Blinding light burned my eyes when I flung myself into a sitting position.

"Helen!" Kaley climbed onto my bed as the room came into focus. I covered my eyes, wincing at the sea of white flooding into the enormous room from the windows. I blinked until I could make out my sister's face before me. Zane and Lucas stood before a long line of beds with pale green linens.

At the end of the room, Eliot hovered by a large, arched entryway fashioned of braided branches, talking quietly with an Evergreen Host soldier. They both stilled when the Queen of the Pines came in wearing a dress made entirely of clamouring silver bells.

Above the branch entryway, a wooden sign was pegged

to the wall:

Rooms of Healing and Butter

"Butter...?" My throat was too dry for the word to make any sound as it escaped my lips.

I took in a deep breath. And then I cried like a baby.

My sobs weren't quiet; I was sure even the queen heard me. But all the brightness of the room couldn't wash away the vision of what I'd seen.

Zane felt his way over to the bed and dragged me against him. "What did you dream about? You were shouting in your sleep!" he whispered against my ear.

"I saw them—the believers. The ones who disappeared," I croaked.

"Ragnashuck." He brushed a hand up and down my back, and I noticed the queen watching us from across the room. She began heading our way.

"They're in the Dungeon of Souls. That's where Night-flesh is holding them," I blurted before the queen was close enough to hear, and Zane stilled.

"Frostbite," Lucas swore. "Isn't that where the witch would bring—"

"Yes," Zane answered bitterly. "It's a trap, Helen. Nightflesh wants you to try and save them."

"Maybe I should!"

"No, no, no, no, no, *no*." Lucas shook a finger. "That's a scotchy idea, Trite."

Zane pulled back to look at me. Electric blue spots flickered in his eyes like a lamp trying to turn on. "We find the pieces of the Triad. We use it to create more orbs, and we try to rebuild an army of Carriers to fight Nightflesh. That's our only chance at winning."

"We don't have time to do that anymore."

Bells clattered at the foot of the bed and Lucas and Kaley stilled. "Leave us."

Zane's jaw tightened, but Lucas tugged the fabric of his shoulder to lead him away. My gaze followed them to the branch entryway. Lucas cast me a look on the way out and patted his fork-and-knife-stuffed pocket, but the Queen of the Pines dwarfed me in her shadow, stealing back my attention.

The queen drifted around my bed, her eyes as gray as rock. The wax candles in the wreath atop her head were unlit now. Silvery strings wrapped the garland, and flecks of gold clung to the pine needles. For a split second, I imagined grabbing the Crown of Pines and running. My fingers twitched, but I dropped my stare to the queen's kohl-lined eyes as she tilted her head.

She looked like her brother. Despite the contrast of their gold-versus-silver eyes, she and Edward had the same jaw and dark hair. An embellished, metal ring hung from her nose today.

"Who did you hear, yesternight?" she asked.

My mouth went dry. I glanced off to come up with something, but she spoke again. "I hear him also," she whispered. "The blackness knocks at the door of my mind day and night. I worry I won't be able to resist him much longer."

I opened my mouth a few times, but no response came. I thought I'd misheard her.

"He's followed you here." Her low voice pebbled my skin, but I nodded in agreement, clutching my bedsheets.

"How do you resist him?" I rasped.

Her gray eyes burrowed into me, and I shrank beneath the weight of her stare. "I don't know, Lady of the East."

My gaze darted up to the crown resting atop her head—*Elowin's* crown.

The Queen of the Pines rose, her bell-covered dress clinking as she moved. Cutting me one last glance, she left, her four Axemen following her out.

I tore the sheets off my warm legs and stood. In the window above my bed, I saw the reflection of a girl with swollen, bloodshot eyes, wildly messy hair, shaking hands, and a frown. It was a familiar look.

Screams erupted from the hall, and Eliot raced through the entryway gripping a butterknife like he was ready to use it. I stumbled back against the bed, but when he reached me, he held out his hand.

"A Ruby Legion division has reached the castle," he said. "There's a quarrel outside!"

I was too stunned to move, so he grabbed my hand and pulled me from the healing rooms. Eliot shoved past nurses, ducking us against the wall as a dozen Evergreen Host soldiers raced by.

"If they hadn't taken our frostbitten Patrol staffs, we could scuttle off a good measure faster," Eliot muttered as he tugged me with him.

"We're running away?"

"We can't stay *here*—"

A low, eerie creak filled the hall and Eliot stopped. It sounded like a sinking ship, collapsing beneath too much water pressure. Eliot's gaze slid down the hall to where a pair of Evergreen Host soldiers had stopped too.

"What was—"

I shrieked as a monstrous, human-sized snowball punched through a window, spraying glass and snow. Eliot grabbed my waist and pinned me against the wall as another snowball hurtled, slamming his shoulder and nearly taking him with it. I grappled for Eliot's hands, holding tight as it ripped past. The soldiers at the end of the hall leapt out of the way as the snowball exploded against the wall.

"Where are the others?" I asked, searching the hallways.

"They were posing as frosbitten *guardsmen*, Trite!" Eliot snapped.

"What does that mean?" I asked as he pulled me toward the smashed windows.

"They were forced to go fight!"

It sank like a boulder in my gut.

"Eliot—" He lifted me and *tossed* me out the window. My exposed flesh hit cold snow as shouts and clanging metal filled my ears. A shadow appeared over me, and I flung my head up. I screamed at the crimson cape flapping in the wind, but Eliot's boots landed before me and the butterknife flew from his hand, striking the Ruby Legionnaire in the eyes.

Eliot kicked him in the ribs and hauled me to my feet, pulling me toward the woods. I looked back at the castle entrance where the Queen of the Pines swung a silver sword, her bells rattling and her soldiers a nest of green robes around her. Two Ruby Legionnaires dropped to the snow at her feet, and she turned on another.

"Wait!" I screamed at the sight of Kaley holding a meat fork toward an advancing Legionnaire. She cried something, and Zane leapt onto the Legionnaire's back, dragging him down into the snow. Past them, Lucas swung cutlery.

I bolted for them. "Helen!" Eliot shouted after me. I didn't hear him follow.

The snow was littered with crimson capes, abandoned bows and arrows, and empty wooden armour where Rime bodies had turned into snow. I counted ten Ruby Legionnaires still fighting against the hundreds of Evergreen Host soldiers creeping through the woods.

Kaley saw me—she reached for my hand. "Helen's here," she called to where Zane panted over the unmoving Legionnaire in the snow. He lifted his head to squint at the light, revealing a bloody cut staining his lip.

"Bring him to me!" A shrill, wild voice cracked over the forest, and the battle hushed.

I realized the last of the Ruby Legionnaires had been defeated, apart from *one*. The Legionnaire was wrestled through the woods toward the queen and tossed into the snow at her feet.

"Your king is a coward," she rasped. The Legionnaire climbed to his knees, and a slow, wicked smile found his face. The queen ignored him and addressed her soldiers. "The Crimson King means to tire me out before the Silver Jubilee Renewal. He thinks sending a division of his Ruby elites to our castle doors will give him an advantage. But he's wrong, and when I kill him in a few days' time, his armies will be forced back, and his heir will cower at my name." She slammed her fist against the bells at her chest, and the Evergreen Host growled and shouted in agreement. Energy buzzed through the woods. But I'd met Tegan, the first Red Prince. And I had a feeling he wouldn't be afraid at all.

I caught the Ruby Legionnaire looking at me. His brows tilted in, recognition flickering across his eyes. Warmth touched my cheeks, and I slid an inch behind Kaley, but his eyes darted to Zane padding over to me, and I knew the sight of Zane would confirm his suspicion.

"Do you know who she is?" the Ruby Legionnaire nodded toward me, grabbing the queen's attention. The Legionnaire's smile returned, and I sprang forward to yell over him, to deny whatever he was about to say next, but a gust brushed past my shoulder—an arrow spiralled through the wind and plunged into the Ruby Legionnaire's copper armour.

I stifled a squawk. The Legionnaire gasped as silence crushed the clearing. A heartbeat later, the man burst into a flurry of snow.

Evergreen Host soldiers erupted with noise; the queen's eyes fired to where the arrow had come from. But I stared at the empty crimson cape floating to the ground, snow trickling away like shaken salt.

"Emissary." The queen's voice was cold. "You've killed my prisoner."

I turned, glassy eyes landing on Eliot. The bow was still raised in his hands. "Maybe I didn't like the way he threatened my *wife*." His large lips were tipped down.

The queen stared at him several seconds too long. But she hardened her jaw and shouted, "Soldiers, station yourselves around the castle grounds. No one leaves. Anyone who attempts to will be executed as a deserter."

My hands had trembled for hours. Eliot never came up to our room.

I paced until Kaley came in carrying two dresses. There were cuts on her knuckles. "The elves are cleaning up downstairs," she said. "There was a wedding scheduled for tonight. The queen wants to go ahead with it."

And since we can't leave, we have to attend, was what she didn't say.

We didn't have makeup, but Kaley twisted my frizzy hair into a braid. She tossed a jade dress my way with tulle spurting from the skirt like an upside-down fountain of stiff slime.

Kaley's wood armour was gone; she fashioned a slender turquoise gown. I couldn't guess how she'd gotten her hands on the dresses, but with her dark brown hair and green eyes, she looked pretty. I, on the other hand, looked like I'd just crawled out of the sewers.

We walked in silence through Timber Castle. Cold wind rushed down the halls through the shattered windows. "We're being watched," Kaley said.

I glanced back and sure enough, two burly men drifted around the corner a second after we did.

Kaley led the way to the spiral staircase, newly embellished with dangling streamers of lights. The pin-point-size bulbs hung like a curtain of stars, brilliantly kissing the staircase with the glow of a false sunset.

At the bottom, Eliot waited, back in his silver jacket with the missing button. I spotted Zane and Lucas further off.

Zane was rigid until I reached him and spoke. "Guess

who? It's your favourite grumpy Trite." His shoulders re-laxed, and I reached to take his hand to lead him out, but a man with a dozen wood rings appeared between us.

"Lord and Lady of the East," the man addressed Eliot and me, "The queen would like you to begin the dance this eve to welcome the bride and groom."

I looked at Eliot, who looked back at me. The hand that was meant for Zane dropped back to my side.

But Zane smirked, twisting the cut on his lip. "I wish you good tidings with your *dancing*," he said as the man left.

"I bet you're just tickled you don't have to watch." I took my coat from Kaley and shoved my arms through the sleeves.

"Quite the opposite. I'm heartwrenched I can't see you thump around the forest floor like a rampaging toddler."

Biting down on a smile, I tried to reach back and swat him but Lucas caught my hand and shook a finger. "Tisk, tisk, Trite. Smacking a blind folk is scotchy manners."

"So is telling someone they're a bad dancer." I tugged my hand back.

Zane laughed, and despite our situation, the sound of it warmed the room. I let myself smile.

Outside, Eliot studied me with a bothered face. The air was crisp and sharp, needling cold into my collar and brush-ing a shudder up my spine. I nearly toppled off the sleigh when the polar bears took off toward a clearing on the castle grounds.

"What's the deal with you and Cohen?" Eliot asked when we were flying over the snow. "Even during the season past, I couldn't figure you two out. Rumour was you had a strong Patrol-Carrier bond, but I didn't think it was…"

I looked over at him; his curly hair whipped in the wind. "Was what?" I shuddered against the chill.

But Eliot shook his head. "It just makes things… com-plicated."

I blinked. And then I laughed. "Eliot Gray, *you* make

things complicated."

"How do I know he can defend you if his frostbitten feelings are muddled?"

"Eliot, you're not my Patrolman anymore. Even when you were, you were awful at it," I said. "Somewhere in the Midnight Forest, Mara Rouge is still laughing about that," I added with a mutter.

Eliot's shoulders tightened, but he sighed. "I'm trying to figure out what's happening to you. You lost your wits right in the middle of a feast. Maybe your energy spent pining after *him* is why."

I could have slapped him.

"Well, Eliot, right now me *losing my wits* has nothing to do with why I want to kick you off this sleigh."

His laugh surprised me. "Ragnashuck, let's forget it. I know things are scotchy but try to have a pinch of fun tonight. It is a wedding, after all."

A wedding.

Like the wedding he would have attended when he was going to let me marry Quinten.

They turned me.

Digging in your heels to resist Nightflesh will only break your legs.

I looked ahead, spotting a canopy of branches sprouting bouquets of feathers above a long table with carved trays of antique cutlery.

I felt the queen's cold eyes on us as Eliot led me through the clearing for the dance. When the flutes and drums started, we tip toed through the snow and Eliot turned me where I needed to go. Others joined in, and to my relief, the spectacle of the Emissary and his wife was lost to the multitude of swaying couples.

I found myself scanning the treeline for a boy with electric eyes. I spotted Zane making small talk with some guests while stuffing his face with gingerbread snaps and icing.

Eliot huffed, and I realized he'd danced us to the edge of

the floor where Zane was announcing how he once took down a gruesome snowsquatch just outside this kingdom.

"If you want to dance with Cohen, you have my merry blessing." Eliot passed me off in Zane's direction, and I raised a brow. "It's not like I'm really your husband, Helen." He cast me a flat smile and slipped into the crowd of guests.

I looked at the people gathering to listen to Zane's tall tale, and I shook my head in disbelief. "Save some of that gloriousness for a dance," I suggested, and he stopped talking. He licked the icing off his lips and felt for the table, ditching his plate, a smirk forming.

"Forgive my scotchy manners, but it seems I've impressed the Lady of the East," he said to his audience. Zane took a step forward, and I linked my arm through his before he started wandering in circles trying to find me.

"They loved my merry story. Shame on you for stealing me from them," he said.

"They all left," I lied. "You were just telling your story to the air."

"You're just jealous." He tugged my arm to bring me closer. "But it's nice to hear you with some cheer after the attack this morning. I…" He bit his injured lip and the laughter fizzled away. "Helen, I didn't know how to find you when they came. I could only do what I was told and hope that Eliot had gone back for you."

"I know." I scanned the couples for Eliot. "But I'm fine."

"Are you?" Zane asked.

"Am I what?"

"*Fine.*"

The silence went on too long as I opened my mouth and closed it again. "I'm fine."

Zane tilted his head in my direction. He took my sides and I tried to navigate us, but we still brushed up against other couples, got in their way, stepped on toes, and everything else clumsy and awkward. With each new bump, Zane's smirk widened.

"It's too bad you can't see. If you could, you'd realize I'm a *great* dancer now," I said.

His grin cracked wide open. "Lying Trite."

"Show-off Rime."

He twirled me beneath his arm.

"Grumpy," he whispered into my ear.

"*Rude*," I shot right back.

"Hmm. I suppose that's fair." He caught my waist when I came around and we slowed to a stop. His amusement faded, a breeze slipping between us. "Liar," he said again, letting the word hang in the air.

I stared, my smile disappearing too. "Hypocrite."

Zane's jaw shifted. "Why am I a hypocrite, Trite? You're the one who keeps telling me you're *fine* when you haven't been for a good measure."

I looked down at the snow.

"I know you went to the Hall of Knowledge in the Scarlet City. And I know you attacked Jolly Cheat because you were so upset about what you found there," I said. "I know *you're* not fine either."

Zane's face changed. The silence that followed was heavy.

"My troubles are *personal*," he finally said.

"So are mine."

He shut his mouth, the flickering candlelight reflecting off his cheeks. Couples glided around us when we didn't move.

After several moments, Zane released a heavy sigh. "Bloody Wanda," he muttered. His fingers slipped off my waist and fell to his sides. "You're right. I've kept a measure of things from you," he said. "There are some things about me I hope you never bloody find out. It's a scotchy mess and I want to sort it out on my own."

"I need to sort out my thing on my own too."

Zane's brows were tilted in, but the rest of his face relaxed. "I'll stop nagging you about your personal troubles then, Helen. But you're not quite right in the head, and I can't figure out why."

I glanced off. "I wish everyone would stop saying that."

He hugged me against his chest, his arms warming my shoulders and the familiar song of him drifted into my ears. "Anyway, I'd be lying if I said it didn't bring me a pinch of cheer to know I beat Cheat, fair and square."

I fought an untimely smirk and my cheek rounded against his chest. "Careful, Patrolman. He's probably hiding in a cave, plotting a new way to try and destroy you."

"I certainly hope so. I'd love to toss that ashworm into the snow a time again."

The wedding music resonated through the forest: heavy drums and wooden flutes. Giggles reached us, and I spotted Kaley and Lucas. There was a twinkle in Lucas's topaz eyes when he spun Kaley around and caught her again.

Zane locked his hands behind my back. I imagined we were back at the factory, dancing with the dwarves amidst the scents of the midday feast. I wondered if this was what happiness was supposed to look like: Lucas whispering things—completely wicked things, likely—and Kaley pinching her lips together, seeming determined not to give him the satisfaction of a laugh. Despite my better judgement, the sight gave me a hope I'd promised myself I would never entertain again. It made me imagine staying here. It made me wonder if Kaley would stay here, and if Grandma would come. The old woman could spend her days knitting scarves and blankets with Theresa.

My gaze wandered to the queen sitting in her high-backed, twig chair. The candles in the Crown of Pines were lit, flickering in the breeze that sifted through the woods.

If it ever became safe enough, Kaley, Grandma, and I could make lives here.

But I wondered if I'd be able to leave Winston behind.

The second time I'd met with Stephen—the church guy in Waterloo—it was because I'd brought him a coffee as a thank you for the day he found me sopping wet on his church's doorstep. I'd wandered into the beautiful building early in the morning and found it in a state of quiet serenity. The sunrise glow brushed in through the stained-glass, warming the benches in the sanctuary. Particles of dust glittered in the air like brassy confetti, silently drifting about. I'd admired the scene for several minutes without moving a muscle. It was the most peaceful I'd felt in months.

"You're back." Stephen appeared from a hallway carrying a box.

I pulled my gaze from the glorious room and settled it on him as he slid the box onto a pew and came to meet me.

"I just came to return the favour," I said, lifting the coffee toward him and hoping he didn't hate the lidless paper cup I'd found in Sylvia's kitchen.

On the walk to the church, I'd grown worried the coffee had gone cold, but Stephen guzzled it back and came up for air beaming. "This is amazing. Am I tasting…orange? Where'd you get this?"

"I made it." An awkward shrug. "Freshly ground beans, a pinch of sugar, a squeeze of an orange slice, a sprinkle of cinnamon…"

I glanced up at the gilded cut-outs across the front of the balcony. Each panel had its own artwork, and it reminded me of the copper pictures that had hung on the walls of Mikal's home.

"Those were put in by the original builders back in 1875," Stephen said when he noticed me staring. "They're hollow behind the panels. The early pastors wanted to be able to store things in them, but most people nowadays don't even realize they're cupboards." He paused to sip all that was left of his coffee. He went on to say a few more things about the church building's history, but I found myself picturing this sanctuary full on a Sunday morning, with quiet hymns being sung into the sky, and a cool breeze coming in through the wide-open doors at the back.

"Do you have any family in Waterloo?" Stephen's question pulled me from my daze.

I really hated it when people asked that question, but I answered anyway, "I have a brother and a sister who both live around here: Kaley and Winston. Kaley lives with me, and Winston..." I shrugged. "Lives somewhere."

"Somewhere?" Stephen cocked a brow.

"He took off in December." I looked away, eyes falling on an end table with a particularly interesting doily.

But Stephen's face changed. "Do you mean Winston Bell?"

My attention snapped back. The look on my face must have told Stephen enough, because he set his coffee cup down on the end table and folded his arms.

"Have you...do you know..." I wasn't sure I wanted to ask, not that I could spit out a proper question anyway.

"Um...yeah, I know him. Our church serves at a soup kitchen downtown for the homeless. He's come in a few times."

It took me a few tries to digest that word.

Homeless.

I bit my lips together, refusing to let it sink in, refusing to let it grow roots in my heart. Those roots would sting when they were ripped out again.

Winston needed to take charity from a church to be able to eat?

I couldn't tell Kaley; I wasn't sure I had the stomach to even say the words out loud. I didn't even want to think them:

Winston would rather be homeless than live with us.

CHAPTER

THE THIRTEENTH

*T*wo creatures drifted through the underground tunnels of the Dungeon of Souls; long, lanky limbs,
shredded burgundy robes, and large, pure black
eyes. They whispered things to the believers on their way,
sometimes in other languages, showing off rows of crooked
teeth. They passed the cages like shadows, offering false
hope and bribes. I'd never seen anything like them, but I
somehow understood what they were saying. One word
burned in my mind as though warning me they were close
by: Feastbeggars. Feastbeggars. Feastbeggars. Run.

The sight had been enough to make me trip over my own
feet. I turned to escape when another voice lifted down the
line of cages: shrill, raspy, female. I stilled, recognizing it.

Heart hammering, I crept back toward her voice. A rock
rested around the corner, and when I crouched behind it, my
stomach dropped.

Gnomes grabbed the shoulders of a fair-featured boy with light hair and old flesh burns. They dragged him away from a cage where Wanda Thermichael screamed threats and shook the spindles with white knuckles. A gnome smashed a club against the bars, but still, Wanda yelled, and yelled, "Bring him back! Bring him back! You frostbitten monsters! Bring him back!"

Kilen kicked as he was hauled away. I stepped after them, my insides screaming as loud as Wanda's voice, overwhelmed with the need to do something. Fire burned through my limbs. I hated that my body wasn't really here; that my hands were useless.

Rattling bars and roaring voices filled the tunnel. I turned, filled with the terrible realization that Wanda and Kilen weren't here alone, and I whimpered.

Cages packed with Patrolmen lined the tunnel. They yelled toward where Kilen had disappeared. They banged against the cage doors, some with bloody knuckles. I spotted Timblewon's fuchsia hair as he shouted, and Mirkra slamming his forearm against the bars to try and break through.

Frost crawled around the bend, reaching down the spindles and pinching Mirkra's skin. He cried out and ripped his arm back. Feastbeggars swept into view, their black eyes settling on him.

Like a parting sea of ghosts, half the feastbeggars rushed for Mirkra, half to raging Wanda.

The dream was torn from me before I saw what happened.

I couldn't leave my bed in the morning.

Eliot came into the room with hot cider and tried to have a conversation. I didn't speak a single word. He stared at me for a long time before leaving again.

Minutes later, he came back with Zane.

"She's a frostbit statue," Eliot said. "She was merry last night. I don't know what happened."

Zane crawled onto the bed and padded his hand along the comforter until he bumped my leg. "Helen?"

I settled my stare on him. His eyes had grown brighter overnight.

"We need to get out of the Green Kingdom." My voice cracked when I finally spoke.

"Agreed. I'm not sure why we're still bloody here," Zane said.

"We're getting a crown," Eliot piped up from the back of the room, arms crossed. "And we'll be executed as deserters if they catch us trying to leave, in case you frostbitten forgot."

"We'll get the crown another day," Zane said.

My fingers laced together; I looked down at my chipped nails. "Nightflesh has the Patrols. That's why they never made it home to the factory after they went looking for us," I told him. "I saw them in the Dungeon of Souls."

It was madness to try and leave.

It was madness to stay.

Lucas went on a hunt for the Patrol staffs through Timber Castle, asking nonchalant questions of the staff. In the meantime, Eliot took me for a walk outside to scout out an escape.

Zane and Kaley walked arm-in-arm behind us. Every time I glanced back, they were deep in conversation. Zane's pointed hood was up, shadowing his face and making it impossible to read his lips.

"If we go through that forest," Eliot nodded toward a

grove of thick-trunked trees, "we'll end up in the village where I found you and Cohen. From there it's a sprint to the border. If Leutenski can come up with our Patrol staffs, we might make it." I leaned into his grip on my arm to keep steady, still lightheaded after my terrible sleep. But I nodded to show I'd heard.

They turned me.

They turned me.

They turned me.

It was like a gong going off in my head. No matter how much ground Eliot and I gained, I couldn't stop hearing him say those words.

"Eliot," I said, and his head tilted toward me. "Where is Asteroth?"

He shrugged. "I have no idea."

"None?"

"None, Helen. He scuttled off four quarters ago and hasn't been heard from since."

"Have you seen anyone else from that side?"

Snow trickled down from the sky, landing on our coats as he took his time answering. When he did, his voice was low like he didn't want the others to hear. "I was…cast out of their company. They don't trust me," he said.

They…

I glanced at him, but he was looking straight ahead. His blue eyes seemed off; like they were fighting to stay lit, fighting not to melt to turquoise. My senses prickled at the sight.

They turned me.

"Eliot, I still can't decide if *I* can trust you," I admitted, and he pinched my arm against him. "You haven't even told me what you've done this past year. I want to believe you're on my side, but something is telling me you're not."

He huffed. "Fine. After your…*Midnight Forest trial* in the season past, I went to get Elowin's attention at the border of the White Kingdom. I went to try and make amends," he said. "It's what Harmony would have wanted."

I blinked up at him. "You tried to see Elowin?"

"Yes. And he ignored me. The White walls didn't frost-bitten budge. He's closed off from Winter, truly. Just like Nightflesh said he was."

That dawned on me, and I yanked my arm away. Eliot spun to face me and when I looked at him, I saw a storm brewing in his green-blue eyes. Zane and Kaley stopped a few paces back, and I studied Eliot as he struggled to keep his irises from turning to liquid seas.

"You're lying to me right now," I realized.

"Helen," Eliot said, taking my shoulders and biting his lips together. "You gave me a task to earn your trust. Let me complete it."

"Don't you get it?" I whispered. "Forget the crown, Eliot. No one's coming to save us here—the Patrol has been captured. The crown doesn't matter anymore."

"It does matter! I'm not a frostbit spinbug. I know a desperate plea when I hear one. You asked me to get you that crown, so I'm going to get it."

I stared, at a loss for words. My reeling thoughts went to Cane and the drum. What if we escaped the Green Kingdom and returned to the factory to find that Cane had held up his end, and I'd come back empty handed? This had been my plan, and I was a stone's throw away from the second piece of the Triad. Maybe it was crazy to let this opportunity pass.

I rubbed my eyes and glanced to the canopy of the nearest tree, imagining curling up to sleep beneath it. But I knew if I did, I'd end up right back in the Dungeon of Souls and rest wouldn't find me anyway.

THE

STORYTELLER

A MIDDLE–ISH INTERRUPTION

A spark once dormant now glimmered in Kaley Bell's chest. The girl with the birdsong voice still could not pinpoint what it was that stirred exactly, waiting to break free. But she knew it was there, ever whirling in her heart, silently tugging her onward so she might follow.

"Leave all you have and follow me." Since the day she had said yes to that whispered invitation, the Truth had been with her, even in sleep.

Which was why she found it riddlesome that Helen's sleeps were so agitated.

Back in the pocket with the ancient, living books, Kaley had read a thing or three of value: The Golden Rule. The Narrow Gate. The Tree and its Fruit. But never had she read an instruction telling her what to do if someone held tight to a thing which forbade them from getting well. On those late eves that Kaley had crept down the hall and spied on her be-loved sister in their aunt's dwelling, she had found Helen reading, humming, and drinking steaming beverages, but *not* sleeping.

This was why Kaley uttered the words to Zane Cohen as they walked along, arm in arm, "We should discuss what we're going to do about Helen once we get out of here."

"Yes. I suppose we should," the Patrolman replied.

The spark in Kaley's chest agreed.

CHAPTER

THE FOURTEENTH

The walk up the spiral stairs to my room left me dizzy.
I was asleep as soon as I fell on the bed. I cried in my
sleep.

I dodged feastbeggars while I searched for the Patrols.
When I found them, Mirkra was slumped at the back of his
cage, and they'd cut Timblewon's beautiful fuchsia hair
down to stubs. I shouted at a gnome for approaching them
with a poker stick. Like before, the gnome paused with a con-
fused look. I waited until he turned, and I punched at his
soggy, gray nose, even though I knew it would affect nothing.
I was so startled when my fist collided with something

hard, that I jolted awake.

"I'm just going to take it," Lucas was saying. "I'm going to jump off the dining table in plain sight, grab the crown, and I'm going to run until they tire of chasing me—" His words hitched when I gasped and sat up.

Kaley dropped the handful of nuts she'd been holding for whatever game the three of them were playing, and she came to my bedside. "This is *unreal*, Helen. You can't go on like this," she said.

My tired eyes slid closed, ears ringing with the calls of the Patrol.

"We need to get back to Porethius," Zane said, standing and tossing his game pieces onto the stump.

We were back in the sunlit healing rooms. The scent of peppermint saturated the air—some variation of mint pie. I tried to decide if I could eat, or if the thought of food made my stomach turn.

"So let me snatch the crown and we'll run for it, like I said." Lucas scooped up all the nuts and dragged them toward himself as if that somehow meant he won the game.

"I told you *I* would get it. And it's about frostbit time you all told me why you want the Crown of Pines in the first place." Eliot's voice cut through the conversation and Lucas's head lifted in surprise. Apparently, no one had heard Eliot come in.

"It would be a record-breaking prank," Lucas lied.

"The Patrol doesn't hold records for pranks. Nor do they condone *stealing*," Eliot said.

"Ah. Well. You got me." Lucas grinned.

Eliot slumped into Kaley's empty chair. "Tell me why you want it, and I'll get it for you. Tonight." He was looking at Zane. "You need me to. Admit it."

"Gray," Zane sighed. "I don't *want* to dislike you, you know. You just make it so bloody easy."

"Likewise. But it doesn't change the fact that we're both dedicated to the same person. We're both her Patrolmen, whether you like it or not." He nodded toward me.

"This rubbish again." Zane shook his head.

Eliot's jaw tightened. "I'm not going anywhere, Cohen. I might not be fighting for you, but I am fighting for *her*."

"Good grief," I muttered.

"Are you boys done your hissy fit?" Kaley folded her arms, the wood armour at her shoulders knocking together.

Zane and Eliot exchanged a look, and it was clear neither of them knew what a *hissy fit* was.

The room darkened, and a cold wind lifted through the space, brushing against the windows. I raised my hands to find frost on my fingertips, spreading in patterns down my fingers and over my knuckles.

My hands trembled. "He's *back*!"

I ripped the sheets from my bed and snatched the pillow to use as a shield as darkness sucked every trace of sunlight from the room. I could no longer see the others—hollow holes appeared where they'd been.

"Don't you see, Carrier?" His deep, bone-shuddering voice echoed, and the smell of iron and blood filled my nostrils. *"All of this* is *about my duel with you..."* The last words rang in tune with Mara Rouge's voice as though she stood before me. Screams pierced the air: high, deep, hollow, sharp. My pillow fell to the floor and my palms slammed against my ears.

"Stop!" I begged. "Please, let them go!"

"Helen!" Zane's voice spiralled through the darkness, and like a light flicking back on, all the shadow and wind vanished.

I blinked, lowering my trembling hands, holding back the tears burning in my eyes.

The room was bright, and the trickle of chatter from the hallway breezed through the space along with the smell of mint pies once again.

Zane pulled me against him, surrounding me with his arms before I could register anything else. His heart pounded against me, his tune slipping from his chest.

"Don't let him in," he begged.

My own voice was raw. "I'm so tired, Zane."

Zane was shaking. "Helen, your sister is right. You can't go on like this. I don't know how Nightflesh caught your ear and eye without you letting him in, but this needs to stop."

A single, salty tear slid from my eye and soaked into Zane's jacket. I saw nothing but blurs of colour, until Eliot sharpened in my view. He stood as still as the animal wood carvings at his back, eyes wide, face pale.

I peeled myself off Zane. Eliot's deep, turquoise gaze locked with mine and I realized: he'd seen the darkness.

Eliot's face changed as he seemed to realize in the same beat; he shook his head. "It's not me," he swore. "I'm not letting him do that to you."

"You're a liar," I rasped. I tried to take a step toward him, my shaky hand flying out to catch the bedpost when my head spun.

"Helen, *please*." Eliot took a step toward me, but I raised a hand to stop him.

"You need to get away from me, Eliot."

Eliot's eyes burned like embers: a green and gray hurricane. "You're blaming the wrong person. And I'm tired of getting blamed for every ashworm thing that happens to you."

"I haven't been able to think straight ever since I let you in! Either you're tricking me, or Nightflesh is tricking *you*," I said. "You didn't really go to the White Kingdom, did you? You weren't trying to make things right with Elowin."

Eliot's hands fell to his sides, a flit of anger darkening his irises. "I did go. But not to make amends with him."

I lifted a trembling hand, leaving it there for him to take. "Eliot, break away from Nightflesh. Elowin will take you back," I said.

A beat of silence heated the air. Eliot didn't blink.

"Nightflesh owns me. There's no escape from the

Beast." I tried to protest but he went on, "And I don't want Elowin back. What kind of a king lets his people be killed? Why did all those Carriers have to die, can anyone tell me that?" he asked. No one spoke, and Eliot looked to Zane. "Doesn't it bother you, Cohen? That Elowin let Thomas die? For nothing?!"

Zane's jaw hardened, and Lucas looked down, tracing a finger over his pocket.

"Fine." Eliot's mouth tightened. "I'll leave after the feast tonight. If you've decided you want to send me off after all I've done for you, Trite, I won't bother you for the rest of your frostbitten timestring."

Eliot marched from the room, and I stared at the branch entryway long after he was gone.

His last promise tugged at my heart.

CHAPTER

THE FIFTEENTH

I tried to raise a green-tinted glass of cider to my lips with trembling hands, nearly spilling it on my lap. I left the glass on the tabletop after that, watching as the pine-wrapped woodsmen and woodswomen came to take their places around the feasting table, branch-antlers piercing the night sky. The Evergreen Host stationed themselves in the shadows at the edge of the woods, the evening breeze fluttering their emerald capes as they leaned their weapons—axes, bows, and sheaths of arrows—against the trees.

Even in my lush, fur coat, I shivered. Below the chatter and loud storytelling, I heard the cries of the Patrolmen in my ears like they were around the table with us. I heard Wanda screaming. I heard Kilen shrieking. I heard Mirkra banging on the cell bars.

Zane's hand crept beneath the table and slid over to take

mine.

"I wish you could tell me a story," I whispered to him, staring at the dark parts of the forest with glassy eyes.

"I'd spend the rest of my timestring telling you stories if it would fix you," he said. "We'll slip away tonight, Trite. We'll go back to the Chocolatiers."

Eliot stepped into view across the clearing. His silvery coat glittered in the moonlight as he sat with a frown. He stared at the prickly, olive centrepieces.

Candles were lit to begin the feast, cider was poured, and the shouting grew in volume as the folk tried to overpower each other. Drums and the clanging of cutlery echoed through the forest.

Minutes into the feasting, I realized Eliot was looking at me. He hadn't taken a bite. Neither had I.

His low voice met my ears. "There's a tree with orange leaves and golden sap, thirty strides that way." His sapphire eyes flickered to the left. "Make sure *you* find it first."

My brows tugged in as Eliot rose from his seat, eyes sinking to dusty turquoise. Lucas rose too, as though wondering if he should follow. Eliot brushed past elves serving platters of fruit skewers, his curls bouncing. He snatched a Host's bow leaning against a tree, along with a single, emerald-feathered arrow, and he disappeared into the darkness.

"What in the fluffy frostbite is he doing?" Lucas dragged a butter knife toward himself, scanning the trees where Eliot had vanished. One second went by. Then two. Three.

Finally, Lucas sank back to his seat.

"I've got a scotchy feeling," Zane admitted as Lucas hauled a mouthful of pumpkin pudding into his mouth.

"Take it as a victory," Lucas mumbled past the glob. "Maybe we should go now before he comes back…" But his voice trailed off and his eyes widened.

My gaze snapped to the shadows where a single arrow spiralled through the darkness toward the table. The loud chatter of the Greens faded from my awareness, and my stomach dropped as the arrow pierced the garland of the Queen of the Pines's crown, ripping the wreath off the queen's head. Lucas spat his pudding; I watched in awe as the arrow carried the Crown of Pines through the night, disappearing into the trees.

The entire table erupted in shouts. Host soldiers grabbed their weapons and raced into the woods, guessing at the location from which the arrow had come. The Axemen launched from their seats to chase after the crown, batting branches out of their way.

"Find it!" the queen screamed; gray eyes wild.

All at once, everyone at the table stood, tossing napkins, cutlery, and pudding.

...orange leaves and golden sap. Make sure you find it first.

Good grief, Eliot.

We dropped our spoons and escaped the table, jogging into the hazy trees. People rushed past in every direction. Zane's hand fell onto Lucas's shoulder as Lucas led us through the dark. The table's candles faded at our backs.

Lucas detached from us, veering in the direction Eliot had told us. A second later, his whisper sailed through the darkness, "I found orange leaves!"

The silhouettes of tree branches cast black patches over the starry sky. I could vaguely make out Lucas's form climbing the trunk and reaching into a gap. "Ragnashuck," he said, pulling something out and hopping down to hold it beneath a patch of moonlight.

I blinked at the Crown of Pines. The emerald-feathered arrow was still lodged into its side.

"How did Eliot get the arrow to carry it?" Kaley whispered.

"Well, darling, it's a nifty trick I learned in my early seasons—"

"Save it for later, Lucas." Zane tugged him toward the woods, but the wreath's candles burst to life, jolting us to a halt. We looked at each other. Against the dim night, we *glowed*. Shouts boomed through the darkness as everything in the woods turned for us.

"Well. Frostbite," Lucas muttered. "Yes! What a relief! We've found it!" he shouted to the half-dozen Evergreen Host soldiers flocking us.

Clattering bells sang through the pines as the queen's garland dress brushed over the snow. In the glow of the crown's candles, her gray eyes were liquid bullets. My gaze followed the crown as Lucas passed it to her Axemen.

"The Emissary of the Second King of the East has fled." Ice layered her words. "I'm inclined to believe he meant to take this from me." She reached for the crown, holding it up. But her liquid stare fired over to me. "You're thieves. You meant to take my blessed crown and flee, like your husband."

"He's not my…" I quickly realized outing that lie would make the situation worse. I shot Lucas a desperate look, my eyes saying it all—*Get Kaley out of here!* Lucas glanced at Kaley, seeming to calculate his odds.

"Arrest them. They'll be tried and executed as traitors of the Green Kingdom." The queen's voice sliced through the air, and my gaze fired back to Kaley.

The Queen of the Pines placed her crown upon her head. With one last stone-cold look, she left, and we were seized by the Evergreen Host.

CHAPTER

THE SIXTEENTH

Stephen had raised an eyebrow when Kaley and I wandered into the church building two months ago, carrying an extra coffee.

"Hi, I'm Stephen." He introduced himself to Kaley and waved a hand toward the nearest pew. "Feel free to sit down."

He slid into the seat in front of us. "I'm glad you came back," he said to me. "It's been a while."

"My grandma made us come," I admitted, and Kaley jabbed me with her elbow. "We're not going to stay long. I was just wondering about our brother. It's been almost a year since we've heard from him, and I don't even know if he's still…"

Stephen offered a slight smile. "I'm happy to help, but I don't really have any information to give you. I haven't seen him since we last spoke."

"Oh…"

"Thanks anyway," Kaley cut in. "Sorry to interrupt your day. Can we repay you with a coffee?" She held out the extra one we brought.

Stephen chuckled. "How about a coffee *tomorrow morning*?" he suggested. "And a date after that?" His eyes flickered to me.

I felt a flush cross my face. Kaley's gaze moved between the two of us, and I felt like she wanted me to say *yes*. But I didn't know what to say. Why in the world was Stephen asking me when Kaley—the pretty, athletic option—was here? I avoided my sister's intense, green gaze, wishing she'd mind her own business.

But Stephen laughed. "Don't worry, Helen, your face is telling me enough. I'm not insulted. Disappointed, maybe, but that's how life goes, eh?" He patted the back of the pew, thankfully still smiling about it.

I released a horrendously fake laugh and Kaley grimaced. "I'd still like to be friends," I said, and Stephen chuckled again.

"I'd like that too. You have a certain light in you, you know. Usually, I'm pretty in tune with these things, but for some crazy reason I can't seem to figure out exactly why yours is the way it is."

My smile had been real after that. If only he knew.

Stephen glanced at Kaley and studied her curiously. Maybe he saw some of that light in her as well. "That's how faith works though. Even just a spark is enough to shatter the darkness when it's got a hold on you."

I had brought him coffee the next day. And the one after that.

My eyes stayed on Kaley until we reached the Green prison—a village of wood-beam rooms with no windows. Thick chains hung over the path like a metal jungle, locks dangling where lanterns were supposed to be. The wood smelled wet, like a humid summer night, and my thoughts drifted back to my summer spent pouring over the story of Day and Night, humming that obnoxious song that was supposed to summon a Guard of Doors.

"Split them up." The Axeman's voice was a dagger.

Zane and I were wrestled one way, Lucas and Kaley another. My gaze broke from my sister as I was shoved into a log room with splinters sprouting from the walls, decaying wood rotting in the corners.

The ceiling was made of sparse wooden slats, revealing tiny stars peeking through the foggy blanket of troubled, gray sky. The clouds promised a pending storm.

Zane dropped to sit against the wall. "The Patrols will come," he said. "They'll figure out a way to escape the Dungeon of Souls, and they'll come for us."

"You didn't see what I saw." I sank down beside my Patrolman, my coat puffing around my face.

"Don't give up yet, Helen."

Without warning, a spoon flung over the wall of our cell and landed in the snow at Zane's feet. But the most unexpected part was that Zane *laughed*. I stared at him in surprise. I watched my Patrolman blink a few times, then pick up the spoon. He held it up like he was looking at his reflection. "I'm starting to see shadows and light, Trite, and dull colours." He stood and threw the utensil back over the wall.

"Ow!" Lucas bellowed from his own enclosure across the path.

I smiled, but it fell away when I looked back at the log cage, the slat ceiling, the prison.

"I've been in the dark too long," Zane went on. "My sputtlepun scotcher is ready to muddle some Green buttons. This isn't the end for us, Helen..." His merriment fizzled away when he found me staring off. "What?"

Instead of explaining myself, I cleared my throat and started to hum. I'd only had a sip of cider at the feast, so the tune was raw and dry, but I carried it until I felt someone *watching* me.

"Helen...?" Zane said again.

I opened my eyes to find a small hole in the air, a golden iris peeking through.

Obb may have cursed—it was muffled as the hole peeled open wider. The white-bearded man's entire face pushed through, hovering like a balloon. Zane was wide-eyed and frozen at the room's wall.

"What is it now, girl? Don't you know I have things to do?" Obb's bushy brows tilted in.

"I know you serve Elowin even if you can't admit it," I said. "Elowin's last Carrier is about to be executed in the Green Kingdom, and the Volumes of Wisdom, wiped out."

Obb's face soured. "I'll not get involved either way," he promised.

"Then Nightflesh will win, even after I've warned you."

Obb blinked impatiently. "It's not possible to make a door to Winter *inside* of Winter. And even if I could do it, I wouldn't."

"Then how are you doing it now?" I challenged, climbing to my knees.

"This is *not* a door!" His face reddened. "It's a peephole! And I'm breaking the rules by talking to you through it. Be gone now, girl." Obb's white beard pulled back through the opening.

"Don't leave!" I couldn't get the words out before the hole plugged and every trace of the man in the navy tent vanished.

I slumped back against the wall, kicking my legs out. My stinging eyes slid shut.

"What are you doing?" Zane's tone was accusatory.

And after all my months and efforts of trying to restore everything, I lost it.

"Why is it so easy for you to ask that question?!" I shoved myself up and Zane shuffled back. "You asked me to stay in Winter, but when I suggested you come to the Trite world, you *laughed.*"

"Helen, I—"

"Do you want to know why I looked like garbage when we met in Waterloo? *That's why!*" I growled. "Because everyone's making me choose. Even *you* aren't willing to help me find a door!" I was almost screaming now, sure even Lucas and Kaley could hear.

I realized my face was wet. I blinked through the blur, trying to slow the blood pumping through my veins.

Zane was dead-still for a heartbeat. He finally dropped his gaze to the snow, jaw tight. "Well, it's about bloody time you admitted what's wrong," he murmured.

Snow descended on a chilly current, piling up in our cell.

"I can't keep being separated from this pace. From you. From all of it," I said.

When Zane lifted his graying, dismal eyes, I thought he would explode. "So, I'm part of the problem? Because of our bond?"

I glanced off, throat dry. "It doesn't matter anymore. We're in this mess because I made an irrational plan that's going to get us killed."

He moved closer, boots dragging through the snow. "But you weren't wrong, Helen. The Volumes don't offer parables for no reason. Ragnashuck, bringing the Triad of Signs back together might be possible with those clues. Trust me, I should know."

The dip in Zane's voice was odd—I studied him as he chewed his lip like a little boy who was about to get in trouble for bad behavior.

"What do you mean, *you* should know?"

He fiddled with the buttons on his jacket. "I have a troubling idea about where the third piece of the Triad is." His throat bobbed. "I mapped those snowseas from dawn to dusk. Even as a child, I steered the ships to learn the sea's tricks. So, I know them well. But I also know there's a thing or three out there worse than your greatest nightmares."

The image of Zane steering a ship as a child was one I'd never be able to scrub from my imagination. "Pirates?" I asked.

"No. There are things a good measure worse than pirates in those snowseas," he whispered, a flash of navy darkening his eyes before he tilted away.

My fingers dug into my hair. "Why didn't you say something before?"

"Because the price for what we need will be costly, and I think I'm the only one who can pay it."

I studied his fidgeting fingers, his stolen glances at the sky. "Why does it have to be you?"

Zane paused to shake the snow from his hair and brush it off his shoulders. I thought he wouldn't answer, but he finally said, "The snowseas don't forget things, Trite. And I gave them a lot to remember."

I grabbed his restless hands, bringing him still. Zane's blotted eyes flickered back and forth between mine. He raised his sleeve to brush the remains of moisture from my cheeks, feeling his way around the curve of my jaw, squinting. His lashes flickered down toward my mouth, and a ribbon of warmth moved through my abdomen.

A dinner fork spiralled over the wall and landed in the snow beside us. I released the breath I'd been holding and reached for it when the lock on our door rattled. A deep voice came from the path. "Take them one at a time to be interrogated. Do the Rime-blood first."

My hand halted and my gaze fired to Zane.

THE

STORYTELLER

THE EIGHTH INTERRUPTION

Gathadriel Mithnus was the fairy sort to listen, obey, and heed the signs. But never did he run from a fight, for it was not within his bones to fear the spirits of darkness that whittled away at Rime souls.

He rather enjoyed quarrelling with them, truly.

But on this occasion, he never intended to face off with the legion that swept up from below the snow; long limbs and whispers of curses upon their dry, thin lips. Headed to fetch a Trite, he was. But he had been surrounded, and so, fetch a Trite he did not.

For seven straight sunrises he battled the feasting spirits in the snow, until the skies grew dim each eve and after. The creatures had snapped at his tattooed flesh, catching a rise from his flaming symbols. 'Twas a war not fought in flesh and blood, but by spirit against spirit. They tore at his wings, bit at his ankles, and spit falsehoods against his truths. Even so, Gathadriel defeated them; two hundred and fifty plus five feastbeggars had turned to black stains of ash upon the glittering white snow, marking the floor of the Glass Woods like burn patches.

Upon glancing at the Winter skies, the fairy counted back his days. Much could have happened in seven days' time. So, Gathadriel inhaled a breath of cold wind and defeated dark spirits, and he trudged back the way he had come, to alert Porethius of these new creatures.

But when Gathadriel arrived at the factory with its metallic song of working machines, he took inventory of the beating hearts and moods in the air, and he discovered that Porethius's presence was far away.

Gathadriel looked out at the night with a speck of trouble on his brow, the scarcity of souls a great weight upon his shoulders.

"Edward!" The fairy's dark skin pulled tight as he turned and marched through the factory, searching the dim halls for his assignment.

In the back of the meeting room, the fairy found the Green once-prince tucked away in a corner, sitting with his arms wrapped about his knees. Gathadriel halted. "Are you ill?"

Edward lifted his eyes, heavy with pink and a leaden spirit. "I have hardly slept since you left," the once-prince admitted. "All is wrong, Gathadriel."

A knock on the factory doors drew the fairy back out to the main room where a short, well-aged man with a white beard had let himself in. The man carried a velvet suitcase much too large for any measure of journey, studded with gears and trinkets.

"Doorkeeper." The fairy edged across the floor, studying the ancient ally he had not crossed since the beginning of time itself.

The aged man blinked his golden irises. "Where is Porethius-Prunella-Sugar Plum?"

Gathadriel straightened. "I will speak in her absence,"

he said.

The Guard of Doors tapped a finger against his suitcase handle. Then, seeming convinced, he said a thing that brought the dwarves, the Chocolatiers, and Edward Haid out of hiding—all of whom had been spying from the shadows.

"I come against my better judgement," the aged man clarified to start. "But even so...I bring poor news of bad tidings about a thing I have seen across the wintersphere."

CHAPTER

THE SEVENTEENTH

A bruise purpled Zane's jaw when they brought him
back to me. I didn't have time to ask what had happened before they grabbed me by the fur of my
hood. Zane spun, but the heavy door slammed shut between
us.

My fingertips tingled on the walk to a snowy cove behind Timber Castle. The gray Winter skies toiled overhead,
swelling and darkening to a murky sea. I jumped at a *pop* in
the forest.

I was shoved toward a stump-chair next to a table and
told to *sit*. The Evergreen Host questioned me about being a
Trite, about my knowledge of the King of the East, about my
desire for the Crown of Pines.

I admitted as much as I could: No, Eliot Gray was not an

emissary, and he was not my husband. Yes, I was a common-blood. When asked how I'd entered Winter, I cracked a smile and said, "That's a long story."

A woman with intense, olivine eyes watched from the side of the cove. Every so often, she hummed, and the snow quivered. I felt the sensation of needles pressing in the sides of my head, and I squirmed in my seat. My hands slapped the tabletop when I couldn't take it anymore. "Stop!" I begged, blinking through moisture.

"Melody..." the Queen of the Pines emerged from the shadows, twirling a silver dagger and eyeing my shaking fingers.

The olivine-eyed woman paused her song, but the foggy breath from her lips curled toward my skin, leaving a trail of prickles. I worried they'd done this to Kaley.

"Try another one," the queen insisted with ice-and-stone eyes.

A cruel smile formed across the singer's mouth, and she parted her lips. This time, the hum carried words. It was like they were embedded into the tune, playing through my mind:

> *You'll have a place around our table mount*
> *All the food you like*
> *Plums and sweets, cakes, and pies*
> *All the food you like*
> *Come and join the feast*

Something tugged in my abdomen. Deep hunger growled, and my gaze tapped off the cove's surfaces, looking for the food she spoke of. I imagined a great feast, a colourful display of sweets, cakes, and pies. My empty stomach groaned, and I wrapped an arm across it.

A platter appeared before me and I sprang back from the table, tripping over the stump. My eyes widened at the glistening white apples, the bowls of ice berries with drizzled syrup, the steaming pile of herbed meat, and the hot cup of soup.

"Is that...real?" I whispered, inching closer on my knees.

The queen appeared past the platter, the needles of her dress sharpening into view. "Feasting. Gluttony. Greed. That is how my people are controlled, common-blood," she admitted. "I just keep feeding them."

My eyes wandered to the singing woman. I watched her lips barely move, vapour spilling from her mouth. "It won't work on me. I'm not greedy," I objected, but the queen's palms hitting the table caused me to jump.

"Yes, you are," she said, and my vision filled with bright light bursting around a rectangle. My breathing raced as the rectangle shifted, the creaking of an opening door filling my ears. Through the opening I saw a familiar hallway—and *Grandma*.

My grandmother grabbed the wall for support, tilting a framed portrait of Sylvia and Quinn. She dropped her cane, her hand flying over her chest.

"Grandma!" I screamed, but the door slammed shut. "Wait, please let me go through—"

Tears fell on my fingers as the door swung back open, slicing my words. A boy appeared; his shaggy blond hair was drenched from the pounding rain where he sat against a brick wall. He was alone until a man encompassed by dark, curling smoke approached and knelt down. The boy lifted his head, revealing the face of my brother, but on a skinny, poorly dressed body I hardly recognized. The man murmured and held something toward Winston. It looked like a needle, and my chest tightened. As soon as Winston accepted it, the darkness around the man spread into ribbons like serpents, all rounding on where Winston was curled into a ball.

"Is this a real door?" I cried. "If it's real, please let me go through..."

The entire scene vanished, leaving me back before the

queen. The singing woman's song became a screeching set of nails on metal, and I cringed.

There was no ripping of fabric in the heavens, no light bursting over my path, no paint-like colours swimming in the air, or white birds with rainbow eyes. But I dug deep for an old memory of being tempted once before in a dark forest, and to a being of music and light that had found me then...

"Stop." My threat halted the last note on the singing woman's tongue. "Or I'll start singing back." My lashes lifted, my eyes narrowed, my orb heated beneath my shirt.

She looked at me like I'd turned into a bear. I raised my trembling hands, gold and silver words forming across my flesh down to my fingertips. I could have cried. I wanted to shout at the words, *"Where were you?!"*

I stood, coming around the stump, eyeing the queen.

Suddenly, the queen grabbed her dagger and sliced. My hand flashed up and ice tore from the ground, a cold handle latching around my wrist as the shards constructed a shield. The dagger slammed into it, and she gaped.

I did too.

Our eyes met.

An eerie tune tore through the cove, filling my head with flickering visions of the rectangle door, and my stare fired to the singing woman as mutated, gray flesh covered her face. A bone-shuddering growl ripped from her throat, releasing a swarm of flies that blotted out my light like a dark mouth coming up from the ground to swallow me.

I didn't remember passing out.

My heels landed on damp stone. Wails of fallen faith

chilled my skin. Everything smelled of rain, rot, and death. It was too dark to make out forms, but the appetite of the feastbeggars was palpable through the tunnels.

I extended my hands—this was it. This was my chance to free the believers...

My face fell.

The gold and silver words were gone.

I flipped my hands around to see, but both sides were the same: plain, pale skin.

I looked around the tunnel, blinking at the dark turns.

Wake up, Helen! *I tried.*

A sound scraped around the tunnel's corner, and I flattened against the wall.

"She's here!" A collection of echoing whispers rushed right and left, coming from everywhere.

"Find her!" The same slew of a thousand whispers.

The scent of sour gnome flesh filled my nostrils, and I slapped a hand over my gagging mouth. Shouts bent around the tunnel. I felt needles—in my head, on my skin, stabbing my heart.

I slid down the wall and pressed my palms against my eyes. "Wake up," I tried again. "Wake up!" My nails dragged down my cheeks.

When I dropped my hands, my eyes fixed on someone, and a scream drove up my throat.

Asteroth Ryuu's silver eyes had turned black. Gray patches spotted his skin; his once-diamond white hair was stained with black speckles like burns. He was silent, staring like a lifeless doll. I trembled as I used the wall to stand.

"Found you." His beastly whisper sailed into my chest. Asteroth's mouth hadn't moved.

I ran, catapulting around the corner, jogging up a set of stairs, following the shouts from those in iron bars. I slowed by a shredded curtain where a tall, black stone reached high into the darkness, covered in carved names. Many of the names were stroked out, but two rested at eye level inside a deep, engraved circle:

Summons of Death for:
Edward Green
The coward
&

Cane Endovan Crimson-Augustus
The renounced

Pounding footsteps filled the tunnel, and I leapt through the tattered curtain, tripping down a triad of stairs. I skidded to a halt right in the middle of the Patrols' cages.

Cells on either side of me erupted with surprise, questions, and cries:

"Carrier!"

"Trite! Run!"

"Get out of here!"

I spun to the boys in raven-black and lifted my hands, trying to summon the power I knew was in my veins. I shook them.

Feastbeggars crept toward me in torn robes, reaching with crooked fingers. But smoke drifted into the tunnel, and they halted. Their onyx eyes swam. "The master has come!" Their whispers rushed like wind as they bowed to someone behind me.

Mirkra cried, "Run!" and a feastbeggar pounced toward his cell.

I couldn't move.

Nightflesh was silent, like he wasn't breathing.

My watery gaze fell to my Revelation Orb flickering light beneath my shirt. A quiet hymn touched my ears; a tune I knew.

"Zane?" I rasped, spinning. I blanched when I realized

what I'd done.

Hidden in the darkness, a tall shadow watched me from behind a metal helmet.

I gasped awake, the warmth of my orb dissipating at my chest. Someone held me, the scent of pine and mint flooding my senses.

"What did they bloody do to you?!" Zane yelled.

I blinked at the log room, the slat ceiling, the hanging chains. I flung around and pressed my ear against Zane's chest, listening for the sweet, slow tune. A hot tear spilled away as my fingers curled around his jacket.

"Helen, I thought you'd been whipsteamed to death when they tossed you in!" Zane's arms tightened around me; I could feel his heart slamming against my cheek.

Slowly, I unpeeled my fingers. It took me a few tries before I was able to speak. "You got treated worse than I did," I rasped. "I don't have any bruises."

Zane grunted. "They didn't hit me to make me talk, Trite. They hit me because that soldier spoke to me in a scotchy, condescending tone. So I slapped the snooty pine sipper."

I laughed through a mix of tears, lip quivering.

Zane tugged me off him and held me out, squinting to look me over. "Lucas and your sister are still untouched. I've been tossing cutlery with the sputtlepuns since you left. The fork and spoon keep coming back, so they must still be over there."

As he said it, two pieces of brass cutlery soared through the gaps in our ceiling and clanked off the log wall.

I crouched and dragged the spoon to myself. "I saw *him.*" My voice dipped. I bit my lips together so I wouldn't whimper like a child. "Nightflesh."

After a long moment of silence, Zane picked up the fork and twirled it slowly in his fingers. He dropped to a knee and tilted the spoon in my hand so that I could see myself in the warped, oval mirror.

"It's no brush," he said, holding up the fork, "and I'm no Apple Dough. But if it'll bring you a pinch of cheer, Helen, I'll fix you up best I can."

Zane took a lock of my frayed, knotted hair and began combing through it.

He told me short Winter tales while he worked. Over the hours, I watched his almost-dimples appear in the reflection of the spoon, until the dark skies drained to a hazy gray, hinting that morning was crawling over the forest.

"All done," he said, crawling around to see his work.

"How do I look?" My voice was still raw.

Zane stared for a moment. His gaze dropped to the fork on his lap, and he twirled it with dexterous fingers.

"Time to check on the sputtlepuns." He stood and hurled it back over the wall. I handed him the spoon, and when he tossed it over, we waited.

Sure enough, the fork and spoon sailed back a few minutes later.

CHAPTER

THE EIGHTEENTH

Blasting horns woke Zane, sending birds shrieking in
the trees and flapping off into the distance.

"What the bloody sea snake..." he muttered, un-
curling from a ball. He used the wall to drag himself up, rubbing his eyes.

I'd stayed awake, watching the early morning shadows
fade and blue skies trickle in, smothered by the constant gray
clouds trapping Winter under a spell of smoke. I'd pinched
myself every few minutes so I wouldn't drift off.

Heavy thuds filled the path outside, and the lock to our
room clanked. The door flung open.

"Out." The Evergreen Host soldier had a braided beard,
and a wreath of branches in his hair.

I obeyed and Zane followed closely. A body hit me,

nearly knocking me off my feet. "Ragnashuck, you scotchy saltslugs! *Watch* it!" Lucas shouted at the man who'd thrown him.

I looked back for Kaley and her green eyes locked onto mine. "We heard you get taken by the Host last night," she whispered ahead. "I couldn't sleep."

"Silence," a soldier shouted, and Kaley obeyed, eyes darting to her shuffling feet.

We were led up the path through snow-dusted woods to a wide, open-top arena made of upright logs. A door lifted upward like a hatch, and the soldiers nudged us through.

The arena was filled with thousands of people viewing what appeared to be a business meeting.

"The Council of Pines," Lucas whispered.

The Queen of the Pines rested upon an intricately carved throne, her green gown draping over the willow branch arm-rests. The Council of Pines sat in a crescent around her.

Across from them, on a bed of frost-kissed dirt, stood Edward Haid.

I stopped walking.

Edward's dark hair and gold eyes made him look young, even with the speckles of silver in his hair. At his back stood Gathadriel, the ally that was supposed to have gotten Kaley out of the Green Kingdom.

The queen listened to Edward speak, her face stone, but her stance looked as fragile as glass.

Gathadriel's gaze flickered to us when we were pushed ahead. Edward's hands clasped and unclasped at his waist.

"I've brought my prisoners, as you requested. Now, tell me your plot before I cage you with them."

"Ever..." Edward's deep voice carried—the arena was dead-quiet. The royals' voices were magnified like they spoke into microphones. "Grant me the opportunity to make a thing right with you."

Gathadriel's wings bristled, and he studied the crowd.

"You may speak of your intentions, Brother. But I do not

have to listen," the queen warned coldly.

"In one day's time, you'll face the Crimson King in a battle he has already won once," Edward said. "But it is *my* birthright to fight the Crimson King. To be slain by him, if it comes to that."

Gathadriel's jaw hardened, his tattoos beginning to quiver.

The Queen of the Pines stood. "You have no birthright anymore."

"You're right." Edward raised both hands. "But I know what will happen to this kingdom if you're turned back into snow."

"You think I'll lose?" Vicious rosiness brushed the queen's cheeks.

"I think it's a chance you shouldn't have to take. I wish to make a deal to fight on your behalf at sunrise."

"Edward..." Gathadriel cut in; he was at Edward's side now.

"Wait, Fairy."

The Queen of the Pines's dagger-voice seemed to brush up Gathadriel's back. He reluctantly turned back to the queen, nodding once, then swept out of the way. He whispered to himself, eyes squeezed shut.

The queen reached for a long, branch-like scepter and dragged it down the dais with her, scraping the wood. She stopped, inches away from Edward.

"This kingdom will not accept you as its king if you win," she promised.

But Edward nodded. "I don't intend to steal your crown."

"Really, Brother? I thought my crown was exactly what your allies came to steal."

Edward's gold eyes darted up in surprise. "You were always intuitive, Sister." He stole a look at us, and I felt his glance drive all the way down into my toes.

"The Crimson King will turn you to pinespittle," the

queen said. "And I'm insulted you think I need your aid. But you are right about one thing—this dying kingdom needs me. So, I'll take your deal."

Her pale hand came out. I saw Gathadriel flinch, but he didn't intervene. Edward looked at his sister, and he took her hand. "Deal." His whisper was almost lost to the wind.

"But I know you, Brother," the queen cut in. "You will run." She dropped Edward's hand and turned her back on him, climbing to her throne as the arena erupted with noise—sticks banging against chairs, silver bells ringing, and cheers flooding the breeze.

Edward's gold stare followed the queen up the dais, his shoulders relaxing. He nodded.

But I gawked at the Green Prince. The Crimson King enjoyed killing his enemies as much as he enjoyed licking pudding off a spoon.

Edward Haid exited the arena through a tunnel. He snuck one last glance back at where the queen lowered onto her wood throne, and I recognized the look on his face—it was how I looked at Kaley, and Grandma, and even Winston.

Back in our log cells, I watched Zane play cutlery-catch with Lucas over the walls until I couldn't keep my eyes open any longer. While I slept, I heard the creatures of darkness laughing at this turn of events.

PART V

THE

STORYTELLER

THE NINTH INTERRUPTION

K aley Bell's thumbs danced in a twiddly circle, around
and around and around and around and around and
ar—

Lucas's hand flashed out and smacked her thumbs with
a look that indicated he was a mere pinch from turning madder than a calling wicket.

"Sorry," Kaley mumbled, pulling her hands away from
his and stuffing them into her pockets.

A fork hit a slat above their room and spiralled down, its
prongs stabbing the snow. The spoon followed a moment
later, and Lucas caught it before it would have pelted Kaley
in her fair, pink mouth.

"Cohen's aim is getting scotchy," he said.

"Maybe he's getting tired," Kaley offered.

But Lucas's smile appeared. "Cohen doesn't get *tired*." Though, the Patrolman's topaz eyes lifted to the wall's heights where the spoon had come from.

Before them, depictions of maps and clues were drawn into the bed of crunchy snow, the butterknives still wet from being used. Kaley nudged the edge of her most recent map drawing, filling in the border with a dollop of flakes to make it disappear. They would be forced to ruin their artwork soon, lest the Evergreen Host discover it and read its wisdom.

Lucas watched the toes of her boots drag.

"I'm ready for a nap, Trite. All this studying isn't my cup of cocoa," he said.

"I know." Kaley's eyes fell to the sketches. "But it's important for you to memorize these maps."

"Why is that? I haven't the mind to replace you as the *library-being* if something happens to you." He paused. "But you already know that, don't you?"

"If we escape this mess, I need you to find something for me."

The Patrolman raised a brow. "I knew you were hiding some big plans in that pretty head."

"You can't tell Helen," Kaley said, forehead creasing. "She's not herself."

Lucas's face twisted. "Gah!" He threw up his hands. "I hate keeping secrets."

"I need you to find an island guarded by fairies. It's called *Orphan Island*."

Lucas sighed and snuggled in deeper against his seat. "Orphan Island, Trite? I hate to shush your pebble talk, but that island isn't real. Even the pirates mapping the snowseas will tell you that."

Kaley picked up a butterknife and began a new drawing. "It is real. I saw it on a few maps."

Lucas rolled his eyes. "Yes. But it was never in the same place, right, Trite? No one can find it because it doesn't exist. It's an old Winter story about a magic coast where lost, lonely children are carried to live merrily together."

"It's as real as any place in Winter. It's in different places on those maps because it's always moving. That's why even those who claim to have seen it can never find it twice."

Lucas craned his neck to study her. "Ragnashuck, you seem to care a good measure about what happens to us Rime Folk. Has it not crossed your pretty little Trite mind that you could leave us to our own demise?" Lucas did not give her time to reply. "And what makes you believe I'll do a thing about any of this once you're gone?"

She tilted her head. "I hope you're joking."

Lucas released a heavy, howly, huff sound. "Yes, fine, I joke. But I'd like a payment, nonetheless. Especially since you're asking me to find a place that doesn't exist." Kaley did not hide the rolling of her green eyes. "I have a thing in mind," he added.

"Great."

The Patrolman's dangerously wide grin caught her eye. "I think I'd like a kiss."

Kaley backed away a pinch. "A *what*?"

"Oh, don't muddle your mittens, darling. Not a big one, just one the size of a button would do." He pulled something from his pocket, and Kaley blinked at Eliot Gray's pearl button she had tossed into the snow a measure of days ago.

"How about a trade?" Lucas offered, holding the button out.

"I don't want Eliot's button." Kaley tried to flick the pearly bead away, but Lucas drew his hand back.

"Fine, Trite. I forbid you from kissing me. And you get no button. I'm sure you're secretly heartwrenched."

"I'm positive it's the other way around." Kaley picked up the spoon and threw it over the wall. Lucas followed suit and hurled the fork, much higher than her throw. Not that it was a contest.

A moment or three passed before he spoke again. "Do you want to know why I'm certain that island doesn't exist, Trite?" he asked.

When Kaley rolled her head against the log to look at him, she found Lucas chewing on his lip, smile gone. A starburst of rust-orange flooded his irises, and she lifted her head from the wall.

"Because I was a lost child, with nothing and no one. And no island fairy came to rescue me."

Kaley's lips parted, but no words came. Lucas's gaze dropped to his butterknife. "So, you see, a place like that cannot exist." He flung the butterknife into the air and caught it again by its dull blade.

Cool air slipped into the log cage, and Kaley hugged her legs to herself, tracing a missing island on her knee with a finger. Far in the distance, a creature howled at the moon. "Maybe you were never rescued by the fairies because you were always meant to be rescued by someone else," she said, bringing Lucas's attention back. Something strange crossed the Patrolman's face. He stared off, a finger lifting to brush the scar on his face.

New snow puffed o'er the walls, sprinkling upon their canvas of drawings. The fork and spoon made their return, plummeting into the snow between their feet. A time again, the pair took the utensils and hurled them to carry on the game.

"Lucas," Kaley said.

"Darling?" His voice was quiet, but he offered his lovely smile.

"I have to ask more of you than to just find the island," she admitted.

"Is that so?" Lucas drew out the pearl button again, rolling it along his fingers to imply what it would cost her.

Though Kaley would not kiss him for that preposterous button, the action threatened to make her laugh.

"If we get out of this disaster, I need to go to the White Kingdom border," she said.

Lucas made a peculiar face. "A good measure of self-declared saints have made that walk, Trite, but they don't always like what they find. What's muddled your soul?"

Her gaze cast to where the fork and spoon had disappeared over the wall. "I need to fix something I broke."

"Ragnashuck, Trite." Lucas rubbed his eyes. "Don't you ever get tired of scheming?"

"Not when it comes to something like this. So, will you come with me?"

"Well. Frostbite, alright." Lucas shoved the button into his pocket. "Why not?"

"And I need to see that note you stole from Eliot Gray," she added. "You can't hide it from me forever."

Lucas shifted in his seat. "Ah. That scotchy, little thing."

"Why haven't you shown it to me?"

"Well, because at first I thought Eliot wrote it about *you*. But now I'm certain he wasn't thinking of you at all."

Kaley's brows tugged in. "Lucas, if you don't show me, I'm just going to wait until you're sleeping and steal it from your pocket."

But Lucas snorted a laugh. "Good luck finding it!"

"Lucas," she pleaded.

"Yes, yes, darling." He reached into a concealed pocket and drew out the folded slip of paper. Kaley had to admit, she never would have found it there had she gone snooping.

She took the note, but Lucas held onto it a pinch longer. When her gaze flickered up, the topaz of Lucas's eyes dipped to rust-gold, but he released the paper, and Kaley unfolded it.

The note was not a sonnet or a letter, rather, it was a simple word:

211

Trite Trite Trite Trite
Trite Trite TRITE TRITE
TRITE TRITE TRITE
TRITE

It appeared twenty plus eight times more, scratched into the paper with black ink that splattered the page's torn edges.

Kaley slammed the note shut, folding it and pushing it back against Lucas's chest.

"Helen," she whispered, the name raw on her tongue.

Slowly, Lucas returned the note to his pocket. "I would think as much."

"What's Eliot's problem with her?" Kaley asked.

"I imagine he's grown obsessed. I saw a Patrolman's sense of duty twist a time or three in my early seasons. It's what happens when someone turns away from the Truth and loses their purpose." Lucas tied a ribbon to seal his pocket shut. "But I can't decide if Gray has become obsessed with *saving* Helen or *destroying* her to end his misery. And the worrisome part, Trite," Lucas turned on his knees to face Kaley, "I don't think he's decided which one he's set on, either."

CHAPTER

THE NINETEENTH

A ll night I thought about Edward Green. The morning
came too fast.

The clearing for the Silver Jubilee Renewal
thundered with shouts, bells, and wooden flag poles pounding against the crystal floor. Half the space was interspersed
with crimson fabric and cherry headdresses, and the other
half with emerald capes, branch antlers, and wooden armour.
The sides roared at each other, waving flags and spewing
hatred across the glassy rink reserved for the kings to fight
to the death.

It had taken us an hour riding a bear-drawn sleigh to arrive. My hands were bound, as were Zane's. I didn't see
Lucas and Kaley. I scanned the clearing at the kingdoms'
boundary where the trees curled in like claws, and snow
ripped across a distant, windy field, trying to spot Edward.

As we were led to our seats, I wondered if the Red royals
would recognize me across the rink. Zane and I were wedged
between spectators on sloped, log benches, surrounded by

Evergreen Host soldiers.

Garland-wrapped figures emerged from the forest shadows like phantoms led by the Queen of the Pines's sleigh. An emerald cape flapped at her back, intricately carved armour holding it to her shoulders. Wings of kohl adorned her piercing eyes where she took in the howling crowd of onlookers. The Crown of Pines was lit atop her head.

"Cheat's here," I heard Zane say over the ruckus of the queen's white bears snarling at the descending reindeer. The Crimson King stampeded across the sky atop his holly-covered reindeer, followed by Prince Tegan, Prince Forrester, and the rest of the Red Princes.

They landed on the ice with thuds, the reindeer releasing sharp screeches across the clearing. The polar bears roared back as the Queen of the Pines swept onto the rink.

"Cheat probably doesn't even know you're here," I said.

Zane blinked rapidly, squinting. "Yes, he does."

It took me a second to locate the embellished madman. I found Jolly Cheat in his pure white magician's outfit, long coat, and wild bell-hat. He was looking directly at me, and he winked. I shifted in my seat. I hadn't seen him since he'd shoved me into the Midnight Forest last year.

Jolly's nickel gaze shifted to Zane. The madman reached to tug the hood off the woman beside him, brushing aside a handful of her pecan hair to whisper in her ear. My throat swelled at the woman's pure white eyes and the black ashworm tattoo on her exposed neck. A slow, cherry-red smile found her face.

Zane was a sculpture of ice beside me.

"Season's greetings." The Queen of the Pines's magnified voice carried over the clearing and I sat up straighter, straining to see as the shouting died down. The Crimson King's copper suit of armour glistened in the sun, a bloodred cape rustling in the wind at his back.

He drew a long, golden sword. "Season's greetings, Queen," his airy voice responded, drifting over the ice from his side of the rink. "Is that fear I see in your eyes?"

The queen's stone-cold gaze didn't waver. "Fear is folly. I carry only a hunger to watch you turn to snow."

Roars burned over the armies in red.

"Shall we see which of us meets that fate?" A beam of morning sunlight tore over the king's blade when he raised it.

"I have no doubt you shall, King, but I petition an allowance for a substitution. However, I only offer the petition as a courtesy; my substitution will participate by rights of his heritage."

The queen's Axemen parted at her back, and out marched Edward Haid in the wooden armour of the Evergreen Host, a silver blade in his grip. Gasps erupted over the rink, and the Crimson King's sword dropped to his side. "I give you the Prince of the Pines. And after he defeats you this midday, King, I will meet your sons in battle, and I will relish their deaths too."

The Queen of the Pines extended a hand adorned with oval wood rings and nutshell-plates. "Shall we bind this substation allowance? Or do you fear my brother?"

A slow, wicked smile spread across the Crimson King's face, his blackened plum eyes glowing. He smashed his copper gauntlet against the Queen of the Pines's leather wristband. "Deal. It would be my *pleasure* to rid the snowglobe of your brother."

The moment the Crimson King dropped the queen's hand, he raised his gold sword and speared it into the ice as the Axemen abandoned Edward to the rink.

"It seems I've finally caught you, boy," the king's voice scratched. "How riddlesome, that after all your seasons of hiding from me, you would choose to evoke your kingship *now*."

Edward offered a weak smile. "I'm not a boy anymore, and you are an aged man."

"Aged with experience spilling blood," the king rasped.

"I came to fight a queen today, but it seems I'll be settling for a Green coward."

Edward's smile fell, and murmurs rippled across the clearing.

The Crimson King ripped his blade free from the ice, spraying shards at Edward's eyes. The golden sword sliced the wind and Edward bent back, catching himself on his palm and shaking the debris from his face. The Crimson King raised his blade over Edward's chest, gripping the handle with both hands, and Edward tilted as the blade plummeted. His gaze darted to where his own sword had flown across the rink.

The crowd leapt to their feet, screaming and waving flags as the Crimson King slammed Edward around the rink. The hilt of the golden sword struck Edward's forehead and he tumbled to a knee, but he ripped a dagger from his boot and stabbed the king's thigh.

A crackling growl filled the clearing, and Edward kicked off a ledge to slide on wood poleyns out of the king's reach.

From her high chair, the Queen of the Pines wasn't blinking. Her fingers gripped her armrests.

Edward staggered to his feet as the Crimson King's smile returned. He tilted his neck from side to side, cracking it.

"That was good practice. But I think I'll usher in *my* substitution now."

Edward's dark brows tugged in as the Reds shuffled apart. Someone was shoved through; wrists bound, mahogany hair disheveled. "I wish you good tidings in your fight to the death, boy," the Crimson King said to Edward, and my stomach dropped.

Shouts rattled the benches as Cane lifted his dull, burgundy eyes, blinking against the bright sun through bruised eyelids. He spotted Edward standing opposite him on the rink, dressed in wooden armour and holding a wide, silver sword.

THE

SILVER

JUBILEE

RENEWAL

THE TENTH INTERRUPTION

'Twas a deafening silence that ruled the witnesses of the Renewal. Edward's flesh was solid marble, his heart a hammer, his will, crushed glass.

Cane's purpling bruises matched his deep gaze, which he locked on Edward.

The Crimson King's golden blade was shoved into Cane's fingers, and Edward's sword grew heavy in his hand. Cane's bindings were cut, and Edward took a step to meet him. But they did not come more than a measure of paces toward each other.

The ivory-haired Red Prince smiled cruelly from the rink's edge, along with the rest of Cane's brothers. A measure of the nobles laughed.

Edward cast Cane a bleak smile. "It seems they got us, Brother," he said.

Cane turned the golden sword in his gashed hand. He

glanced back at the Reds like he might hurl the weapon into their multitude. "I'm sorry, Green. I couldn't outrun them."

Edward offered a small nod.

"Begin the Renewal!" a folk from the emerald banners screamed, and that was it—a thousand voices began chanting as two fairies landed in the crowd, faces ashen. Porethius's hand found Gathadriel's.

"It'll be alright, Red," Edward said. "Remember that you are loved. Perhaps not by those ashworms in crimson capes, but by One who matters more."

Cane blinked, brows drawn, and Edward smiled as he glanced at the familiar banners with his family's crest, at the Green villagers, at the wreaths. He recalled his early seasons chasing Ever through Timber Castle and tossing glass beetles in her hair.

"Green?" Cane dragged a step closer.

Edward glanced up, settling on the Red once-prince's face. "Greater love hath no folk than this; that he lay down his life for his brother," he quoted, dropping his blade and pulling a set of medallions from his pocket.

Cane's burgundy eyes narrowed—he inhaled, but 'twas too late. For, from the first moment Edward had seen Cane across the rink, Edward knew this was his cross to bear.

Popping erupted through the clearing when the Green Prince slapped the medallions together, and a spring of snow blanketed him in white. And as the flakes unleashed their fury, Cane's shouts, along with the other sounds of Winter, died fast from his ears.

Quietness came with the light that followed. Edward's spirit was approached by a warm, familiar prayer who lit the way, beckoning him with a giggle, a pleasant flit, and a flirt. And Edward Green found the Truth he had known was by his side since the day he had uttered that prayer by the fountain.

For the first time in many seasons, peace came flooding in like a warm hand to welcome him home.

CHAPTER

THE TWENTIETH

Witnesses were screaming. Even the sneering Red
Princes at the sidelines had dropped jaws now. I
was on my feet, moving toward the rink, pushing
through garland-wrapped men and women with my bound
hands, Zane on my heels. The Evergreen Host didn't try to
stop us—they stood like statues; gazes fixed on the rink.

Their long-lost Prince of the Pines was dead.

Cane dropped the golden sword and bounded to the pile
of snow on the ice. A Ruby Legionnaire slid from the Reds
to intercept him, but he was ripped back by Porethius Plum.
The fire in her violet eyes could have set the snow ablaze.

Cane swept to the snow pile, tufts of white floating,
sticking to his jacket.

"Bring him back! Elowin, his work isn't done!" Cane
begged. "I still need him! *Kingsblood, bring him back*!"

The spectators grew quiet, all listening to the pleas of the
surviving prince of the Renewal.

"He loved you like a brother." The Queen of the Pines's

whisper brought Cane's face up, his tears glimmering in the morning light.

"More than my own brothers."

My stare flickered to the Red Princes. Prince Forrester's eyes tightened, his fingers flicking to the blade hilt at his belt. Some of the young princes still chuckled in victory, but a shrill tweet reverberated from the trees, and the princes' gazes lifted to a glimmer in the heavens.

Forrester jumped in surprise, his blade tumbling to the snow as hundreds of silver-winged birds spiralled in from the forest. They filled the branches above with a canopy of silk feathers, a low hum thundering in their beaks.

The Queen of the Pines watched with glassy eyes. "If Edward loved you such a great measure, then his work is done. Let him go to the next kingdom to be with his True King," she said, and Cane blinked through tear-stained lashes.

The birds' melody grew like a funeral choir, paving the moment with birdsong until the snow Edward left behind erupted and wisped away in the wind.

The birds hushed. They began to disperse, one by one.

Cane stood on wobbling knees and extended a bruised hand to the queen. "I'm sorry for your loss," he rasped.

They looked at each other in silence. Then the queen took Cane's hand. "Likewise, Prince."

After a moment where everyone seemed unsure of what to do next, Red nobles began to leave, cheering and waving their flags. Reindeer lifted into the sky with shrieks, their horse-scent showering us below. But one from among the Reds stayed behind.

Jolly Cheat watched me from the crowd. Nobles brushed past him, making their way to their sleighs. Cheat wasn't glaring anymore—his mouth was twisted, his brows were bunched, and his intense stare made me strangely mindful of my grimy hair and sunken eyes.

He tore his nickel gaze away and turned to leave with

the others, his red and black overcoat disappearing amidst the capes and dresses.

"What shall we do with the prisoners, Your Majesty?" A voice drew my attention back to the Queen of the Pines. A spear-tip poked my back, and I hopped forward, catching Cane's wilted, gray-purple gaze. Zane tried to follow, but they held him back.

The queen lifted the Crown of Pines from her head and studied it. Then she extended it to me. "It was his by right. And it seemed he wanted you to have it," she said.

I was too stunned to accept the gift, but Cane took it and rested it on my hand until my fingers curled around it. A steady flow of power began to beat in my veins, like the crown was giving off a pulse. The queen marched to her sleigh, flanked by her Axemen and the Evergreen Host, and only Cane and I remained on the rink.

"Kingsblood," he whispered.

"I'm sorry." Guilt pressed on my stomach. "I'm so sorry."

Cane's throat bobbed and he glanced to where Edward's body had been. "I can't lose anyone else, Carrier." The burgundy in his irises darkened. "I..." his eyes slammed closed, "I *hate* losing people."

My eyes stung. "So do I." The crown felt warm in my grip.

"Helen!" Kaley called over the rink. Peeling my stare off Cane, I reluctantly turned to find two-dozen dwarves seated on the log benches, and Apple with a glistening tear in her eye. I huffed in relief, smiling weakly as I moved for Apple, wrinkling my nose at the faint scent of smoke in the air.

My fingertips buzzed as I tapped them, counting. It was such a small group that was left.

Frost crisped my fingers and I stopped. A ribbon of darkness floated into my vision. "No..." My hands flashed out before me as everything turned pitch black. Smoke and screams slithered into my ears and lungs, and I stumbled to my knees as a whirlwind tore at my hair. A loud, barbaric laugh echoed in circles, roaring in my ears.

"And soon they shall all fall..." The deep voice coiled around my bones. *"Cane Endovan-Crimson-Augustus. Apple Dough. Zane Cohen Margus-Bowswither..."* The names burned like a brand against my brain, and I screamed.

A light flickered at my chest; my orb struggled to push back the darkness and make a path, but the claws of blackness dove in and smothered it.

An arm burst in, tattooed symbols glowing as it ripped the blackness apart with a double-bladed weapon. Porethius's eyes were lavender stars in the dark; she spoke in another language with words I could *see* leaving her lips:

לָסֶגֶת נָחָשׁ לְצַיֵּית אֱלוֹהִים

The darkness screamed in my ears, blasting me with smoke, and I choked. My hand clasped my throat until cool air brushed my lips, and I inhaled, filling my lungs until it hurt. The blackness recoiled, fighting with every slithering limb until the white landscape of snow and trees returned.

The blaze faded from Porethius's eyes. I thought she'd be furious that I came to the Green Kingdom, but I saw compassion as she extended a strong hand. I blinked, stuck on those words she'd spoken. I didn't know how my mind had translated the symbols, but chills tightened my skin as the words sunk in:

Withdraw, Serpent! Obey your True King.

My fingers were cold when I took Porethius's hand. I smelled sugar and plums as she pulled me to my feet. Zane's electric eyes burned like azure wildfires. He approached, exchanging a look with Kaley.

"You opened your heart to Eliot Gray," Porethius said. "Your timestring is being tugged this way and that."

I scooped up the Crown of Pines from the rink, clutching it to my chest. My legs trembled and tiredness rushed through me.

"Come on, Helen," Zane took my cold fingers and dragged me to him, holding me tighter than ever. I realized he had a Patrol staff when he broke into a skate over the snow, around the log benches, and into the woods.

Fred Dough's sleigh waited in the bushes. Theresa was already on board, extending her arms to receive me when Zane lifted me on. He hopped in too, and Kaley sat across. She stared at Zane, who stared back at her.

Soft mint and pine encompassed me when my Patrolman wrapped an arm around my shoulders. I fell asleep to the rhythm of his breathing and the sweet song in his chest, with the Crown of Pines across my lap.

THE

STORYTELLER

A TRITE-ISH INTERRUPTION

Emily Parker was a Trite with a measure of qualities; the greatest of them being her stubbornness. With a strut in her step, and a shout tucked into her throat that she had saved for the appropriate moment, she trudged through the Waterloo snow in ankle-high boots not at all appropriate for the measure of slush on the sidewalks. With a huff and a hoot and a frothy cough, Emily made her way to where her dear friend, Helen Bell, had once told her a train had visited.

When Emily came past the brick shops, she studied the empty lane and the farmers' fields a pinch and a dip beyond the city. She spun once. Then she turned a time again, slower.

"Hello?" she called into the space.

The wind whistled its amusement as it sailed through the shops' alleys—the only response poor Emily Parker received at all. And so, she cleared her throat a time again.

"Hello?! Winter people?" she shouted, louder this time. "I know you're around here!" The Trite tightened her coat's collar, clutching it to herself. "Invisible-Winter-people? I need a ride, please!"

A snort echoed down the lane from a pair of youthful Trites passing through, and a blot of warmth found Emily's cheek.

"I'm not crazy!" she called at them. "I'm doing something important, for your information!" Emily tightened her coat again as the Trites shuffled off with a quicker step.

Emily sighed. "How do I open my eyes to see you wintery people?" she muttered to the wind.

"Easy."

Emily jumped when a voice came from behind her. She twisted, finding no one.

When the voice returned, it was at her back again, as though it had moved. It came against her ear, with an accent thicker than any she knew—almost indecipherable.

"Blink twice," it said.

Emily stilled.

With a double flap of her lashes, the Trite felt the cold air shift, changing directions. She turned toward the voice and was struck to find a young man looking at her through husky, turquoise eyes, fashioning a proper jacket and a sleek top hat. A silver chain dangled at his hip, and he pulled out a pocket watch to check the time.

"You're a pinch late for your reservation, Miss Parker. But I think I can make up the time," he said in that same thick drawl. But Emily had hardly heard the fellow; her eyes were fixed on something else.

For, behind the young man sat the most marvellous train.

CHAPTER

THE TWENTY–FIRST

I awoke as we reached the factory. Apple slid from the sleigh first and shed her olive-green cloak, pulling a handful of bangle bracelets from her pockets. Porethius dropped from the sky, slamming onto the front step with Cane in her grip. He detached himself and wheezed. But he took a long breath and straightened, smoothing down his mahogany hair before opening the doors. He staggered to a stop the moment he entered—Apple almost walked into his back.

A young woman stood in the dimly lit main room of the factory, her honey-blonde hair pulled to the side in a twist. Apple's gasp filled the chocolatey air as everyone flowed in.

By a mountain of rose-chocolate squares, Holly Kissing's hands were clasped behind her back. Or *Scarlet Strange's* hands, rather.

"You got out," Cane said to her.

Scarlet shifted her footing and nodded. "I brought this." When Scarlet pulled the ruby-red drum from behind her back, Cane huffed a dry laugh, but my lips parted.

"Kingsblood." The Red Prince met Scarlet in the middle of the room. "I'm merrily ubbersnugged," he whispered, receiving the drum and handing it back to Kaley, since I already held the Crown of Pines.

I blinked at the items in our hands, hardly believing they were real. Kaley cast me a subtle smile that said it all: that two Trites had managed to do something we had no business setting out to do.

Almost.

My gaze shifted to Zane. I watched the electric-eyed Patrolman scuff his pecan hair and lean his Patrol staff against the wall. He glanced into the empty factory balconies, and I imagined he was thinking about the young Rime souls in raven-black who used to fill them.

I didn't remember which halls I'd used when I searched for somewhere to nap. My bones felt on the verge of cracking, my muscles threatened to liquify. I could hardly think about anything but sleeping.

When I awoke hours later, a glittering, blue ceiling stretched above me with a copper chandelier of raindrop-diamonds dripping from glassy threads. I stared at the artwork reaching down the walls, depicting an array of white animals: antlered creatures, doves, lions, deer, and polar bears.

I laid my head back down and breathed a sigh of relief, inhaling the comforting smells of chocolate and nuts. When a shuffle sounded in the hallway, I sat up, smoothing down my hair. I cleared my throat to alert whoever was out there that I wasn't sleeping anymore.

Apple appeared with a deep-brown smile and a twinkle in her eyes. She carried a tray of treats. "Good morning, friend." She placed the tray on the coffee table.

"Thank you." I rubbed my eyes. Then I rubbed my eyes again. It didn't seem possible to still feel tired, but my body wanted to lay back down.

I took a handful of truffles and popped one into my mouth. "*Mmm*," I moaned. "I wish I could have these with me all the time." I eyed another.

Apple smiled. "I'm always just a season away, friend. I'll wrap some and send them with you for when you have to leave."

I slowed my chewing and dropped my gaze to the tray.

A raven-black jacket appeared in the doorway. Zane's eyes were that same muted tone as before, and I made a face. "What's gotten into you?" I asked, nodding to the truffles. "Eat something. You look like you're about to tip over."

"I'm fine," Zane said. "We need to talk."

I glanced at Apple, but she only shrugged. So, I stood and wiped my mouth with my sleeve, stifling a laugh when Apple scowled.

Zane led me through a network of spindled metal hallways and into the large, hollow main room. The sound of the chocolate waterfall filled the space. Kaley emerged from another hall; a backpack slung over her shoulders. I realized she was coming with us when Zane went outside, and she followed.

"Good grief, you two. What's going on?" I asked the moment we met cold air.

Zane glanced at Kaley. "Trite?" he said.

Kaley studied me. In my sister's forest-green eyes, I saw a look I didn't understand.

"We had a good plan, Helen. We got two out of three Triad pieces. But I also have my own plan," she said.

I huffed a phony laugh. "Okay. What's so bad about *your* plan that you had to keep it from me?" I stole a glance at Zane but he was quiet.

"Helen, I watched you burn out for months. And even after coming back here, you're still not better. I think what you need is *rest*." Kaley swallowed. "Even Lucas knows when to go on sabbatical."

"What are you saying?" I hugged my arms to myself.

My sister took a deep breath. "You tried to force your way back here when you weren't supposed to." She took one of my hands in hers. "But this isn't just about that. It's also about Eliot."

She lifted her hand, palm up, and I felt a tug in my spirit. It dawned on me what she was offering to take, and I pulled my hand from hers, horrified. My gaze fired to Zane, but he was looking off.

"I'll give it back in a little while," Kaley promised. "But you need to cut off Eliot's bond."

"And Zane's in the process!" I called back, unable to fathom this idea.

"Yes," Zane finally spoke, dragging his electric eyes to me. "And mine."

"How can you even..." I shook my head, clasping my fingers around the orb that had belonged to me for three of the most important years of my life.

"Trite, as long as Eliot is pledged to the Beast, he's a link between you and Nightflesh." Zane bit his lip, reaching to push my messy hair out of my eyes. "I need to fix you, Helen. This is how I do it." He dropped his hand.

"Edward said that the greatest form of love is to lay down one's life for their brother—or *sister*. You've been taking care of me long enough. For once, let me take care of you," Kaley said, open palm waiting.

In my mind's eye, I saw the Queen of the Pines's door between worlds, creaking open and letting the light of Sylvia's hallway spill through. I didn't know if it had been real or an illusion, but if she had offered to give me that door, I would have taken it. Shame on me, I knew I would have.

Stinging warmed my eyes. I felt like I had years of sleep ahead of me to make up for the months I'd lost. I lifted the glass orb whose gold and ivory centre brushed up the sides, still blemished by that dark, smoky crack from the collapse of Wentchester Cove.

"I just want to sleep," I admitted.

"I know," Zane whispered.

I stared at my sister's outstretched hand. And all the tension I had stored up in my shoulders began to drain. Though it felt like giving away a part of me, I unclasped the necklace and passed over the important treasure that Harmony Hucklebunk-Reyes had once given to me.

"This transfer of responsibility is official," I rasped, recalling those first words a Rime Folk had said to me in the streets of Waterloo.

Kaley's fingers wrapped around the glass sphere. Her brows tilted in, her eyes becoming distant. She whispered something, and I looked at Zane, then back at her. I leaned in to try and hear. "Kaley?" I didn't know what she was doing, or what she was looking at. It was like she forgot where she was. But a second later, her eyes darted back to me, and she blinked. Then, she smiled.

I was about to ask who she was talking to when the sharp blast of a horn filled the air, causing us to whirl. Those in the factory spilled out the front door; Old-Jymm dug out a spyglass and held it up, squinting out across the horizon.

"It's the train!" he yelled.

"By the sharpest wind, what is Cornelius Britley doing all the way out here?" Apple asked, tugging a pocket watch from her dress folds. I recognized it as the one Timblewon stole from the ringmaster at the circus. "And so dreadfully off schedule…"

The train was moving faster than I'd ever seen it; wind off the engine blasted over the snowdrifts as it rolled to a stop, violet sparkles littering the ground. The moment the gears stopped spinning, the golden-arched doors swished open, and I made a face.

"Emily?"

My friend emerged beside Cornelius Britley, who

kicked out a metal staircase attached to the train.

"Helen!" Emily rushed down the stairs. Her chest rose and fell as she pursed her mulberry-purple glossed lips. "I know this is bizarre, and you told me to stay away from here for my own safety or whatever. But...it's your grandma." Emily tapped her long, painted nails together as she paused to catch her breath. "She's in the hospital, and I didn't want anything to...well, you know. I didn't want something to happen while you were *gone*."

My lungs constricted. I saw it all over again—Grandma in Sylvia's hallway, dropping her cane. But it couldn't have been real. Everyone I knew who went to the hospital either died or fell into a coma; my grandmother was too alert for that place.

"So anyway, I didn't want her to be alone, and obviously I don't know her that well so it would be weird for me to go there," Emily went on.

I closed my eyes. "I have to go," I said.

"It should be you, Helen," Kaley agreed. "She's always been closest to you."

"You're not coming?"

Kaley slid the orb necklace over her head. "I have something important to do."

Stifling my objections, I grabbed my sister's hand. "Make sure you're back across that intersect before it closes," I said.

"Wait...*Helen*..." Zane appeared in front of me with a wild look on his face. "I just..." His fist came against his mouth like he was trying to shut himself up. "It's too bloody soon. I thought I had you for another ten plus two days," he blurted through his fingers.

I took in his bright, Rime eyes, memorizing how he looked this year so I'd never forget. "Bond or not, I'm going to miss you until it hurts," I said, and Zane's shoulders dropped.

The factory door slapped open again, and Apple flew

down the stairs carrying an armful of boxes bound with ribbons. She handed me the assortment. "Now, they're all labelled, of course. And don't eat them all at once—that'll muddle your stomach. And—"

"I'm sorry but I promised the train guy this wouldn't take long," Emily butted her way in, taking half the boxes.

Apple sighed and cast me a glossy-eyed, dark chocolate smile. "Safe travels."

Cane and Scarlet watched from the stairs with Fred and Lucas. Lucas cast me a wink.

It was hard to believe that these few were all who stood between Nightflesh and his rulership over Winter. I'd never forget this moment. I'd never forget these faces.

"Come on," I said to Emily before I changed my mind.

With my arms full of truffles, I boarded Cornelius Britley's train, ignoring the cries and objections of my heart as I left Winter's greatest fight in the hands of those at my back.

THE

STORYTELLER

AN INTERRUPTION

'Twas a vision, no shinier than a silver spoon, no larger than a mustard seed, that had filled the mind of Kaley Bell the moment her hand had received that ancient stone of glory: a spherical orb of revelations and Truth.

The resting spark within her chest took off, ready to embark on the mission of a saint. With fire in its gallop, and a screech to ruffle the veils of darkness in its path, it thundered across Winter's winds into the Dungeon of Souls with the speed of an arrow, slicing through the laugh of a witch oozing up from the floors.

In the vision, Kaley watched the spark light the dark tunnel. She tasted a sweet flavour which urged her to breathe a message in a different tongue.

"Fear not. I bring you good tidings of great joy." Her intercession soared into the hearts of the believers where gold and colours had become weak. And she added, "Elowin *watches*."

Boys in blackbird coats climbed to their knees to behold the spark, and other believers down the hall rose on wobbling legs. The spark whispered, "Greater is he who sits upon the True throne of Winter, than he who lives in the gutters and shadows."

One folk cheered, and then another, until the volume of the believers sent the feastbeggars slinking back into the crevices of abandoned tunnels.

"Glory to Elowin!" one such believer chanted.

"Elowin is with us!" another one said.

"We are not alone!"

"We are not alone!"

"We *are not alone*!" they cried.

Kaley could not shake the chants from her ears even a measure of days later.

'Twas youthful Lucas Leutenski who found her standing atop a hill, peering into the whisking snow. The air was white for a great distance.

"Are we almost there?" she asked, thinking of her beloveds across the intersect. But Lucas drew around her, an impossibly wide smile lingering on his closed mouth. He was a measure taller than she, and Kaley was forced to lift her head to meet his gaze.

"I have no apprentice, darling, which means I'm free to take on a charge. And you now need a guardian, so since I'll certainly be your first choice, I'd like to state my conditions."

"You'd like that, wouldn't you?" Kaley said. "I choose Zane."

Lucas laughed. "No, you don't. You choose me. So, back to my conditions—"

"You wouldn't be able to keep up with me, Lucas Leutenski," she said. "No offense."

Lucas blinked as she settled her gaze back on the whitish landscape. He moved in to cut off her line of sight, capturing her in his shadow. "You don't know me well enough to realize that putting that little bit of *challenge* in your voice only makes me want to do it more," he tilted his head, topaz eyes swimming, "*darling*."

Kaley bit her lips so she would not crack a smile, but when Lucas glanced past her into the haze of flakes, he stilled. The Patrolman grabbed the staff from his back as a curly-haired figure emerged from the whisking snow.

Eliot Gray wore a silvery coat no longer; a long jacket hugged his body now, a shade of black that looked dangerously close to raven feathers.

"How far is it to the White Kingdom?" Kaley whispered as Eliot approached them with a chipped Patrol staff in his hand.

"Too far to outrun *him*," Lucas replied as blades of ice emerged from his weapon.

Eliot stopped at the foot of the hill and raised a hand. "I came to help," he said to Lucas. "And to apologize. I have information on Nightflesh, and Asteroth, and what they're planning. I can't go back to them now that I've left, they'll turn me to snow. Please, Leutenski, I know the rest of the Patrol have been captured and you and Cohen are all that's left. Let me help you."

"How did you find us?" Lucas eyed the once-Patrolman, and his presumptuous *jacket*.

"I followed your footprints. I got to the factory shortly after you left."

"And Cohen didn't run you through?"

"Cohen wasn't there." But Eliot's gaze flickered to Kaley. He had an unusual look. "What...*happened*, exactly?"

"Is your chest feeling a little cold these days, Gray?" Lucas taunted, and Kaley zipped her coat up over the orb.

But Eliot sighed. "Leutenski, I know where this path will lead in a day's time. Please, let me come. Elowin is the only one who can help me now."

Kaley's insides thawed, and she thought of the spark of hope in the Dungeon of Souls. "Let him come," she said. "But hurry up, Eliot. I plan to arrive by nightfall."

"Whaaaaaaaaaat?" Lucas rounded with wide eyes to look her right in the face.

"He's just going to follow us anyway." Kaley turned to head down the other side of the hill.

"Not if I whip his scotcher," Lucas articulated through his teeth.

Eliot rolled his eyes as he walked past to join Kaley, and Lucas scrambled to catch up, wedging himself between the two. He cleared his throat. "Prepare to be serenaded the *entire* walk, Gray."

Kaley and Eliot both cringed when Lucas began to sing.

And so, they set forth—Trite, Patrolman, and once-Patrolman-perhaps-maybe-a-Patrolman-again, skating toward that great barrier beyond which the kingdom of light and colours awaited. Where those who had passed on had found themselves alive again, and those who once were lost, now were found.

But as they reached the great barrier to the dwelling place of Truth himself, Lucas took Kaley's fingers and tugged her to a halt.

"Someone's up there," he whispered, drawing Eliot to glance ahead also.

Two figures battled in the snow before the wall, jumping as high as the sky itself, slashing with wood and ice.

"It's Zane!" Kaley realized, pulling forward, but Lucas tightened his grip.

"Stay back, Trite," he instructed. Lucas slid down the hill and inched toward the pair cutting and slashing and heaving and jumping.

"That's Jolly Cheat with him," Eliot whispered as he followed. They were close enough to hear the pumping threats, the screaming hearts, the grunts of hits being taken.

Zane slashed his staff, drawing a spiralling worm of ice from the ground and sending it plummeting over the Court magician. Jolly hacked back, turning it to glassy dust. A patch of swollen flesh covered Jolly's brow, and Zane's lips dripped with red.

"They're going to turn each other to snow," Lucas muttered, drawing his own Patrol staff. The movement caught Jolly's attention.

Eliot did not draw his weapon.

Suddenly Jolly threw his head back, and a crazed laugh echoed to the sky. "Come! Come, Leutenski, you young thing. Let us all have a merry brawl."

Zane's head snapped toward where Lucas stood, and he blinked, shaking the fog from his eyes. "You finally bloody made it," he called at Lucas. "Cheat's been hunting you since you left the factory! It's been a footrace to the border!"

"A footrace I won." The madman twirled his staff.

"You old snoot," Lucas called back to Jolly, marching over with his weapon at the ready. "You think you stand a chance against three sputtlepuns?"

But Jolly's nickel eyes flashed, and he leered. "The odds are more even than you think."

Lucas paused his marching. And he sighed. "Frostbite." With a wheel of his heels, he turned in time to block the hook of Eliot's charging weapon.

Kaley watched them, her hands balling into fists. Glancing at the barrier, she dropped her backpack and broke into a sprint, aiming for that glittering white wall whose light was warm, and welcoming. Her spirit lifted as she slid to meet it—

It nearly turned her nose to a snub when she smashed against the wall, and she bounced back.

The four combatants stopped as ripples of lightening snapped across the barrier. They looked to Kaley, and all at once, the four folk rushed in her direction. Jolly summoned a wave of ice teeth that lunged over where Kaley lay. Zane tried to break it with a wall of snow, but Eliot collided against him.

Lucas though, he made it.

The youthful Patrolman threw himself atop the Trite, abandoning his weapon in the snow.

Kaley's heart pounded as scraps of black fabric ripped from Lucas's back where the wave rolled over him. The Patrolman gritted his teeth—the frost's fangs tore his skin, splinters of ice stained with Rime blood tumbling off.

Kaley gaped as Lucas squeezed his eyes shut. After a heart pumping second or three, she reached into the pocket of Lucas's jacket and stole a thing; a pearly button which he had stolen from someone else. And as the ice roared in her ears, she lifted to press her warm lips against his.

'Twas a simple kiss, one no larger than an ink pen's point. But Lucas did not want a simple, modest, teensy-tiny kiss.

His watery eyes blinked back open, and he kissed her back, pressing his mouth properly on hers. The snow settled around them, but only when Lucas was satisfied did he pull up to let her breathe. Kaley gasped and blinked, then blinked a time again.

Three figures stood over them. When Kaley shook her mind clear, she found three rather confusing looks:

Zane Cohen looked ready to burst. Perhaps that one was not so confusing.

Eliot Gray looked bothered.

Jolly Cheat though, he looked *worried*. But the most peculiar part was that none of them were fighting any longer. Past them, the barrier shifted with a burst of colour, and the boys turned.

Groaning bounded down the wall—like the echo of a turning ship—and with a surge of glassy light, a tunnel tore open. Dust of gold coiled at the edges, and a warm breeze rushed through.

Zane helped Lucas to his feet, but none spoke. For, standing in the mouth of the tunnel, was Elowin.

Zane tumbled back to his knees. Awe, and a thousand plus a thousand more feelings lingered in the air as the Patrolman peeled away his gloves with shaking fingers.

Colours and songs drifted from the King of Truth, words of wisdom glided o'er his flesh. Bronze, green, and purple tones made a kaleidoscope in his eyes as he looked at them one by one. But his gaze rested upon Zane.

"Can I...Can I see them?" Zane's voice rose with a deep ache.

A warm spirit moved along the snow. "You cannot pass through until your time." Elowin's words sounded like the rustling of leaves in a soft breeze, or the trickle of water over rocks. "Thomas and Mikal will stand to receive you when that day comes."

Jolly looked as though he had been slapped across both cheeks—blots of flush touched his flesh, and his eyes were penetrating and wild. He stared past Elowin as though he was seeing a ghost down the tunnel.

But Kaley had not come to make a way for others to ask for what they should not have. She approached the tunnel but did not enter.

"I..." she began, piecing her thoughts back together. "I came here for Helen. I want to give her a chance to start a life at home." The inky laps of colour coming off Elowin danced in response.

"I know this is a strange request but..." Kaley fiddled with her fingers. She was suddenly quite aware of the electric-blue-eyed Patrolman at her left. "I want Helen to forget about Winter," she said.

Sure enough, Zane's head snapped toward her. "You bloody what?"

"Not forever," Kaley clarified. "Just long enough for her to rest, and to forget her fears."

"And exactly what *measure of time* are you asking for, Trite?" Zane stood and drew a step closer.

Kaley turned back to Elowin. "Let her forget until…" she paused, her finger tracing the pearly button in her pocket, "until a Rime Folk returns her memories with a *kiss*," she decided.

Everyone looked at Zane, who blanched, and Eliot grunted in disgust. Lucas grinned.

"That's all. We'll go now, but please ask Helen if she's willing to let go of her memories so she can get the rest she needs," Kaley said. She clasped her hands together to stop her fidgeting.

The warm breeze ruffled her hair and flitted over the snow toward Zane, releasing a whisper.

I have heard. Elowin didn't speak the words, but his music promised it to Kaley's heart.

His multicoloured gaze settled on Eliot, and this time Elowin spoke aloud. "Remember, forgiveness and redemption are only one prayer away."

There was a pause; a gust skated across the snow, twirling into Kaley's collar. Then Jolly Cheat started to laugh; a loud, crazed, chilling hoot that tore Kaley's attention to the magician. It seemed the sort of laugh that might carry on forever, except that one from the group brushed by like a shadow, the cackles drowning out his footsteps.

A silver dagger slid from Eliot Gray's pocket, and Kaley shrieked at the blackness of his eyes as he sailed past her and thrust the silver blade at the True King of Winter.

Elowin did not move as the weapon plunged across the boundary. The moment the blade entered the tunnel, it liquified, and Eliot halted as it melted over his fingertips with a sizzle. 'Twas Eliot who shrieked now, and as he tore his hand back into Winter, the metal froze and clasped to his flesh.

The following moment hung in stillness, the once-Patrolman's cries echoing o'er the gales in the distance as he held up his silver-tipped fingers.

"Ah," the madman in red finally spoke. Jolly knocked his staff against the barrier, igniting a fresh array of lightening. "I see nothing I try will work here. It seems we'll have to wait for another eve to settle our score, Patrolman," he said to Zane, taking one last sidelong glance at the tunnel entrance. Jolly reached for Eliot's collar and dragged him toward the hills. "Run, spinbug. Before they decide to catch you."

The two sailed off into the whisking storm while the tunnel began to close, its creaking competing with the howling wind as it moved to separate the living from the truly living, once again.

"Thank you for meeting with us!" Kaley called into the shrinking gap, and Elowin's whisper-song offered one comfort more before the tunnel sealed:

I am with you always, even on the darkest of eves. You are not alone.

Kaley found herself reaching for Lucas's hand as the barrier smoothed out, the creases disappearing and the warm wind along with it. A dot of blood stained the youthful Patrolman's thumb, and she swallowed. Perhaps he was her Patrolman after all.

"Take me home now, Lucas," she said.

CHAPTER

THE TWENTY–SECOND

Grandma was wrapped in the knit Theresa had given her last Christmas. It was the first thing I noticed when I came into the quiet hospital room where my cousin Quinn was sprawled in the corner on a chair, flipping through photos on her phone.

"Finally," Quinn muttered when I approached Grandma's bedside.

Without another word, my cousin stood, grabbed her purse, and tapped out of the hospital room on her flats. I sighed when she was gone, feeling a mild urge to punch Quinn in the face for no real reason. But I nearly jumped when I looked down and saw my grandmother's eyes open.

"Is she gone yet?" Grandma whispered.

I made a face and glanced back over my shoulder. "Yeah."

"Thank goodness. I don't think I could have pretended to be asleep any longer. We ran out of things to talk about hours ago." Grandma tried to peel away the knit with shaking hands, and I moved to help.

"What happened?" I asked, eyeing the machines around the bed. I stole a look at her medical chart that had conveniently been left in a clear pocket on the wall.

"Oh, you know, dear. Old age finds all of us." My grandmother smiled, but I knew it had to be something serious if she'd been dragged to the hospital. The woman would have rather climbed a thistle-covered mountain in bare feet than climbed into a hospital bed.

The room was quiet until a doctor asked from the other side of the curtain behind me, *"Do you want to rest, Helen?"*

I didn't know how the doctor knew my name, but I huffed a laugh. "More than anything," I answered, turning. I scanned the room, and leaned to peek around the curtain, but the doctor must have made a quick exit.

"Hmm?" Grandma asked. "Did you say something, dear?"

"Uh…" I made a face at the empty room and came back to her bedside. "Nope."

The sound of rattling loose change filled the doorway and Grandma froze. "Is Quinn back?" She tried to tuck herself back in, but the smell of freshly ground coffee beans told me it was someone else.

Emily started talking even before she was visible around the curtain. "I know what I want to do with my money," she said, coming around with two paper cups in a tray. She slid one out and handed it to me. I could have hugged her.

Grandma peeked one eye open with a confused look like she wasn't sure if she should keep pretending to be asleep or not. She wasn't wearing her glasses, so I imagined she was trying to guess who Emily was.

"What have you decided to do with all your money, *Emily*?" I asked to help the old woman out.

Grandma smiled and closed her eyes after all, leaving us to our "private" conversation.

Emily pulled out her phone and began poking the screen. At first, I thought she forgot she was talking to me, but then she flipped it around to show me what she'd been after. "We're going to open a café. I've been typing out all those coffee recipes you were coming up with when you thought I wasn't listening." I blinked at the notepad app on her phone, filled with ingredients and directions. She pulled the phone back and flipped to a new screen before showing me again. "And this is where we're going to do it. I need a place to live and a job, and you want to make coffee drinks, so it's perfect. This cute building on the corner is for sale. I think it used to be a breakfast diner or something, but there's an apartment above the store."

A quiet snoring sound drifted up from Grandma, and Emily hushed her voice. "Let's talk outside," she nodded to the hall.

I smirked at my grandmother, but I stole one last look at those daunting medical charts on the wall as I followed Emily from the room.

We took our seats in a row of brown chairs and Emily pulled out a notebook and pen.

"You really want to gamble your money on my business intuition?" I joked, tugging the flap of my coffee lid open to take a drink. But I paused as a strange sensation came over me. I looked around, but no one else was in the hall apart from Emily and me. My fingers drifted to my chest, and I rubbed it as coldness drained away, a new feeling I couldn't identify taking its place.

I blinked my dry eyes, and for a moment, I considered curling up on the brown chairs to go to sleep.

"I don't have ambitions, and I'm not super smart like you are. But you have dreams and a brain. So...I may have already put in an offer on the shop."

My gaze shot over in surprise. "That's...actually amazing..." A slow smile overtook my face and she laughed.

"I know, I'm the coolest friend you have," she said, and

I decided not to point out that she was the only friend I had. "I can't wait to show Kaley when she gets back."

My brows tugged in. The sensation returned, and my finger traced over my heart. I felt like I'd forgotten to lock Sylvia's house when I left or something. "What do you mean?" I asked, taking another sip of coffee. "Where'd Kaley go?"

Emily rolled her eyes. "*Ha*. Ha." She yanked up the flap of her own coffee lid and took a chug. "By the way, I think that magic train guy is cute, though I couldn't understand a word he was saying."

I blinked at my friend. "Okay," I laughed. "What train guy?"

"Ugh, *stop*, Helen. You're so bad at jokes. Anyway, about our café—I think we should call it *The Steam Hollow Corner Café*, since it's on the corner, and we could make it like that little place you visited in the intersect that you loved."

I feigned a laugh, but I was shaking my head. "Emily, what in the world are you talking about? Seriously, are you alright?" I put the back of my hand against her forehead to check for a heightened temperature, but she shot me a look and swatted my hand away.

I didn't want to say aloud that a viable explanation was a delusional disorder—especially if her sleep was irregular—but after her years in a coma, I didn't want to take any chances either. "Maybe you should see a doctor while we're here."

Emily's face changed. "No...Helen..." She drew back.

"It's okay, Em, I know you're not crazy. Sometimes these things are out of our control. Let's get you checked since we're here anyway?"

Through the hospital room window, Grandma stirred. I rubbed my eyes, sure a nap for myself was in order. "She's awake. I should be in there." I stood. "Let me know if you decide to see a doctor before you go, and I'll come with you." I opened the door, but I leaned back to say one last thing. "And I think the café is a *great* idea. Let's do it."

I left Emily in the hallway chairs with her hands dropped to her lap, staring straight ahead.

In the room, I dragged Quinn's chair to my grandmother's bedside as a nurse came in and added a sheet to the clear pocket on the wall.

"Any chance you could keep an eye on my friend? I think she might not be sleeping well, and I read that poor sleep can result in irrational decisions, or even obsessive tendencies if she's not careful," I said to the nurse, nodding toward Emily through the window. But when I looked to where Emily had been sitting, I realized she'd left.

I sighed and patted my pockets for my phone so I could call Kaley, hoping she'd be up to checking on Emily whenever she got back from...

My hand slowed at my pocket, and I blinked.

I couldn't remember where Kaley went.

EPILOGUE

A Week or Three Later...

A branch of cloud covered the evening skies of the Trite world; cloudy fingers reaching o'er the city of Waterloo like the hand of a soggy, grayish sea ghost.

Zane Cohen eyed it as he stood on the sidewalk's snow-dusted edge, anticipating an oncoming storm. He slid his hands into his pockets—rough *Trite* pockets, inside the scratchy *Trite* coat. A common toque also covered his Rime ears, which drooped off the top like a lazy, ugly thing, refusing to hold a pointed shape as any good hat or hood should.

He leaned to look down at his bland boots with plain laces and rubber soles. There was also no curl in them, whatsoever.

A large, Trite vessel rolled to a stop on the road before him, and Zane nearly jumped at the sharp hiss of its brakes as it arrived.

"Ragnashuck," he muttered to himself, glancing both ways to ensure no one had seen his almost-jump. In doing so, he spotted a peculiar fellow waiting for the vessel's door to slide open. The fellow had a rather familiar arrogance to his tall, slender stance.

Zane turned, bright eyes narrowing on the hood which did not cover the folk's face well enough. The Patrolman's fingers flew over his shoulder to feel for his weapon but found only air. He balled his fists instead.

But when Jolly Cheat turned his head as though sensing he was being watched, his nickel irises settled on where Zane stood. And it was then that Zane realized; Cheat was in Trite clothing, also.

Jolly studied Zane for a measure but did not cast him a gloating stare, nor a warning look, nor a threat of any sort. He simply offered a modest nod of greeting, and possibly, of farewell. That was all.

In fact, the madman was not aiming in the right direction if he had come to seek out Helen Bell. Zane's gaze flickered to the lit sign on the vessel, which read:

TO CONESTOGA

Jolly redirected his silvery gaze to the vessel door when it opened, and without another glance back at Winter, he climbed aboard and disappeared behind rows of reflective windows.

Zane watched until the vessel rolled away into the first sprinkles of snow descending upon Waterloo. He could not guess where *Conestoga* was, but he imagined the poor souls of the village were in for a scotchy treat.

With a deep breath, the Patrolman began his march through the piling snow on the sidewalks, trying to remember that the common folk could see him now, and he could not simply walk through them. 'Twas a pinch of an adjustment to weave around the unmerry Trites hauling bags and packages and loading them into nearby vehicles.

They were all so very boring and blind and busy, with lazy hats and flat boots.

When Zane reached the end of the block, he paused by a familiar lamppost whose bulb had burned out.

Yes, this was the place.

With a deep breath, he faced the corner shop where a soft glow against the fogged windows indicated someone was inside. A sign was taped to the glass, depicting the hand-written words:

Coming Soon:
The Steam Hollow Corner Café
Help Wanted

The weaponless Patrolman fiddled with the buttons of his scratchy coat and peered through the frosted glass. He spotted a Trite girl hauling a box from the back and setting it atop a table. She had the plainest hair and the dullest eyes. But she looked like she had slept well. And anyway, she was perfect in every way that mattered.

The Patrolman's mouth curved into a smile as he realized he hadn't the faintest clue how to get a job.

A pinch and a dip away, an aged man leaned over his trinkets, tightening a wheezpin with his twisty-tube, and peering at the tiny metal parts through his spectacles. When the wheezpin fell out, he sighed and dragged a hand down his white beard.

The flap of his navy tent swished open, rattling the star

chimes overhead, and he started as whispers filled the shelter—ones of promises, blasphemies, and lies.

He sat up straight and pulled off his spectacles. "What do you want?" he called toward the flap. "I have work to do."

A cold breeze brushed the man's arms as someone entered—not a circus clown, nor an acrobat, nor a dancing elf. But a body encompassing the darkness of night.

"Asteroth," the aged man cussed. "Or should I greet the one who really possesses this body? Which of your ancient names shall I use? Night Beast? Serpent of the Eve? *Night-flesh?*"

The once-prophet's long, diamond-white hair was tangled, his flesh wrinkled with gray patches. He had lost weight since the season Obb had spotted him as a young, sputtlepun scribe of the Red Palace. "You have wasted your time coming here. I am a Guard of Doors no more. And even if I was, I wouldn't help you do such a despicable thing, and violate the rules of... "

Asteroth settled his hollow, dark gaze on the aged man, and Obb's throat constricted. He looked to the tent flap but jumped to discover gruesome, wispy creatures in torn burgundy fabric blocking his path. 'Twas from them the terrible whispers came, and Obb felt bile rise from his aged stomach as he beheld the abominations of this new age.

When Asteroth Ryuu spoke, it was with a voice not his own. "Choose your fate: death or obedience?"

With tight skin, Obb made his choice. "Death," he said in the face of evil.

A beast stared through Asteroth's eyes.

"Wrong," it said.

THE STORYTELLER:

A WINTER STORY

Nestle in, if you will, and let me tell you a pirate's tale...

Once upon a Winter's eve, Zane Cohen was quite little. Though, not little in height or anger, but little in spirit—a spirit no larger than a nut, no heavier than a feather or fishbone, yet just big enough to upset the scales of those around him.

The Rime boy was not like the others of his crew, nor his blood relatives who whispered spells into the air. And so, little Zane Cohen built a wall of steel 'round his young heart, and 'round his joy, locking it deep where it could never come out to play.

Read on, then. See it for yourself.

MERRILY MERRILY

LIFE IS LIKE A DREAM

FIRSTLY

There was not enough snow in all of Winter to wedge between Zane-Cohen-Margus Bowswither and Tigris Oran-Mathsideon to create sufficient distance between the two. Born rivals, they were, even at a dozen seasons old.

Before a sky bleeding scarlet and succulent orange, Zane stared across the deck at Tigris's twinkling smirk and the iron in his narrowed eyes. The boy's obsidian hair was soggy with perspiration, but he seemed otherwise well; fit for a race. Healthy enough to bury Zane's glory at the bottom of the snowseas.

Unfortunately for Tigris, Zane was excellent at races, and he very much hated to lose.

With folded arms and a sweet wink at his foe across the deck, Zane went over the rules of the race in his mind—rules that had been changed at the last minute by his mother who stood by to watch.

It was a true season's-end miracle that she was present at all. His mother—the prophetess, vision seer, and *steerer of the ship*—had become the interim ruler during this freezing quarter until a new captain was selected; a title which should have been Zane's birthright, but his mother was too mystical and scheming to simply hand such a position over. Reasons ranged from, *"It's not yet time,"* to, *"You're still too young,"* plus, *"I cannot bloody see what you're hiding from me!"*

To be Captain of the Kelidestone was every-bloody-thing. The Kelidestone was a mighty, fearsome ship with bloodred sails—meant for gliding over open seas, chopping through ice-topped lakes, and plunging across the snow dunes by the windmill-wheels hugging the bottom that could be rowed from inside. Zane's hands belonged at its helm.

The prophetess had come to watch the race, but she had not spoken a word to Zane since she'd ascended from be-lowdecks where she had spent nearly a full quarter summon-ing her energies and scribbling visions on parchment. She had not sent for him in all that time, either.

Tigris, however, had been summoned a good measure of times.

In a pinch, his mother would see how foolish she had been to parade Tigris around before the crew; the captain she "foresaw" to inherit the ship in his future, as was spoken to her through a vision. A future not put in stone—but one she would surely craft the way she wanted.

The waves raged in hunger, spurting through gaps of bro-ken ice the Kelidestone had shattered to make space for the duo of pirates to swim. All for this game of theirs. All for this race that Tigris Oran-Mathsideon would lose.

"Are you yet ready, sputtlepuns?" Sembleton held an ice-shredded scrap of flag in his fist that had once boasted a bone skull with a frostlilly as its mouth but was now too mangled to make out.

The ice below cried and groaned as the last of it was snapped and dragged away by hooks and chains to make a large hole for entry into the dark snowseas.

Sembleton raised the tattered flag to the wind, giving brief life to its tendrils, and Zane crouched to dig the heel of his boot against the deck. It was time to show Tigris what a minnow he was.

"Wait." The prophetess raised a hand, halting the theatrics and the game.

Zane slid his frosty gaze to the woman, eyeing the dark serpentine tattoo reaching up her neck into her pecan hair.

With convincing grace, the prophetess rose from her seat and glided over the deck to where Zane stood. Tigris eyed them carefully from his spot, feeling left out, no doubt.

Zane stood tall again, wishing only to remind his mother how much he had grown these last seasons.

"Steelheart." A smile cracked at the furthest edge of her red-painted lips. Her hand came against his forearm, patching over his permanent ink symbol that informed all he crossed that he belonged to this crew.

Zane's eyes darted down to that hand.

"I wish you good tidings in your race," was all she said.

Zane fought a grimace at the sight of her wild eyes which were paler than normal today. "I don't need your well wishes. But I wonder what will happen to poor Tigris when I beat him? Do you think the crew will still want him as their captain after I scrub the seaweed floors with him?"

Those pale eyes flickered. "Careful, Steelheart." The whisper was sweet, but a warning.

Zane released a laugh. "I bloody better be. I have no doubt you're counting down the sunsets until you can turn this crew on me and carve a bone dagger into my back," he growled. "Leave me to my race, Mother. Watch me beat your champion."

Silence. Zane could almost taste the fury leaking from the woman.

"As you wish." A gloat.

Zane eyed her as she sauntered back to her seat across the deck, the necklace of bones at her throat clapping together with a ruckus.

"*Go!*"

At Sembleton's roar, Zane spun back to find Tigris bolting across the main deck.

With a grunt, Zane sprinted after his rival and hopped the rail, falling far and fast toward the needles of ice stabbing from the shattered, frozen blanket of the snowseas.

He twisted his body to avoid the spikes and straightened into a dive as he hit the water, gliding beneath the bitter waves like a bird arching through a rippling sky.

Numbness bit at his nose and extremities—a feeling that might render most to panic. But Zane had come to win and prove to his mother that she did not get to adjust his future with a mere flick of her fingers whenever she liked.

A low groan rumbled through the water and Zane grinned, a brush of icy current leaking against his teeth. Through the weeds, he spotted Tigris diving into the frosty marsh in search of a pure black pearl. It was a gamble to test the weeds, as sirens often came out to play when the plants were disturbed.

But he knew his own way around the marsh and knew where to best look for a pearl.

Paddling around the weeds, Zane scanned the dark sea floor for signs of a gem that might have spilled away from the sirens' troves. As the seconds slipped by, Zane paced his energy so he might hold his breath longer. He imagined he would transform into a handsome, icy merman soon.

Another grin found him at that thought.

A shuffle in the marsh halted his search. He wondered if Tigris was in trouble, if the sirens had found him. As Zane peered into the slimy grasses and sponge, he did in fact see Tigris. But Tigris was not in trouble.

The young sputtlepun was reaching into his pocket. He drew out—

A black pearl.

Cheater.

Zane abandoned his search and headed into the weeds. If Tigris intended to swindle a win, Zane would steal the pearl right from the boy's hands and deliver it to his mother with a smile.

Tigris's silver eyes rose as Zane slashed away the weeds between them. The boy's grip tightened around the gem, and he drew a dagger, halting Zane's pursuit.

No weapons during the race—rule number four.

They floated there for a heartbeat until Tigris's hoary gaze dropped to the tattoo on Zane's arm. A slow sneer followed.

Odd.

Zane's attention drifted to his forearm. He'd barely had a chance to sort out his curiosity when a sea-shuddering current barreled into him and tipped him off balance. Tigris too went spinning, falling into the blackest pit of the marsh. Zane stared after the boy until the current came again—a punch of a wave against his flesh that sent his skull colliding with the jagged underside of the Kelidestone.

"Bloody frostbite!" His underwater curse let in a mouthful of water, and he batted his arms to steady himself.

Tigris swam like a panicked gull to the surface, the pearl still clutched in his grip. Zane blinked against the bubbles, peering through the black sponges muddying the water and through the tendril of red—

Red...?!

Zane's eyes fired back to his tattoo, to that spot on his forearm where his mother had touched. And he saw it—the slight prick into his flesh where his blood leaked from. He hadn't felt it beneath his mother's hand.

His growl was drowned by the third current that plunged against his body and pushed his back against the daggered wood of the ship. He thrashed as the water fought against his pinched mouth, against his nostrils, trying to make its way in and drown him.

Zane kicked off the ship and paddled for the hole in the ice where Tigris had disappeared. There was no game to play anymore. Something was down here in these weeds. Something that perhaps his mother had known was waiting.

He clenched his teeth as he saw how the trap had been laid: his mother's careful touch, Tigris's planted pearl, even Tigris having a dagger on him when he should have been searched by Lother before the race.

His own crew. His own mother.

They would all frostbitten suffer for it.

Zane slapped a hand over the needlepoint cut in his tattoo and kicked for the hole above that now seemed much too small and far to reach. His mind burned through every spell he knew, which he spit toward whatever creature hunted him below.

But he already had an idea of what sort of monster had awakened in the bowels of the snowseas. One that would smell his blood. And one that would never forget it once it did.

SECONDLY

The octosiren was half the size of the Kelidestone; its fangs longer than Zane's own legs. It slid from the blackest cave of the snowseas, spilling bronze and brass treasures over the sea floor. The creature rushed to circle Zane like a serpent, its sharp scales tipping out to pierce his flesh as it closed in.

I smell you...

The octosiren's cold whisper drove into Zane's chest and turned the dull colours there to ash and cinders.

I smell you too. Zane jested back, though he wasn't sure the creature could hear him, or if he had the same sort of speech as this *thing* in the water.

But a low, cruel chuckle told Zane the monster had heard him.

Zane slid his eyes closed. He would die here like this—in the pit of the snowseas. Perhaps it was where he was always meant to meet his fate; a fair payment for all his pillaging in his earliest seasons. Pillaging that had killed his spirit at first, made him ill and sent him into the corner of his cabin to tremble at night as visions of his evils haunted his dreams. He had learned to sing himself to sleep, and he had taught himself to read to pass the worst of times. But it had not been enough.

Under the water, Zane's supply of air ran out. The pale colours began to swim in his chest, his heart writhing for life he did not have left to give. And so, a measly prayer for forgiveness of his misdeeds slipped into his mind, to an old being of legend he did not believe in, one that might spare him a pinch of mercy in the afterlife for his crisped soul. A being he had read about in a book or three stolen from a coastal village he had destroyed to please his mother.

But an idea struck him as he was nearly encompassed by the octosiren's long, black tentacles.

Might we make a deal? Zane's gaze slid over to seek out the octosiren's dreadful face.

If an ancient miracle awakened and allowed him to escape this fate, Zane swore he would kill Tigris for this. Their rivalry had settled on the side of dangerous over the seasons, but this…this was a new level of backstabbing.

Interesting, the thing said back. *But now that I've smelled you, I'm sure I'll crave your blood incessantly.* The creature quivered. *Your blood smells of mint and the forests above. And…anger. Pure, undiluted anger.*

Fine. Zane swallowed, his chest burning like open flames. *Hunt me for the remainder of my timestring if you must. But even so, I'd like to make a deal.*

And what do you wish to bargain for? the thing asked.

Well. I'd rather like to live today.

The red and orange sky had melted to gray and purple when Zane climbed the ladder and tumbled to the deck of the Kelidestone. Cries of surprise lifted from nearby crewmen at the sight of his saturated, shivering body.

"Frostbite!" Sembleton leaned to see Zane for himself. "We saw the octosiren's fins brushing the ice's underside!

How did you escape?"

But Zane's cold blue stare slid across the ship to Tigris. To his mother, who stood tall at the cheating boy's side. "I have my secrets too," he said.

The prophetess stared with those unwavering, pale eyes. In her own dark, subtle way, she looked pleased that he had found a way out.

"Well done." Her voice was barely a whisper.

Zane rolled to his feet, fighting the shivers driving against his bones through his wet clothes. He stared back at his mother, bottling the fury that tempted him to shout at the woman and toss Tigris back into the snowseas to face the octosiren himself. But, instead of exploding with the anger that had gained him a pebble of respect from his crew in recent seasons, Zane marched across the deck and stood eye-to-eye with the prophetess.

"I don't know what you're up to. I don't know what game this is. But leave me bloody out of it."

That same curved smile tugged the edge of the woman's red mouth. It was infuriating, and so Zane left for his cabin, craving dry clothes and a warm blanket.

"You lost the race, Steelheart." Her voice trailed after him. "The crew will not be forgiving of that."

THIRDLY

Tigris Oran-Mathsideon was a bad apple. A time or three, Tigris had left critters in Zane's bed to keep him awake at night. Zane had growled in annoyance on the mornings he woke with red bites peppering his torso. But he always retaliated, and he always did it well. Zane's clever mischiefs forever left Tigris more enraged and swearing revenge.

It had been a contest of pride in their earliest seasons. Now, it was a contest for the hearts of the crew. And Zane was exhausted from fighting for their attention when most days he wasn't certain he still wanted it.

After he had shivered for hours and tossed back and forth in his hammock in a fitful sleep, he rolled to his feet to face the night. Soreness lingered in his cold bones. He dragged on his warmest coat to storm through the ship and find something to drink that might numb the pains in his muscles, quiet the voices in his head, and ease the loathing in his heart.

Fear's cold touch dragged up his spine as he imagined what might happen to him the next time he dared to poke a toe into the snowseas. He tried not to think about the creature below the surface who claimed his blood smelled of cheap pirate-mint and *anger*. The creature that would follow this ship wherever it went, waiting for Zane to slip up and test the water.

The deck was nearly empty when Zane stomped up the narrow stairs, but even Brox and Mollbane went silent as the son of the prophetess clattered his way over the deck boards, kicking aside bottles and baskets of fruit until he reached the full bottles of fermented ice-berry juice.

They would consider it a sputtlepun temper tantrum, but Zane didn't care.

"A bit early for that, don't you think, Steelheart?" Mollbane muttered from across the deck. Zane turned to the man, taking in the pirate's bristly beard and half-sagged eyes. A man bitten with the curse of age.

"Do you want to quarrel, Mollbane?" Zane tested, uncorking the bottle against Mollbane's warning.

But Mollbane grunted, sizing up Zane's youthful, sputtlepun frame. "Your lassie is on board. Flew in off the cliffs last night. Might want to stay clear headed for when you face her."

Zane's hand froze on the bottle's mouth.

"Sentra..." he spit her name, wary of saying it loud enough to stir the Winter winds, "is here?"

"Consider yourself warned," Mollbane snorted and strutted off.

For a breath or three, Zane stood under the Winter stars, staring out at the hazy horizon black with night and sleepless curses. "Bloody ashworm," he muttered, shoving the cork back into the bottle and turning to hurl the entire thing into the snowseas. "Bloody conniving, spellcasting *ashworm*."

He stormed into his mother's cabin. And lo' and behold, there she was—Sentra. The girl's ink-black hair and even blacker eyes tightened the skin on his shoulders as he tried to avoid meeting the beady gaze of the rival pirate.

"What is *she* doing here?"

His mother lounged over her cushioned bed with her feet up.

Sentra growled in response—a feline sound that fit her. She wasn't quite normal, not a colour-blooded Rime Folk. Something dug up from the pits of the snowseas perhaps and given legs and a face. But those pure black eyes...

"I invited her," his mother said.

Only now did Zane realize he was bare chested beneath his open-hanging coat. With a snarled lip, he yanked his coat shut and folded his arms to conceal himself from the two devils before him.

You will marry Sentra Donspellis, his mother had informed him two quarters past when their feud had truly begun.

I certainly will not. Trust me, I'll be dead before I'm seen marrying a demon-eyed, rival captain's daughter.

His mother had thrown a fit of rage, claiming Zane did not care for his crew and that he would never be captain if he did not do as she asked. But Zane refused to be married during the season next when he would be merely ten plus three seasons old. Still a sputtlepun.

Sentra was ten plus seven seasons old and certainly planned to control him after the deal was sealed by their dreadful union. Zane would not do it.

It was why his mother had not spoken to him in almost a full quarter—until now. Until she had wished him luck before the race and pressed a pin into his wrist so the octosiren would smell his sweet blood and become infatuated with it.

The prophetess's *façade* dropped as she glanced at her son in the doorway. Sentra stared at him too, her glare equally as piercing. Even her leathery wings seemed arched in disdain.

And so, Zane smiled.

"I'll leave you unmerry lassies to your ugly scheming." He bowed. "But as always…find a way to leave me out of it." He said the last part to his mother, ice-blue eyes sharp.

She snarled at his back like a polar bear when he turned.

"*Steelheart*." The name rolled off her venomous tongue. "Stop."

The air in the room seemed to change, and Zane was met with the sound of his mother lifting from her cot.

So, they would finally speak, then. Finally sort this out. But when he turned back, he saw that his mother was not bracing for a quarrel.

"I don't answer to you," she said.

"And I don't answer to you," Zane reminded, leaning in to emphasise it. "But when I'm captain, you *will* answer to me. And after you tried to feed me to the octosiren this sunset past, I vow I'll come up with all sorts of dreadful little ways to make you hate your scotchy life on my ship." *The same as what you did to chase off my father*, was what he did not add.

His mother shut her cherry-red mouth. And so, Zane made his exit.

But he did not storm down the hall as he might normally have done. He slid against the wall to listen. And he hated himself for it—that he was so desperate to learn what his mother was doing, to learn what the moves she had been making these quarters were leading up to.

The woman had begged Zane to let her see the secrets of his heart in his seasons, and each time, he had refused. So, she had tried anyway, working her visions and spells to dive into his heart against his will. She had been furious when she realized she couldn't get in—something Zane himself did not understand either but had been all too pleased to discover. The woman claimed a wall of steel existed around his heart.

"That boy is not going to wed me." Sentra's gurgling fish-voice slipped out from the cabin.

"He will. I will bloody make him," his mother cooed. "I need to make this deal. My supplies won't last another season and we've already pillaged the coastal villages we can reach. I need more cutlass wielders. I need a new crew with a hunger for blood."

Zane shook his head in disgust. All this over a few more weapon-hands? He had discovered at a young age that she would do anything to get what she—

"You can kill him after the wedding."

Zane stared at the chipping boards across the hall, not truly seeing them at all.

"You're certain? I don't want a prophetess's retaliation if you decide you regret it." Sentra's voice held no conviction, and Zane's jaw solidified. His fingers tapped his bone dagger as he considered marching back into that cabin and ending their conversation for good.

"My son will not be Captain of Kelidestone," his mother whispered. "Steelheart has no interest in fulfilling the role I made him for, and I won't spend the next twenty bloody seasons putting up with his insubordination."

Whether it was anger or sorrow that touched his stomach with heat, Zane didn't know. But he pulled himself off the wall and walked on light toes to his cabin in silence.

All night he lay awake, ignoring the pile of books stashed on his night table which he would read at times like these to keep his mind from caving in on itself. But he only stared out the oval window at the Winter stars now, singing along to a song his father had taught him as a boy.

"Row, row, row your boat—" His hum took over for a verse when he couldn't remember the words. "–Merrily, merrily, merrily, merrily—Life is but a dream."

He ended the song as it settled in him what he was: unwanted. Someone not worth fighting for. Only an animal to be forced into submission. He was a creature of the seas, abandoned by his father, and hated by his mother.

And one day, perhaps, he would make them all pay for it.

FOURTHLY

Zane marched through the snowy village with heavy boots the next morning, trampling an already foot-print-congested road. Most of the coastal villagers had surrendered, but a few fought back as their homes were torn apart while the Kelidestone crew searched for anything of value. The villagers who rebelled had to watch their wood houses go up in golden flames.

The prophetess stood on the shoreline in her long, silk cloak, the fur of her hood brushing her chin. Her pale eyes took it all in as she was no doubt already counting the worth of her new treasure. A trident rested in her grip—a gold trophy she had once stolen from a siren in the early seasons of her timestring, or so she claimed. It was for show though; Zane had never seen his mother use the thing.

Tigris led a band through the alleys to hunt those fleeing, to steal the necklaces off their throats and the rings from their fingers.

Zane rolled a long necklace of black snowsea pearls over his fingers, staring at them. The string of stones glimmered in the direct sunlight; a gift likely given to a wife, or a daughter, or as a proposal. Easily fetched—unlike the underwater pearls Zane had not managed to find during the race.

A girl with bouncing orange curls had sprinted into her front room and *thrown* them at him, as if the surrender of their most valuable treasure might somehow keep the young pirate demon at bay. Then the girl had fled out the back door after her family.

The leaking kohl on Zane's lids stung his eyes, adding to the irritation from his terrible sleep the eve past. A shuffle of white feathers brushed his cheek and he whacked at it before realizing what it was. Silver twinkled upon the bird's wings. It arched and landed in the street before him.

Zane tilted his head as he studied it. The bird was *very* white.

His mind danced over the value of meat it might provide if he could capture it—not that he felt like selling the meat or even sharing it. Hunger rolled in his stomach, and he took a slow step forward. But as if sensing his dark motives, the creature flapped and lifted back into the air. Zane watched as it joined with a host of others—just high enough above the village to stay out of reach.

When he dropped his gaze, he found a trio of folk in black standing at the end of the street, side-by-side. His brows furrowed.

The three statue-still bodies wore curled-toe boots and tall hooked staffs balanced in their grips that reminded him of large, wooden fishing lures. Two were in their early twentieth seasons if Zane had to guess, and one was middle-aged like Mollbane.

All three were striking. They had no bells or garlands to be seen, but the way they stood together—shoulder-to-shoulder—was as though they were different parts of a single body.

A spark ignited in the eyes of the middle-aged one with butter-toned hair and a beard to match. Zane found himself drawing forward, stalking them like an ashworm in the snow.

As villagers rushed by, Zane kept his gaze on the trio, certain they were about to do something, though he could not guess what. But when the middle-aged man's warm, sunflower eyes dropped to Zane's ice-cold ones, Zane halted. The man smiled, and Zane felt a touch of fury warm his blood.

Was that a taunt?

Zane realized he stood before them now, just an arm's reach away. "Here to defend the village?" he guessed, eyeing the staffs they carried. A twinkle found the silver-nickel eyes of the boy on the man's right, and a slit of striking, white teeth showed when he smiled.

"Ragnashuck, pirate. I'd think you'd know a takeover when you saw one," the boy said, daring Zane to do something about it.

But the middle-aged man cast the boy a look. "Manners, Nicholas. We're not here to make enemies." The man's voice was calm; like an easy breeze on the snowseas.

The boy on the right flashed his devilish grin again. "Aren't we?" he taunted, silvery eyes glimmering at Zane.

Zane looked at the folk one by one until his stare fell back on the aged one in the middle. "Move your merry scotchers," he said with demeaning articulation. "Or you'll be tangled up in those wood hooks and pretty black clothes when I'm done with you."

All three blinked.

Suddenly, the silver-eyed boy threw his head back and released a mad laugh. Zane tilted his head like a crow, deciding he would tackle *that* one first.

The middle-aged man sighed and looked to the sky where the birds circled overhead.

"No need to get hissy, pirate. We're only here to play," the silver-eyed boy wiped a bead of moisture from his lash.

"Alright," the middle-aged man said. "Nicholas. Posineon. Clear the street's edges. I'll sweep the middle."

All at once, the black-cloaked trio moved. Zane's eyes

darted between them as he drew his cutlass, trying to decide which one to tackle as they all brushed past, sketching their staffs over the snow and gliding like melting butter on a fire-roasted fish.

Frustration boiled Zane's blood as the three snuck up on bellowing Kelidestone crewmen who snatched what they could. The silver-eyed boy and his companion blocked blades with skill and tossed the pirates into the snow like flimsy branches needing to be cleared away.

A growl lifted in Zane's throat; he tore after them, reaching the middle-aged man first. His trained cutlass swished by the man's ear, but the man whirled and locked his staff against the cutlass before Zane could strike again.

Then, it was Zane's turn to smile. "You're making a mistake, old man," he said.

To that, the man arched a light brow. "Am I?"

Zane's grin widened. He slashed, chopping a notch into the old man's cane. "Only half my crew has made land. The other half is marching up the beach as we speak," he laughed. "I might be young in seasons, but you could learn a thing or three from me."

Zane expected the man's face to fall, and for the old brute to holler to his allies to retreat, but he did no such thing. He stared at Zane for a measure, his golden eyes roaming until Zane shifted on his feet.

"Like I said," Zane cooed. "Move your merry scotchers." His fingers buzzed against his blade, ready for a fight.

The man's eyes lifted to the shore where the rest of the Kelidestone crew marched in from the row boats.

"Mikal!" one of the boys in black shouted from the street as he noticed them too. In the same moment, Lother sprang from the shadows like a demon with wings and brought his cutlass across the boy-in-black's shoulder.

From across the street, the silver-eyed boy's gaze shot up at his ally's cry.

But still, the middle-aged man did not move, did not unlock his weapon from Zane's where they were knotted together—curved staff against arched cutlass. Even as Lother took off to chase down a villager. Even as the silver-eyed boy fired across the street and rammed Tigris into the siding of a house as the young pirate came to finish what Lother had started.

As if they were speaking on a silent thread, the silver-eyed boy looked up to the older man in question as he took the arm of his injured ally and slung it over his own shoulders to carry him away.

The middle-aged man looked back at Zane though, instead of retreating. "Take Posineon home," he called over the street as it flooded with new pirates.

Without objection, the silver-eyed boy darted between two houses—sliding over the snow on his toes—and disappeared.

Zane glanced to where his weapon interlocked with the aged man's. The sleepless night put fire in his veins, and he shoved with all his might, forcing the man back a step. From there, Zane raised his cutlass to the man's throat as ten plus three pirates filed in to surround him, along with the prophetess who drifted around to watch.

The buttery-haired man dropped his staff to the snow in surrender.

"Welcome to the snowseas, old man. Let's see if I let you survive until sunrise." Zane's mouth tipped upward in victory.

But there was no dismay on the man's face, even as he finally replied, "I am *not* old."

The ship rocked the crew to sleep, the easy sway soothing

Zane's weary body as he stared through the cage at the prisoner the crew had dragged belowdecks. His mother had declared the prisoner to be worth a ransom, should his two allies return. So, they hadn't killed him. Yet.

It was very much like his mother to decide the prisoner belonged to her.

After an hour or three of mocking the middle-aged man, the rest of the crew had drifted away to their cabins, or to the main deck to set sail with his mother behind the wheel, until only Zane and Tigris remained.

"You cheated." Zane finally said it. Even with everything that had happened since the race, he wanted Tigris to know he had seen it.

Tigris's lip curled into a snarl. "You *survived*." The words were so wicked, Zane looked at the boy.

Once, Zane was praised for his pranks and his ability to draw a laugh or three. Now, he had been handed a platter of frustration in place of it. Tigris was always the first to toss a cutting word in Zane's direction or fling a fish at the back of Zane's head to make the men laugh. Zane's temper had become a thing so easily triggered, he was sure the crew placed bets on it.

Tigris's eyes slid over, a gloat stealing his face. "I win, Cohen-Margus-Bowswither. Your ship. Your life. It's mine."

Zane grunted and looked back to the man in the cage who said nothing. It didn't seem as though the old man was listening as he stared through the small window at the snowseas, but Zane had a feeling the old bat had heard every word.

I win. Your ship.

Your life.

But Zane could hold on. Had to hold on. Or he would have nothing. Being a pirate, son of the prophetess, was the only thing he was.

"We'll see," was all he said before Tigris's quiet chuckle

filled the ship's belly. The boy strutted off to command the sails alongside the prophetess where he believed he belonged.

Zane was glaring when the old man glanced at him. To Zane's ever-growing frustration, the man did not even look afraid. Nor did he appear bothered by the ring of purple around his left eye, or the swelling bruise along his jaw.

The prophetess would consider all her options before she decided what to do with the prisoner. She would settle on whichever one filled her pockets with the most gold rings.

As Zane stared into the older man's buttery irises, he found his mind back in that snowy street of the village with the trio in black. He considered how the trio had moved in unison, so quick and without complaint at the brief command of their captain. How obedient they all were. How loyal.

Zane folded his arms as he played over how the silver-eyed boy had rushed in to save his friend from Lother's and Tigris's cutlasses. Zane wondered if Tigris would ever perform such a rescue for him. The bloody pirate would probably stoop down to dig the blade in deeper.

"Who are you?" Zane finally asked the aged man when the silence had gone on too long.

"My name is Mikal Migraithe."

With that shallow answer, the man stood and limped across his cell on limbs still stiff from the beating he had taken from the crew on the way down. Zane watched, bored. He craved a good sleep before he was wakened to serve his shift as lookout. He turned to leave as the others had, but the man's voice stopped him. "You're very angry, boy."

Zane's back tightened like he could feel the man's eyes upon it. And he didn't know why he admitted it, or why he cared to even respond in the first place. But Zane heard himself say, "Yes."

He left the belowdecks after that.

FIFTHLY

The morning sun was blinding. Zane lay out over the crates, shielding his eyes with an arm until a shadow blocked the light. He peeled his lazy eyes open, and a piece of half-rotted fruit hit his stomach.

He gawked and flew to sit up, growling a curse at Tigris. But he did not find his rival when he stood.

Sentra stared at him with her sleek black eyes, unblinking. The deck was mostly empty behind her, and Zane flexed his fingers as he considered how easy it would be to toss her overboard to face the octosiren lingering below the ship. Zane imagined the creature might grow impatient and bite out the ship's belly to sink it soon.

Sentra dared a glance at the snowseas too. Zane prepared himself in case she struck. He would not go over the edge easy, and Sentra was no bigger than he was. But her glassy eyes shifted back to him.

It was bloody impossible to tell what she was thinking behind those horrid black eyes.

"I'm here to warn you," she gargled.

Zane blinked, slow and doubtful. But the tightness in his limbs trickled away as he studied the enemy pirate. "Of what?" He was sure she was about to lie—all part of his mother's game.

"Your mother wants you dead. She's trying to kill you."

At that, Zane slackened, hardly believing Sentra's willingness to admit it. "I know," he said and angled his head. "But why are you telling me? You don't care about me."

But a dangerous smirk found her mouth. "No, Steelheart. No one cares about you." Zane flinched as her finger came up to poke his coat. "Tigris discovered that your weakness is your anger. It's how he was able to get your mother and crew to turn over your birthright."

Zane clenched his jaw. "So?"

"So, you and I are the same. I'm horrid and mean and vengeful," she said. "And my spirit repels people. Perhaps you'd like to feed this crew to me and my father? Perhaps you'd like to donate this magnificent ship to our fleet and help me rule another crew at my father's side?" She pursed her large lips. "Your mother is a cunning ashworm with her deals. But I know you can make deals too."

"How do you know that?"

"How did you escape the octosiren?"

Zane's jaw slid back and forth.

Sentra's unusual eyes kept her from being truly beautiful, but she was confident, and for the first time, Zane saw it as something to be admired. Something he might use to hurt those who had wronged him—starting with his mother. And then Tigris.

"It is a sad day on the Winter snowseas when a mother turns on her own child." Sentra dropped her hand and levelled her onyx eyes on him again. "My father says we cannot trust someone willing to turn on their own offspring. It means they will turn on anyone if the price is right. And I'm inclined to agree."

"I could kill the octosiren," Zane considered. "I could win back the favour of my crew. Take them out from under my mother's rule."

But Sentra let out an unfeminine grunt. "Your mother fed you to that octosiren in the first place. If you can't admit that to yourself, Steelheart, maybe you deserve to die in that beautiful monster's jaws."

With that, the enemy pirate turned and sauntered over the sunlit deck, her layers of skirts fanning out with the sea wind. Zane clenched his molars.

Only Sentra would consider the grotesque octosiren to be a *beautiful* thing.

"I'll be back in ten days plus one to hear your answer." She glanced back in warning. "Don't go anywhere, Steelheart."

Zane's face changed. That had felt like a threat.

But Sentra paused to stare up at the skies. "And those birds..." she grimaced. Zane glanced up, noticing how many white creatures circled above their ship. Some had landed on the rails—he hadn't noticed while he had been napping. Sentra's black eyes dropped back down to him curiously. "They're watching you," she stated.

Zane stared after Sentra until she moved to the edge of the boat and hopped off, her wide, dreadful wings ripping out from her back to take her over the snowseas, scaring some of those white birds away. He envied how easily the girl could come and go. And he imagined what a battle between his crew and hers would look like—with her crew able to fly and land on their deck at will.

He shook the thought from his mind and eyed the birds wreathing the pink skies as he stormed across the deck, deciding he did not care for sunshine anymore.

Bloody, frostbitten Sentra. It seemed even she wanted to use him for something.

No marriage, then. It seemed he would not be forced to wed the enemy after all—but her price was his ship and crew. He was not sure he could stomach the idea, even after how they had turned on him. And Sentra would probably turn him back into snow after anyway.

"I can show you how to handle that." A voice like a river filled Zane's head and he snapped his eyes over to the middle-aged man—Mikal Migraithe.

The man rested on the bench in his cage. Zane looked around in surprise and tried to remember why he had come down here. "Your anger," Mikal clarified.

The man pinched a tiny, white flower with a gold centre between his fingers—a fragile thing in comparison to his muscular frame. There were no flowers at sea apart from frostlillies. Zane might have asked how the man had come by it, but it looked as though there were garden pieces hidden in one of the many pockets of his black jacket.

"I used to be angry too," Mikal said, plucking the last few petals from the flower and dropping them into the pile already scattered over the floor.

Zane eyed him and allowed another step toward the cage doors. "How did you deal with it? How did you make your anger go away?" He could not help but notice that the way this man spoke, and stared, and observed; it was all rather...*quiet*.

Finally, the man raised the petal-less flower, and pitched it to the floor where Zane's eyes followed it. "Verses." Mikal brushed his hands clean of the flower's remains. "Wisdom," he then added.

Zane made a face. "Wisdom?"

"I can teach you some, if you'd be willing to listen." Mikal's gaze flickered up.

But Zane folded his arms. If the kohl lining his eyes was not evidence enough, he was sure the snarl upon his lips would be. "I have better things to do than listen to an old man ramble on about a thing or three."

At the *old man* comment, Mikal stifled a grunt, but he repositioned himself on the bench and leaned back against the cage bars. He appeared comfortable, even though nothing about the ship's cages were comfortable. Zane had been shoved in them a good measure of times during the early seasons of his timestring when he disobeyed his mother, or broke a rule of the ship, or angered one of the bigger crewmates. He could never sleep on those damp, hard floors, especially with an empty stomach.

"What would you do if you could master your anger, pirate?" Mikal asked, folding his arms and displaying trained muscles.

Zane shifted his jaw, wondering why this man bothered to ask. No one ever asked him his reasons. No one bothered to ask him much about anything. "I would take back my ship," he decided. "I would win the affection of my crew."

"Do you *want* their affection?" The man drummed his fingers against his biceps.

Zane shrugged. "I suppose. I don't want to wind up dead or…"

Alone.

Zane slammed his mouth shut, his eyes narrowing in on the prisoner that had already gone too far with his questions. Mikal raised his palms defensively. "I didn't ask you for your secrets, boy. I won't pry them from you. I wish to offer you a solution to your anger. But first I wish to see what you might do with the solution if I give it to you."

Zane did approach the cage now, hands curling around the bars as he stared down at the arrogant ice-weed eater before him. He imagined how he could make this man suffer if he continued his little manipulative game of questioning. Zane could practically *hear* the man knocking against the steel coating his heart, trying to get in, to destroy him.

"Secrets. Everyone wants my secrets," he muttered. "Even you, it seems."

At that, Mikal stood, but Zane did not cower or back away even though the old man could reach through the bars and grab him. "I don't want your secrets," he said again. "I will offer you verses at no cost of a trade to help you with your anger if you want them. That is all."

"That is all?" Zane mused. "You don't wish to make a

deal for your freedom? You don't wish to trick me into letting you out?"

And the man sighed, much like he had done in the street when the silver-eyed boy had run his mouth. "In the early seasons of my timestring, I let my temper flare. I nearly drove away all my beloveds," he said. "So, I wrote verses. I still recite them in my mind, even now. The wisdom keeps my heart steady."

For some bloody reason, Zane didn't think the old man was lying.

"I have my own ways to do that," he said, thinking of the books on his night table. Books he had kept hidden for all the seasons he had been collecting them, since Tigris would howl with laughter if he ever discovered Zane liked to read. "I suppose I study verses too," he realized.

"Is that so? Do you like books, then?" A funny smile tugged at the corner of the man's mouth—as though it stirred a joke in his mind.

But Zane dropped his hands from the cage and took a step back.

A secret. The books were a *secret*. And this man had just dug it out of him—no magic or spells or visions were even used.

"You're dangerous," Zane realized.

Mikal shrugged. "Some might say that. But not for the reasons you think."

"Who are you? And don't just tell me your name this time." Zane's hand padded along his hip for the grip of his cutlass.

"I'm the Commander of the Patrols," Mikal answered, and Zane felt the colour drain from his face.

He had heard of the Patrols—a team raised by powers Zane knew little of. He had never met one, wasn't even sure they existed, until this moment. But confirming stories of the land folk was difficult when the Kelidestone spent most of its seasons on the dunes or far into the snowseas.

Mikal's face glimmered with a smile, his butter-gold beard glowing in the sunlight from the window. "Yes, boy. You can bet your scotcher we're as real as the ship below your boots. And I can show you how to become someone with honour. Unless you think you're better off with the bloodthirsty ashworms on this boat that want you dead."

Zane could not move now. He stared at the man with the golden hair and serene eyes, replaying again that moment in the street when the two others in black moved as a single unit in perfect agreement.

"You want to learn how to control your anger? You want to see what a real family looks like?" the man went on, and Zane found himself moving away until his back hit the wall. "Then come with me." Mikal's eyes sparkled like a light of their own, and Zane was sure he was dreaming it.

"Are you mad?" His own voice was high and wrong. "You're my prisoner. You're not going anywhere, and neither am I. I'm going to be the bloody captain of this ship and you're going to shut your..." His voice trailed off as the man reached for the hooked staff that was leaning against the wall below the window.

"I confessed that I'm the Commander of the Patrols," Mikal said, studying his weapon for just a moment. "And now you know I'm dangerous." His golden gaze flickered back up. "So, do you really believe I would have been taken prisoner by that flimsy crew if I didn't want to be?"

Zane's blood turned cold as the man tapped the heel of his staff against the cage door and it swung open, as though the lock had been picked hours ago.

The man—Mikal—walked out and towered over where Zane found himself shaking against the wall. His hands fumbled for his cutlass, and he drew it, holding it up toward the great man on his wobbling fish legs. "You're my..." Zane choked.

"Prisoner?" Mikal guessed. "Yes, yes." He waved a tired hand through the air and turned toward the stairs. "Time to go, boy."

Zane watched in dismay as the man climbed the stairs at his leisure until his black clothes disappeared through the door at the top.

Zane was a frozen pillar of Rime flesh and pumping blood in the ship's belly until he snapped back into himself and raced up the stairs.

He could *not* let the prisoner get away. He whirled the cutlass in his grip, shaking out of his trance and reminding himself how to slash and destroy. He was a pirate. A bone-snapping, weed-eating pirate. His mother would rage with disapproval if Zane lost her prized trading piece. The crew would abandon Zane altogether; it did not matter that Zane was the one to capture the prisoner in the first place.

His colours burned red and angry in his chest as he realized he had been duped.

The sun blinded him when he plunged onto the deck, but he skidded to a halt at the sight of his *entire* crew standing in defense, cutlasses drawn, staring at this one man with butter-gold hair.

Zane eyed the man's back—right between his shoulder blades. He could sneak up behind him. He could—

"I wish to make a deal with the prophetess of this ship." Mikal's voice was a clean current, a symphony of wild nature. "And I'm in a bit of a hurry, if you all don't mind."

Zane's gaze fired over to where his mother swept down the stairs to the main deck, long, black skirts gliding behind. Her cherry-red lips curled up as she looked Mikal over, likely deciding what she was going to do with him for his outrageous demand that she *hurry*.

"And what sort of deal would you like to make, Commander?" she purred.

Zane blinked. So, she knew then. She had seen what Mikal was when he was captured. No wonder she expected a ransom.

"I wish to fight your best pirate," Mikal said. "You choose

who. And if I lose, I will bring you ten plus two troves of gold rings and fine pearls, which is everything I have to my name. A fair price, I imagine."

Zane cringed at the glisten in his mother's eyes. "And if you win?" It was a hungry whisper. It was then that Zane knew this Mikal Migraithe was truly mad. Most knew better than to challenge a prophetess in the first place, let alone one as renowned across the snowseas as his mother.

"If I win," Mikal limped a step to keep his balance, agony etching between his brows even as he tried to stand tall.

Yes, certainly mad.

"If I win," Mikal said again as he twirled his staff against his palm, "I would like to leave this ship unharmed, firstly. And I would like Zane Cohen-Margus-Bowswither to leave with me if he wishes."

Zane's face paled. "What—"

But the prophetess's mocking laugh cut off Zane's question. "You have a deal," she snapped, and Zane staggered a step back, blood thickening to fire and ice.

The arrogance. The *confidence* in what she thought Zane would decide; that he would bow a knee before her and stay if given the choice. The shock hit him in the gut the same way it had when he realized his arm had been pricked to leak the smell of his blood into the water for the octosiren.

Not only was she willing to give him up for a chance at treasure, willing to bet away her own offspring, she had done it *easily*. Even after all this time, the fortune teller thought she had Zane pinned under her spell.

But she hadn't called him *Steelheart* all these seasons for nothing.

Mikal cast Zane a look of understanding, and perhaps sympathy. By his angle, the man's face was unseen by the rest of the crew. "Only if you want to, Son," he added, leaving the choice in Zane's hands.

But Zane stared.

Son.

A strange mixture rose in Zane's lungs, and he could have sworn he felt cool violet creeping over the bleak shades of gray and fiery reds in his chest. His hand drifted over his heart, and he rubbed his flesh, testing the sensation he did not recognize.

When he glanced up, Mikal, along with the Kelidestone crew, waited with bated breath. His mother's pale eyes were sharp as a bone dagger when she realized his hesitation. He wondered if she wished she could take back how quickly she had responded to the man's deal.

Steelheart, indeed.

For the first time in his timestring, Zane realized he could forget this crew he had tried so hard to keep, this mother who had tossed him away, and the soiled memories that came with them.

The two boys from the trio in the village filled his mind. Their faces had not been wicked or malicious or filled with bloodlust. They had been laughing because maybe…maybe they were happy.

"*Steelheart?*" The prophetess's tone was cold. Threatening. Demanding that he answer.

Zane glanced at the snowseas, the blazing sun above, the crates of fish and rotting fruit and the spilling burlap bags of peppermint. Could he leave this?

Yes, he bloody well could.

"Do it," he breathed, eyes flickering to Mikal Migraithe. The man's staff stopped its spinning the moment the words were spoken. He cast Zane a small smile of agreement.

The prophetess was silent for the first time in Zane's timestring. Poison filled her stare, pale eyes narrowing. "I choose Lother," she spat, the act of the sultry sea witch vanishing.

Lother. Because Lother was the most fearsome of the crew. Lother was the one who had taught Zane to seek, kill, and destroy, and Zane felt that new violet in his chest wither away to gray again. Zane had been trained right into the dirt and sea and snow, which was how he knew Lother was a pillar not easily tipped over.

Zane pulled his shaking hands off his cutlass and clasped them together to witness his luck or lack thereof.

Lother sneered, dragging his hands to the barrel of spare cutlasses, not even testing them to select the best one.

Mikal waited as the prophetess slithered over the deck and extended her hand to seal the deal, the promise of rings and pearls dancing across her unlit eyes, and a spark of worry lingering in the corners that she could not quite hide. Mikal shook her hand, wincing at the stiffness in his arm as he raised it to do so, and Zane watched his fate be passed, just like that, into someone else's hands. His mother's eyes settled on him from where she fidgeted across the deck after the impulsive deal she had made. She was a woman who was meant to see the future, who perhaps had not checked the future of *this* deal.

Lother was a giant in comparison to Mikal's aching, hunched frame as the two readied themselves. One of them would be dead soon and Zane felt a stone of regret sink through his stomach that he might witness this old man's death at the hands of his ruthless former teacher.

But everyone had always fought against Zane. No one had ever fought *for* him.

Until now. Until Mikal Migraithe.

SIXTHLY

Lother prowled like a sea demon, sniffing the fear in the air as he rounded the deck. Not Mikal's, mind you. The man appeared to be utterly unbothered. Mikal waited until the pirate was ready—a respectable act considering no pirate would have granted him the same respect.

The scars on Lother's shoulders gleamed in the late morning sun as he slid off his coat and tossed it in a heap. He kept his violent yellow gaze on Mikal, seeming to decide how he might snap the middle-aged man's bones and wet the deck with his blood.

Zane found himself holding his breath. If Mikal lost to Lother, Zane would have a dreadful price to pay for the risk he had taken. Lashings at the very least. He might be thrown to the octosiren after all.

Finally, Mikal took a deep breath and marched to the centre of the deck to meet his foe, and Zane faltered at Mikal's walk. For, gone was the limp. Gone were the slow moving and stiffness, the weak muscles the old man had convinced everyone he had developed from the beating he'd taken as he was dragged onto the ship.

"Bloody ashworm," Zane whispered, and grinned.

Lother stopped his cutlass twirling, sizing up the man who appeared before him, who held out his staff at the ready and cast a polite smile as a cracking sound filled the air. Frost and ice spiralled out the end of Mikal's tall cane in a dozen silver blades. Zane found himself laughing, to his mother's disdain.

Lother snapped his cutlass across the space, attempting to get a slice in before Mikal was ready, but Mikal ducked like a youth, moved like a sputtlepun, and unleashed strikes like an ashworm taking its bite. Perhaps Mikal was not wrong when he claimed he was *not* old.

The dreadful dance was fast and cold and startling—pirate metal against ice and wood—until Lother's cutlass was slashed from his hand. The pirate's yellow eyes trailed his weapon and he gawked as the foot of Mikal's staff landed in his gut, sending him tipping flat onto the deck. Lother didn't scramble back in panic, though his eyes assured he wanted to; he remained steady for the killing blow.

But the dozen points of ice hovered at the pirate's throat, and Mikal's warm, golden gaze flickered up to the prophetess who was a pale statue by the rail. She glared down at Lother, at her failed crewman.

"I think I win." Mikal's cool river voice blanketed the tension on the deck.

Zane unclasped his hands and found his fingers grazing over his cutlass again; he didn't know why. Didn't know what he would do with it if he was compelled to draw it.

But his mother's dim gaze fired up to Mikal—the man who was meant to be her prisoner.

"You don't win until he's dead," her voice cracked. "Finish it."

Crew members grumbled amongst themselves, unnerved by the command. Zane wondered why the old man didn't just kill Lother and be done with it.

But Mikal stood tall and stared at the woman whose pecan hair fluttered in the sea breeze. He looked past her to where the shore was in view, close enough now to reach by rowboat. "I'll take my leave," he said, clear and certain.

But the prophetess smirked, those cruel, red lips doing nothing to waver Mikal's attention. "My son does not belong to you unless you win, Commander."

Mikal bowed slightly and Zane's heart sank as he wondered if Mikal would agree. But the old man raised himself and a flit of fire burned in his golden eyes. "Your son does not *belong* to anyone. Not even you. The spells you've wound around his heart and soul have loosened." The prophetess's face fell. "And don't try to spit those spells to keep me here, either. They won't work."

A crumpling sound filled the air and Zane's eyes flashed to the snowseas where a path of ice was forming from the coast. It raced over the rippling water like a white banner, reaching for the Kelidestone.

Zane's heart began to thunder with a sound he did not know his body could make. When he glanced at the old man, he realized the path of ice over the snowseas was not being made by him.

"It's your decision, Son." Mikal's voice carried over the deck to Zane as the pirates began to stir. The crew looked to the prophetess to see what she would do, to discover their orders.

That pounding in Zane's chest grew to war drums as he looked to the beach and saw them—the army in black. There were dozens; their crow-black jackets sharp against the white snow on the shore. They had made the ice path; Mikal's allies.

Without another thought, Zane bolted. His breathing hitched as he stumbled down the stairs belowdecks, so riled he nearly missed the door to his own cabin. But he sprang back and tried to think, tried to sort through what he would need. His belongings were few: his books, his bone dagger, his cutlass.

Zane's hands shook as he scraped what he could off the

surfaces of his room into a burlap sack.

When he was finished, he turned for his door. He took one last deep, shuddering breath and looked around at the creaking walls, the tipping floor, the dirty window…the bad memories.

Perhaps he was not running away from it all.

Perhaps he was only running toward something else.

The sky seemed a heavier blue when he emerged onto the main deck. Every crewmate on the Kelidestone had his weapon drawn. Zane looked from one crew mate to the next, then to his mother, who steamed like a burning ship in battle when she saw his satchel of belongings.

"Let's go," Zane heard himself say to Mikal.

Though the ship was filled with enemies, the old man did not look afraid. A knowing smile warmed his face and he nodded, extending a hand. "To land, then."

Zane took the man's hand, not caring if those watching thought it unusual or weak. Mikal hopped onto the rail and Zane followed, and only then did he realize why he would need the old man's sturdy grip.

A long, icy slide down to the snowseas lay before them. Zane's chest tightened at the thought of that ice snapping, of finding himself in the water and being snatched up by the octosiren waiting in the depths.

But Mikal didn't give him time to debate. The old man pulled him onto the rink and Zane's stomach leapt as they slid down the slope. He nearly screamed at how fast they moved—certain he would *never* willingly slide over ice and snow like this again.

A few of Mikal's allies in black had come to meet them; they were halfway across the bridge when Zane overheard his mother's growling voice from the Kelidestone, "Do it!

Kill him!"

"But the *deal*—" It was Tigris, of all mates, who protested.

"I agreed not to kill the Commander. I said nothing of *Steelheart*!"

Zane's blood ran cold as her furious growl roared over the snowseas. He did not have time to spin before the golden trident she hurled into a deadly spiral reached him. But the trident did not spear through his chest.

Zane turned to find three wooden hooks before his face, all snatching that trident from the air and holding it in place before it met its mark.

He blinked at the staffs; Mikal's was not one of them.

"Ragnashuck, she has good aim," one of them muttered, and Zane recognized the silver-eyed boy at his side, gripping one of those staffs holding his mother's heartless blow. "Maybe *she'd* like to join us," he added with a grin to the others, all of whom chuckled—a sound that hit the colours in Zane's chest with a burst.

They dropped the trident onto the bridge and Mikal used his heel to nudge the gilded weapon into the snowseas where Zane watched it sink and sink and sink.

A shuffle of white and silver appeared in his peripheral vision. The birds—those same ones that had been circling above his ship—spiralled toward the Kelidestone. They landed on the rail, building a wall of white feathers between the boys in black and the crew of the ship, staring at those on board with narrowed, beady eyes.

It was the most absurd thing Zane had ever bloody seen.

The silver-eyed boy snorted. "Those pesky critters seem to like *you*," he said to Zane on his way by as he headed down the bridge.

"If you were nicer to them, Nicholas, they'd like you to," another boy spoke up as he followed—Posineon. The other boy from the street; his shoulder was wrapped in bandages now.

And the last boy was not a boy at all, but a girl, Zane realized. Uneven stems of choppy, light hair stuck out from the hood wrapping her head. Her eyes were large and fishlike, and when her gaze slid to Zane, she smiled to reveal a set of crooked teeth. Zane glanced away.

"Wanda, at least *try* not to scare the pirate-folk," Posineon called back at her, and she grunted.

"What's your name anyway?" the silver-eyed boy yelled from where he twirled his hooked staff with long, slender fingers. His grin was a pinch wild, and those white teeth glimmered as much as the snowy shores behind him.

Zane opened his mouth but paused. There was a river of blood on his name, and so much of that name belonged to the woman who had just wanted to see him die, and a man he had barely known who had left him with that woman.

"Steelheart," he decided.

At that, the boy, Nicholas, stopped walking and raised a doubtful brow. Then he rolled his eyes. "Don't be so *dramatic,* pirate," he said, turning back to the shore. "Giving yourself a nickname like a jolly circus jester..." He shook his head. "Who does that?"

Zane glanced once more at the Kelidestone where the birds held their barrier of beaks aimed the other way. For the first time since Mikal had struck the deal, Zane did not feel afraid to turn his back to the ship. To that woman who called herself his mother.

He swivelled on the ice and trotted after the boys in black, Mikal following close behind. The old man slid over the path on his heels, his staff gliding along behind him as though it were the force moving him forward.

Fresh snow sparkled the shore, blanketing the land in white where the rest of the Patrol waited. Two boys didn't carry a staff like the others, and in place of the pure black garments, they wore white coats lined with silver threads.

Though the group in black began hiking up the snowy hill, using their staffs to force the snow to part before them, one of the boys in white remained. He was young. Messy, light-blond hair swept over his head, not quite as tidy as the impressive coat he wore. The boy was no older than Zane by the looks of it; not as old as any of the others in the group. He had a funny smile that blended warmth and cunning— like Mikal's.

The odd boy extended a gloved hand toward Zane, who stopped at the very line where the sea met the snow. All the others, including Mikal, journeyed up the beach, but it seemed this boy was in no rush to catch up.

"I'm Thomas," he said.

Zane studied the hand, looking for a threat. Waiting for the boy to spew a harsh word or three to claim his territory among this group.

But the boy's smile only widened, reaching his bronze eyes. "Ragnashuck, you're going to be trouble, aren't you?" He studied Zane's torn sleeves, the skull and frostlilly tattoo, the kohl ringing his eyes. "What's your name, pirate?"

Zane wasn't sure why this boy had a different spirit than the others, why the twinkle of mischief in his bronze eyes told tales and held promises of rascally fun in the future.

Zane found himself raising his hand to shake the boy's— Thomas.

His name was Thomas.

"I'm Zane Cohen-Margus-Bowswither," he said.

The boy scowled. "Well, ragnashuck, I'll never remember all that. Can I just call you Zane Cohen? Half a name is easier than a whole one like *that*."

A true smile came out, and Zane folded his arms. "Alright," he agreed. "And to answer your question, yes. I imagine I'm going to be all sorts of bloody trouble for your merry scotchers."

Thomas bellowed a laugh, a *real* one that made the colours in Zane's chest glow.

LAST OF ALL

The snowseas had never felt so cold and empty. The
octosiren paced the waters, abandoning its lair from
sunset to sunrise, searching for him: for the boy with
blood as sweet as mint and sap, and as vibrant as the magic
of the ancient Winter woods.

He was not like the others; the boy had bartered and ban-
tered and had reeked of desire to be playful and young. The
others always smelled of salt and sea and sails and greed. Of
dirty metal swords and violence.

The orange and bloodred surface of the snowseas shattered when something plunged into the waters, disrupting its
near silence.

But it was not the boy who returned. It was not the mint
blood the octosiren smelled, but an icy will and the dark,
sticky blood of sin.

Pecan-brown hair drifted around the woman as she descended like a hunting siren, lovely and pale-eyed. She hovered in the seas before the octosiren, who let its grin slide
open so she might witness the sheer length and atrocity of its
teeth.

You are not as afraid of me as you should be, Prophetess,

the octosiren warned.

The woman tilted her head—a predator herself in a way.

I've come to strike a deal, her mind's voice carried on the current.

But the octosiren's smile only grew. *I see.*

The creature began to slide, moving around in idle circles where the prophetess floated in grace. *But I've already made a deal with your son.*

That boy is not my son. Not anymore.

Shame. I rather liked him. He smelled of dreams and promise. The octosiren paused, then added, *And he smelled of an animal locked in a cage for too long.*

The prophetess's lip curled into a snarl. *You will bring him to me when you catch him*, she said. *That is the deal I wish to make. He will return here in the future, during a time when the stakes will be quite high for him. Once you catch him, I want him delivered to me, no matter where in Winter I am.*

The octosiren considered this. *Interesting*, it said. *I suppose I can barter another deal, in addition to the one the boy made, of course. I rather liked his deal.* Another long smile, and the prophetess's face changed.

What did he offer you? Worry slipped into her silent tone.

Your riches. The octosiren's slit eyes travelled up to the surface where the Kelidestone's belly coasted through the patch of iceless waters. *He showed me the precise spot where I must bite through your ship to have them. He negotiated my patience—that I would have to wait until you came down here to barter. And now that you have arrived, my lust for gold shall be satisfied.*

He...what...? The prophetess whirled back to her boat, to her rings...*Why would he tell you to bloody wait for me to come to you?!*

So that you might watch. The octosiren's roaring laugh rippled through the waters as it spiralled once to gain speed, and punched through the bottom of the ship, spilling away timber and supplies, jewellery and rubies.

Half the riches the octosiren ate, gobbling them down in a mighty thirst for all that shines and glimmers, and the other half he let sink to the spongy floor of the snowseas never to be found again.

The prophetess released a deadly underwater scream.

For, even after all her seasons of cleverness and scheming and foresight, the boy of mint and pine had proved to be more clever than she.

BOOKS BY JENNIFER KROPF

A Soul as Cold as Frost
A Heart as Red as Paint
A Crown as Sharp as Pines
A Beast as Dark as Night – Coming December 2022
(Available for Preorder Now)

Carols and Spies, Princes and Pies coming 2023

ACKNOWLEDGEMENTS

To God: I can't imagine doing any of this without you. What a different life this would be if I didn't have you in it.

To my reader: Thank you for reading my story. I've hidden 40 pinecones throughout this book for your enjoyment. Feel free to go pinecone hunting and see if you can spot them all.

I want to thank my husband, Phil, for always stepping up to provide what I needed to be able to make book-magic happen. I'm basically a crazy person, but you make me far less crazy than I could be.

I also want to thank my son, Austin for whom I wrote this book. You are my little prince, even when you're peeing on my lemon tree to "water it" or when I've discovered that you've coloured a picture for me on the bare kitchen table with a Sharpie. Sometimes I worry I'm going to get phone calls when you start school.

I want to thank some of my Enchanted Anthologies co-authors and personal author tribe: Lyndsey Hall, Alice Ivinya, N.D.T. Casale (Nicole), Ashley Steffenson, Sky Sommers (Ilona), Astrid V. J., and Elena Shelest. This really is the dream team. You have all encouraged me more than you know this past year, and I'm so glad we banded together to raise funds for some great causes and became friends in the process. And to all the other friends I've made in the author/writer communities these past years: I'm blown away by the support, and the good people who are in this space. Thank you!

I want to thank Jesse Calder for being the most handy dandy beta reader/content editor in existence and for always working with my preposterous schedule. I'm fully aware that I could not have published any of the Winter Souls Series books without your help. Thanks for the hours and hours of video chats.

I want to thank my editor Melissa Cole and to advise any authors out there who write clean fantasy novels to hire Melissa Cole for an exceptional end product that you can be proud to publish. Find her at *editormc.wordpress.com.* Thank you for telling me that the plural of "reindeer" is still "reindeer" and not "reindeers" and for saving me the embarrassment of writing my heart out to my readers about all the *reindeers.*

I want to thank my amazing audiobook narrator Mia Hutchinson-Shaw for being an awesome human and for doing killer accents that are going to make this series come alive when the audiobooks are released!

Also, I want to thank my siblings, Steph, Melis, and Jesse, for over thirty years' worth of gut-laughs, mildly inappropriate table talk, and for always giving me a hefty load of inspiration for absurd humour to add into my books. And I want to thank all my nieces and nephews for reading my books.

And as always, I need to thank my parents, Jay and Sandy, for reading me books as a child and sparking my obsession with stories. I want to thank my mom for letting me spend my teen years in my room writing pirate stories, and for making me grilled cheese sandwiches and delivering them to me at my desk when I would get into a good part of the story, lose track of time, and go half a day without eating. And I want to thank my dad in particular for raising me to believe that if you don't hop off an escalator fast enough, you'll get sucked into that place where the stairs disappear. I still half-prance off that last step in a scramble every time I'm on one, just out of instinct.

I want to thank all the incredible women, friends, pastors, and youth at Wilmot Centre Church for praying for me over this last decade, for helping to shape me into the prayer nut I've turned into, for making me laugh, and for constantly showing our community how much God loves them.

And I'll stick in a special thanks to Steve Preston (and family) for sending me updates and videos of your kids' reactions to all the plot twists in A Heart as Red as Paint this past Christmas! You guys always make my day.

To Grandpa John: I'd just like you to know that I wrote this book half a year before I had originally planned because you told me on the phone (four months before A Heart as Red as Paint was even released) that you were finished with book 2 and were ready for book 3 now. Haha! Thank you for being my biggest fan.

ABOUT THE AUTHOR

Jennifer Kropf lives in a small town in Wilmot Township in the heart of Ontario, Canada. She writes Young Adult Fantasy novels, devotionals, and has recently launched a line of fantasy-themed journals. She's a mom of three, a wife of one, and she thinks coffee is amazing and tea is downright disgusting.

Find all her books at JenniferKropf.com or join her email list to stay updated on all new books. Visit her website for resources for teachers and book clubs, resources for writers, and other cool things.

www.ingramcontent.com/pod-product-compliance
Lightning Source LLC
Chambersburg PA
CBHW020429030726
47495CB00006B/1725